Praise for *Place Last Seen*

"Ordinary adjectives will fail in their attempt to describe this book, though 'tortured' and 'gripping' are certainly two that come to mind. This accomplished story will ultimately crack a reader's heart, not through the usual mechanisms of tenderness of sentiment but more in the manner by which a shield of granite is fractured by the daily freezing and thawing of the world. Be prepared, be warned: This book will reach into, and touch, your heart."
—Rick Bass, author of *Where the Sea Used to Be*

"*Place Last Seen* is a terrific book—deeply moving without being sentimental, suspenseful without being manipulative. Charlotte McGuinn Freeman tells this story of loss with a voice that is both honest and balanced, in prose that is both muscled and elegant, with a heart that is both courageous and wise. This book is solace and redemption for all of us—those who know grief now and those who know they will one day."
—Pam Houston, author of *Cowboys Are My Weakness* and *Waltzing the Cat*

"Charlotte McGuinn Freeman is an exceptionally gifted writer, to the point that it's almost impossible to believe that *Place Last Seen* is a 'first' novel. Beautifully crafted, written with perfect pitch and authority, and peopled with characters so vivid, complex, flawed, and utterly real that they seem to walk right off the page, it is from beginning to end a true and harrowing tale of a child lost and a family in crisis."
—Jim Fergus, author of *One Thousand White Women* and *The Sporting Road*

"It has been a long time since I've read a novel as structurally pleasing as Charlotte McGuinn Freeman's *Place Last Seen* or one with as many well-drawn, believable characters. There are no villains here, only real people doing their best, and it is a riveting story—suspenseful, complex, and satisfying in the way of all truthful tales. The courage and ingenuity of these people, and the pursuit of their quest despite all the obstacles, made me unable to put the book down. I look forward to reading more from this talented first novelist."
—Judith Guest, author of *Ordinary People*

"Breaking out of the gates with a book like this, Charlotte McGuinn Freeman has a bright literary future ahead of her." —*Metrowest Daily News* (Boston)

"Attitudes toward the 'mentally challenged,' the intricacies of search and rescue, and the terrible randomness of fate are all poignantly explored here.... A cinematic page-turner."
—*Publishers Weekly*

Charlotte McGuinn Freeman

PICADOR USA
NEW YORK

Place Last Seen

A NOVEL

Picador® is a U.S. registered trademark and is used by St. Martin's Press under license from Pan Books Limited.

For information on Picador USA Reading Group Guides, as well as ordering, please contact the Trade Marketing department at St. Martin's Press.
Phone: 1-800-221-7945 extension 763
Fax: 212-677-7456
E-mail: trademarketing@stmartins.com

Book design by Michelle McMillian

Library of Congress Cataloging-in-Publication Data

Freeman, Charlotte McGuinn.
    Place last seen / Charlotte McGuinn Freeman.
      p. cm.
    ISBN 0-312-24227-1 (hc)
    ISBN 0-312-25407-5 (pbk)
    1. Wilderness areas—Sierra Nevada (Calif. and Nev.)—Fiction.
    2. Missing children—Sierra Nevada (Calif. and Nev.)—Fiction.
    3. Family—Sierra Nevada (Calif. and Nev.)—Fiction.   4. Sierra
    Nevada (Calif. and Nev.)—Fiction. 5. Loss (Psychology)—Fiction.
    I. Title.
PS3556.R3839 P57 2000
813'.54—dc21   99-055047
                                                      CIP

First Picador USA Paperback Edition: March 2001

10 9 8 7 6 5 4 3 2 1

This book is for Liza Burton, with all my love.

In nature there are no punishments,
only consequences.

—Jack Kersley,
Training the Retriever

Place Last Seen

Prologue

*M*aggie is lost.

Anne crouches in the trail, listening to this sentence loop over and over through her brain. Her daughter is six years old—blond, brown eyes, Down syndrome, lost. Anne places her hands palms down against the pebbled black-and-white earth and breathes deeply. She's waiting for the white noise to die down in her head, waiting for the panicked shouting of the afternoon to quiet so she can figure out what has happened to Maggie, so she can feel her daughter's presence through the rock, feel her as the dowser feels the tug, the twitch of the stick—*this* way, *this* way.

Richard is gone—hiking out for help. He's worried about the dark, wants a search and rescue team, is afraid if they hesitate, they risk hypothermia, or worse. Maggie's only got a T-shirt and shorts on; it's October, it will get cold when the sun goes down.

He's taken Luke with him, and even as she's scared without them, Anne is perversely glad they have gone. She can hear now; she can hear herself think. She thinks that maybe now she'll be able to hear Maggie.

Anne runs her fingertips across the pebbled black-and-white surface of the trail—Maggie's feet stood here. Maggie's feet, white sneakers, pink Velcro straps. Hiking the trail this afternoon, they had to stop twice so Anne could cinch those straps tighter. Setting her on a boulder, Anne held Maggie's foot and pulled hard on the straps while her daughter twisted away, straining to see the Steller's jay squawking at them from a nearby branch. "Maggie, sit still. Mommy's trying to fix your shoe."

But now, with the sun beginning to slant long and gold in the west, Anne sees only her own hands—blunt nails, long fingers, the nick on her right hand where she'd slipped with the staple gun stretching canvases last week, her wedding band. Anne remains crouched in the trail, thinking that if her hands can *be* Maggie's feet, then maybe Anne can get a direction. Anne concentrates on Maggie's feet. Those feet were here. Her ankles in white socks, lace trim dirty from the hike; her knees, the left one scraped from last week's attempt at the two-wheeler. She fixates on the physical reality of Maggie's body. Her hands seem to sculpt a phantom Maggie in the air—calves, knees, torso. Maggie's body is real; it exists. She is *somewhere*. She may be lost, but she must still have material existence. She occupies space. She can be found.

Maggie's not lost, Anne tells herself, standing up. She's hiding. She does that sometimes, out of crankiness, or when things aren't going her way, and then she gets bored waiting to be found, falls asleep. It happens all the time. Only this time, it happened up here, on the spine of the Sierra, in this jumbled landscape of broken granite and scrub oak, instead of at home, in the house, where they know to look under the bed, in the closet, to listen for Maggie's snoring coming from the clothes hamper.

One hand shading her eyes, Anne looks out over the landscape. She is in a high cirque, three small lakes behind her, jumbled talus falling off the peak to her right, a saddle where the trail goes up and over to Lake Aloha, two smaller peaks to the left. Turning, she looks out over the broken landscape that stretches below her to Wright's Lake, the campground. It's a mess, descending in ledges, boulders scattered and heaped, falling into a scrubby forest of pine and thick underbrush. High on the west flank of the Sierra, she can see out over the foothills, nearly to the coast hills. A great empty gulf of air yawning across the state of California. To Anne, it's terrifying and she feels fear like a great wind rushing up from the flatlands, roaring up the foothills, swirling into and around this high basin like some infernal force.

Her heart races and she can't catch a breath. *Stop,* she tells herself. This won't do Maggie any good; she's got to get a hold of herself. Anne changes her mind; she doesn't want to be all alone up here; she wants Richard. He doesn't panic. He's calm and rational and isn't spooked by things. This was almost bearable when it was the two of them, trying to stay calm, trying not to scare Luke, trying to be the parents. But it's really fucking scary up here all alone.

They were *right here,* Anne tells herself, looking at the faded orange cross painted on the rock. They were spinning, pretending to be fire helicopters. Richard was egging them on while Luke made *whap-whap* sounds and Maggie, lopsided as usual, giggled and kept spinning into her brother. Like that game we had as kids, Anne thought, watching them, the one with the tops and the yellow plastic boxing ring. The goal was to knock everyone else out of the ring. Head thrown back, Maggie was looking straight into the sun, her arms flung out, white-blond hair flying as she wobbled and spun and shrieked. Giving in to the delicious dizziness of spinning, the children fell into a whirl of white granite, green-black evergreens, and religious blue Sierra sky. Anne watched them, then waved to Richard that she was going to set up the lunch. She'd only gone fifteen yards or so to the lake, hoping to snatch a quick moment for a sketch while the kids were occupied, before they needed peanut butter and carrot sticks and cookies.

So where is she now? Anne asks herself as she wishes for the millionth time that she'd stayed here on this spot on the rocks and had never taken her eyes off her difficult missing daughter.

Maggie was right here with that raggedy, too-wide smile; then the next thing Anne knew, Luke was running, panicked—shouting that Maggie was hiding and he couldn't find her. Anne closes her eyes, hands clutching her face as she struggles to banish the visions of *what if*: the afternoon haunted by fears of water, of the lakes; the thought of Maggie falling onto granite, blood running across stone. Anne presses her fingertips against her eyesockets. She knows she can find Maggie if she can only focus. If she can envision Maggie whole and unhurt, if she can get an image of her; if she can do this, if she can make out the details of the picture, she can find her, find the place where Maggie is hiding from her.

She sees only darkness inside her head. Even with Richard and Luke gone, even in this infernal quiet, she cannot picture her daughter lost. She cannot sense her alone in this landscape, cannot imagine where Maggie might exist in this place.

Anne opens her eyes and screams Maggie's name into the wind. Her voice falls puny into the steady updraft from the valley. She shouts Maggie's name again, trying to sound confident, trying to overcome the way the wind snatches the words, empties them and sends them flying out into that enormous terrifying space that is the valley. She's fighting to keep the fear out of her voice, to sound friendly, like the good mommy, the mommy who isn't crazed with fear and anger that her six-year-old, her daughter, who should know better, who *does* know better, Down syndrome or no Down syndrome, has wandered off, is deliberately hiding from them, has gotten lost in this tangled landscape.

Concentrate, she tells herself. If you aren't going to hike out for help, you'd sure as hell better do *something*.

If I can only *think* like Maggie, she tells herself. Dropping to her hands and knees, she tries to see the seductive mirage that drew her daughter off. Moving slowly, Anne crawls across the landscape, scanning for a footprint, a broken plant stem, scuffed lichen. A jay squawks from a solitary lodgepole pine as Anne, on her hands and knees, hunts her child through the brittle granite landscape of the northern Sierra, granite the color of bone, granite that crumbles into windswept sandy soil, granite that won't hold footprints.

MORE PEOPLE, Richard tells himself as he strides down the trail. We have to get more people up here. If they could just get to a phone, get a search and rescue team before it gets dark, before the temperature drops for the night. There are too many boulders, too many trees growing in clumps of two or three, too many gullies and cracks in the pavement-like stone. He and Anne can't search them all, and this late in the season, there weren't any other hikers up there to help out. There must be a search and rescue team, he thinks. People must get lost all the time.

Rounding a switchback, he glances at Luke, tells himself to slow down. He's got that miserable look children get when they're

5

being dragged somewhere by adults, but what can Richard do? They have to hurry.

Looking up through the pines, Richard checks the light and figures they've got probably two, maybe three hours of daylight left. They should have headed down earlier, as soon as Maggie disappeared. But they'd thought she was only hiding. She'd done it before, in the house, once in the Denver airport—she was being bad. It was nearly an hour before they'd looked to the lakes. Maggie hates cold water, but with Maggie, who knows? If she'd been in there the whole time . . . Neither of them had wanted to say it, but it was clear from the way they followed the shore, peering into that deadly blue water. He was in the water before he had a chance to think about that flash of white. Richard shakes his head as if to banish that vision of a small leg underwater, so far down, he couldn't see it properly; all he could see was a form, an outline, and who knew how long she'd been down there? Be rational, he tells himself, and looks up and checks the light, struggling to focus on the bright green lichen glowing with backlight among the dark pines. This is not a disaster. This is just a situation.

Dropping into another steep switchback, Richard sees that Luke is falling farther behind. "How you doing?" he calls up to him.

"My foot hurts."

"It's not far," he tells the boy. "We're almost there."

Richard ignores the black look Luke gives him, but he does slow his pace a little. He should have insisted they hike out after the lake. He knew then that something was wrong, that they couldn't find her alone. He shouldn't have waited. They lost what—an hour, two? But Anne was convinced. She'd dragged them back to the place where the kids had been playing and had

Luke crouch on the granite and cover his eyes. They'd been playing hide-and-seek when Maggie disappeared.

"I'm going to walk off and you tell me if it sounds like the direction you heard Maggie take," she said to Luke. "No peeking—we need to do this by sound to make sure."

"Okay," Luke answered, crouched on the bare rock, his hands over his eyes. Anne went uphill, to the left, and climbed a little outcrop while Richard watched Luke—his body tense with concentration.

"Luke?" he'd asked quietly. "Does that sound right?"

"No, Dad," Luke said through his fingers. "She didn't go that way. I told you—she went down by the dam."

"Anne!" he'd shouted.

She'd run back through the brush, an inquiring smile on her face.

"That's not it, Mom. I told you. She went that way." Luke pointed downhill.

"Okay, okay, I just want to make sure," she said. "Let's try it again. Close your eyes." Luke returned to his original position. Richard watched his wife. She had that brittle, high-energy sheen to her that meant she was untouchable. Richard knew better than to try to sway her. Eventually, she'd wear herself out. But in the meantime, where was Maggie?

Anne walked away, clomping a little for effect, heading not quite toward the dam, but uphill from it. Richard watched with a certain admiration; he would never have thought of going that way, but it looked like exactly the sort of thing Maggie might have done. Oblique. Richard glanced down at Luke, placed a hand on the top of his head. Luke shook it off.

"*Dad,*" he said, annoyed.

"What do you think?" Richard asked, waving Anne to come back.

Luke paused. "That could be it," he said with hesitation.

"But you're not sure?"

"I don't *know,* Dad. We were just playing. I wasn't listening that hard."

Now Richard turns to check on Luke. Behind him, the trail is empty. Dust motes swirl slowly through the late yellow sunshine.

"Luke!" he shouts. "Luke!"

Listening, he hears only a solitary woodpecker working a trunk to his left. *Oh shit,* he thinks.

"Luke!" Richard shouts, and still there is no answer.

Richard runs, panicked, up the trail.

I JUST WANTED light, Anne thinks, walking among boulders, calling Maggie's name into the relentless silence. She'd recently finished a series of small paintings, little jewels based on thirteenth-century altarpieces. They were strange, but when she'd started them, she knew they were strange, that no one was doing work quite like this, using these old forms, ancient techniques of gilding, then incising decorative patterns into the smooth surface of the gold leaf. Opacity was what she had intended, the opacity of metal, of those saturated blues and reds. She wanted the opacity of the materials to reflect what she thought of as the opacity of family life—the way these people in her life, closer to her than anyone could ever be, nonetheless remained on some fundamental level mysterious, never entirely known.

She'd loved everything about the project—from cutting the wooden panels to fitting the hinged diptych and triptych forms together using the old methods. She'd loved spreading on layer after layer of gesso, then sanding it down with ever-finer grades of sandpaper. And finally, laying down the images.

Opacity seemed the only possible artistic response to Maggie's absolute difference, to the fact that down to the strands of DNA in her cells, she was so slightly and yet profoundly different from Anne, or Richard, or even Luke. Anne had appropriated the elongated forms of Russian Christs, the swan shapes of medieval martyrs, the iconographic importance of position and size in order to paint the ordinary mysteries of family life—the tantrums and everyday disasters, those moments of goofy, unexpected joy when someone said something unintentionally funny.

She'd liked the way that iconographic emphasis on size had allowed her to represent the different ways her two children demanded, needed so much in such different ways. She'd gotten worried, though, when the image of Luke had come to her as a martyr out of an old Russian icon. The painting wanted to be what it was, Luke in a rectangular center portrait, surrounded by smaller panels depicting all the times she'd had to tell him to wait, all the times she'd had to leave him to take care of Maggie. But she didn't want him to see it; didn't think it could possibly be good for a little boy to see that his mother had painted him like that. The guilt and uncertainty had stopped her for a couple of weeks. Finally, she'd moved out of her garage studio and found a place in town to work, so she didn't have to worry about Luke stumbling upon something he shouldn't see.

Her show had been a success—she'd gotten a small mention in *Art in America,* in the back section—but now that project felt like it was over for her. She felt as if she'd pushed solid colors and shiny surfaces as far as she could. For a few weeks, there had been nothing in that part of her head where the art lives, but then she'd begun to start thinking about big paintings, about catching that western transparency of space and light that had convinced her, mere weeks after arriving in Boulder for college, that she could never go back to the watery green of the Midwest.

Anne walks across this strange granite that rings like struck china and wonders if she didn't break some cosmic taboo by painting those panels. She wonders if she missed the real danger—not that her children would be wounded by seeing those paintings, but that by sending their images out there, by using them as material for her art, she's somehow tempted the evil spirits of the world, called attention to them. She comes to a boulder group, circles it, checks for Maggie in a small cavespace at its base. Two huge rocks, twelve or fourteen feet high, have come to rest against each other, several smaller stones rolled against them.

Eyeing the thick crack up the backside of the boulder group, Anne thinks bitterly that now maybe she understands why certain cultures refuse to name a child, refuse to praise the beauty of a child out of fear that the very act of cherishing will call down those dark forces that tear all that we love out of our grasp. This knowledge sits in her gut like a stone, nearly doubles her over. *I can't,* she thinks. *I've got to keep searching.* Looking at the crack again, Anne figures she can see from up there. It's been years since she has climbed—she and Richard gave it up long ago—but she used to be good. Reaching up with one arm, she feels the cool rock for a solid handhold, fingers recalling counterbalance, toes feeling out an edge to stand on. This is what she needs, something active and solid. Levering herself up, her arm moving slowly, smoothly for the next hold, wedging a foot sideways in the crack between the two rocks, she balances on that point where the boulders meet and she scans for Maggie—pink, white, a scrap of color—color that doesn't belong in this landscape, a flag signaling the location of her hiding child, her vanished girl.

Anne looks across the two lakes. Linked, they form the headwaters of a small creek that shines along the gulchbottom down to Wright's Lake, the campground, their tent, the car—backseat strewn with Maggie's toys, the pink feather boa she had insisted on wearing the afternoon they left home. It's Anne's fault for dragging them all up here. It's too late in the season—she'd had to call the ranger station to make sure the campground was even still open. Richard had been in the middle of a big project, at that awful stage where it seems like all you do is draw and redraw the building, stand on the site, trying to help the client visualize how great it will be. He hadn't really had the time, but they had managed to duck out of town anyway. She's done this; she's dragged her whole family up here just so she can see the light, and now look what's happened.

The lakes: still, blue, cold. After they went hoarse shouting Maggie's name into the wind, Anne and Richard looked to the lakes. First, they screamed for Maggie, running through the underbrush, circling out from the place Luke last saw her. They deliberately shut the lakes out, not thinking about that terrible possibility. But Maggie wasn't there. She wasn't in the bushes near the heli landing site; she wasn't responding. She just absolutely wasn't *there*. She and Richard looked at each other over Luke's head, trying to be calm, trying to be parental. They decided to take a shoreline each. Visibility was good. Each glimmer underwater, each Coke can clearly visible at fifteen feet triggered an adrenal jolt of recognition: *not* hair, *not* T-shirt, *not* limb. Climbing over talus, Anne couldn't believe that Maggie was in there. If Maggie had drowned, if Maggie was dead, Anne would *know*. Despite the clench of fear in her throat as she stared into that dead clear water, Anne was sure that although she wasn't answering, although she'd disappeared, her daughter was still alive.

Until Richard dove into the lake. It is as if that moment is forever frozen in Anne's visual memory—Richard's feet disappearing beneath the surface, splash breaking the silence, Luke yelling, "*Mom!*"

Anne sprinted. Jumping from unstable boulder to rock, she felt time slow down, felt the talus tilt, heard it clink with the hollow scraping sound of broken crockery, even as she watched Richard come up for air, shake the water from his eyes, flip over, hiking boots kicking once in the empty air before disappearing beneath the surface. She lost her sunglasses, heard them skitter and bounce down into the rocks. Everything was startlingly clear. Anne rounded the end of the lake, leapt off the last talus boulder, and ran across the polished granite of the lakeshore, arriving as Richard, gasping with cold, blowing like a whale, burst through the surface, water droplets glittering like ice, clutching aloft in one hand an old white hat, an old white hat that must have blown off someone's head and into the water, an old white hat he thought was the body of his child.

Richard swam toward shore, breathless from the icemelt lake, clutching the hat, convulsed with fright and relief, still haunted by what he thought was a leg underwater—bluish white, drowned. Anne pulled him out of the water, crouched to encompass the familiar shoulders of her husband, her Richard, the man she's loved since college, the only man she's loved. She rocked him like one of her children while he spat out, "I thought . . . I thought . . . " and she said, "I know . . . I know . . . " and Luke, who's almost nine and is embarrassed by this display of parental affection, stood over them and patted his dad on the shoulder, on the head, on whatever parts of his father's body were closest and said, "Dad, Dad, it's okay. Dad, look, it's just a hat."

And then they looked at Luke and laughed, laughed with the hysteria of people who are really frightened. And Richard reached up and pulled Luke into his arms and Luke squirmed and shouted, "Dad! You're all wet!" and they laughed some more, until they were all three lying in a pile on the shore, exhausted with relief and laughter. Richard shivered once, convulsively, in his wet clothes and the situation settled down on them like fog: Maggie is lost.

Anne, balancing one hip against the top of the boulder pile, looks out over this landscape she has sought, sees light streaming out of the late-afternoon sky, sees it blaze off the exposed granite shoulders of the basin, sees it set the surface of the lakes gleaming a steely silver, and hates herself for seeing forms and colors instead of Maggie.

She turns to climb down from the rock. Blindly lowering herself, foot groping for a hold, a place in the crack where she can wedge her toe, she remembers how she hates downclimbing—the terrifying blinkered aspects of it, never quite able to see where she is going, the frightening tug of gravity as she lowers herself down. This is dumb. That's all they need now, a lost child and a mother who's hurt herself playing rockclimber. From a solid foothold eight feet up, Anne turns and jumps, landing with a *whump* in the stone-hard dirt.

Dusting her hands on the leg of her shorts, Anne turns to look around her. The glare has intensified, and she longs for her lost sunglasses. She's got to stay in the present. She's got to keep looking. To her right, there's a clump of lodgepole—deadfall and three live trees. It looks like the sort of spot Maggie might like.

Maggie could have been sleeping all afternoon. The girl sleeps

13

harder than anyone Anne's ever known, and once she's out, nothing wakes her up. If she's been sleeping, Anne knows, she'll be waking up about now, blond hair stuck to her face, hungry, disoriented, frightened. Anne grows very quiet, listening deep inside herself for a signal that Maggie is out here, that Maggie is calling to her.

As she walks across the bare granite, she hears only the sound of small pebbles crunching beneath the soles of her hiking boots.

LUKE FOLLOWS his father down the trail. Richard is going too fast and Luke has to trot a few steps every so often to catch up with him. The steep trail twists between high shoulders of rock. As they come around the corner by the big rocks where they had a snack on the way up, Luke can see the lake, the campground below. There are people on the lake in boats. He hears a shout rise through the still, late-afternoon air.

They should have stayed at the lake. He and Maggie were making boats out of sticks, and pushing them offshore, and then seeing who could hit theirs the most times with rocks before it sank. Maggie threw a lot of rocks, but they missed; the little stick danced just out of her aim. So she went and got a really big rock, so big that she could hardly carry it, then staggered out on the little spit of land and heaved it into the water with a huge splash and a *thonk* on the bottom of the lake, and they both laughed because it was so funny and because she turned around and gave him that "So there" look. Then Luke went and got one, and it was a contest, who could find the biggest rock, carry it to the end of the spit, and chuck it into the water without dropping it on their toes.

Then Mom and Dad had said, "Come on, we're going to climb to the lakes and have lunch. It will be fun. It's pretty up there." Luke didn't want to go. He wanted to play by the lake. It was all their fault. If they hadn't gone on this stupid hike, he wouldn't have lost Maggie.

He looked for Maggie—really, he did. He followed the creek down a long tunnel of green bushes. He thought maybe she had followed the water. It was when he was edging around that deep pool that the movement startled him, caught his attention. Fish. There were fish in the pool; you could only see them when they moved, because they were the same color as the bottom. Luke crouched to watch. They were tiny, the size of his index finger, and brown. The fish were still; only their fins feathered back and forth to keep them in place. Luke wondered if they knew he was there. Did they think he was a predator? An eagle maybe, waiting to swoop down and pluck them flapping out of the water? He looked around for a rock. He only wanted to scare them a little, so they'd move.

He found a palm-size hunk of granite. It was almost black, and heavy. He leaned over the water. There was a flash of movement, then stillness. Luke was dazzled. The fish had darted for safety before the rock even hit the water. They'd looked like a star exploding. Then it was still again. Quiet. Nothing moved in the pool. Even the leaves had gone quiet.

That's when Luke remembered he was supposed to be looking for Maggie. He shouldn't have looked at the fish. He should have found Maggie.

Luke is nearly worn-out. It's a long way back down and his dad isn't stopping at all. On the way up, they stopped a lot, because Maggie was being a pain. First her shoes kept coming undone. Then she decided she needed to name everything. "Jay!" she shouted at every bird she saw. There is a hot place on the side of Luke's heel where a blister is starting. His father keeps

15

walking and his wet boots make a funny little whistling sound every time he takes a step. Luke wants to stop. He is tired, and they're going so fast, he's getting dizzy on the twisting trail. He knows they need to get to the phone, but his legs ache and his foot hurts and he wants to sit down. He wants a lemon drop and a drink of water. He wants his mother to lean against and look down at the lake and for her to wipe the sweaty hair off his forehead and tell him it is going to be all right. And his father just keeps going. He's getting farther away and Luke has to run to catch up.

Luke's dad turns around. "Come on, Luke. We need to keep going. We're almost there." Luke feels his chest fill with anger and tears and he glares at his father. Can't he see that Luke is tired and hot and his foot hurts?

Luke stumps downhill and the words fall in with his footsteps. My foot really hurts. My foot really hurts. My foot really hurts and Maggie is lost. Maggie is lost. Maggie is lost. My foot really hurts and Maggie is lost.

HIGH IN the talus field above the lake, Anne alternates between calling for Maggie and gazing into the holes between these boulders jumbled on the mountain's shoulder, then scans the area below her for a sign of movement, the flash of Maggie's bright hair or white T-shirt.

Anne had obsessed about this trip all week—planning the meals, getting the gear together, double-checking to see that everyone had their winter sleeping bags, warm clothes, that they didn't forget the stove. She'd been determined—*this* was the family she wanted: Maggie playing by the lake, Luke running to her with some exciting thing he'd found, a rock, a snail, an odd pinecone. She'd thought she had everything covered when she'd packed the car, picked up Richard from work early so they could beat the traffic, get up here in time to cook dinner in the campground, set up the tent.

And last night had been so perfect. She remembers thinking, See, it *was* worth the effort. In the long yellow light slanting out of the west, she and Maggie had walked along the sandy shore of the lake. Richard and Luke had gone off to the bog—they were into stalking these days, a leftover from Richard's childhood spent hunting with his dad. She'd smiled at the vision of tall Richard, skulking through the woods, towheaded Luke behind him, while Anne and Maggie had walked along the shore. The water had been gold with reflected light, and the cool air fragrant with pine. Quietly, with concentration, they'd floated black bits of twig on the surface tension of the water. Anne has always been fascinated by surface tension—by the way molecules cling together under improbably heavy loads.

Maggie's clumsiness meant they'd sunk a lot of twigs, but slowly she'd gotten the hang of it, placing pine needles on the water with Chaplinesque exaggeration, whispering to her mother as if the sound of her voice would break the water's hold. It was in those moments that Anne knew that if Maggie were to wake up tomorrow without Down syndrome, she would be a different child, not her Maggie at all. Anne's fierce pride is that Maggie is *not* a falling-off from some perfect child who might have been, but is, in fact, the only Maggie. Not a damaged Maggie, but the real Maggie.

She is adamant about this. Yes, Maggie is difficult, and yes, she has told the teachers, she disrupts the class and doesn't always understand, or want to understand, the rules of appropriate behavior. Yes, you have to tell her three, four, five times, but it's her right to be mainstreamed with other children and not shuffled off in some dead-end "special needs" class-room. Since the beginning, she and Richard have been deter-mined—it's not what Maggie can't do that is important; it's what she *can* do. And Anne is absolute in her belief that Mag-gie will do everything that other children do—ride a bike, swim, ski, go to school, take dance classes. Maggie is Maggie; she might be different and difficult, but, her mother insists, she is perfect.

Anne wishes she'd brought the binoculars. She's high enough that if anyone was moving down in that little cirque, she should be able to see them. Above her, she hears a pika squeak, and as she turns, she's startled by movement. Her heart sinks as she sees that it is only a marmot, gold fur shining on its belly, standing on hind legs to check her out. Anne closes her eyes and concentrates on the vision of Maggie safe, ankle-deep in water, crouched over her pine needle, a needle that floats in a fading circle of concen-tric rings, rings that disappear as they move away from their source.

RUNNING BACK up the trail, Richard rounds a switchback, nearly collides with Luke.

"Luke!"

"I'm *coming*," Luke answers, looking up at his father with gen-uine surprise.

"Didn't you hear me?" Richard nearly shouts, feeling himself go hard inside against his son.

"No."

Luke makes a circle in the dust with his toe.

Richard takes the boy by the shoulders, hard. He can feel the collarbones under his thumbs, flat wings of shoulder blade against his fingers.

"We have to *hurry*. Don't you understand? Your sister may be hurt. We have to get help."

Richard barely refrains from shaking him; his hands itch to shake those small bones. He shoves the boy into the trail in front of him and swats him once, not hard, on his rear. "Now move it!"

They continue down the trail. Luke sniffles quietly. Richard is all but dancing from the effort not to grab the child by the wrist and drag him down the trail. If he were smaller, Richard might, but this year he has grown; he's too big to carry. They move down the trail, far too slowly, although Luke is clearly limping along as fast as he is able.

Anne balked when he brought up hiking out. "We can find her," she insisted. "She's not lost." He hates it when she refuses to be rational—there were only the two of them—well, and Luke. They'd been searching for nearly three hours, and whether she was hurt or asleep or being naughty for some inscrutable Maggie reason, it was clear they couldn't find her by themselves. "There has to be a search and rescue team," he said, trying to keep calm, trying to make sense. "We need help." Then she wouldn't hike out with them, refused to leave without Maggie. Richard had to agree with her there—the idea of Maggie emerging from whatever hiding place she'd wedged herself into, thinking they'd left her, crying and no one to find her—of course Anne had to stay. He gave her the smaller pack, with water, with warm clothes for herself, and for Maggie. It would be cold by the time he got back. He was worried about Luke, too. What if it got late? They didn't have warm clothes for him.

He'd left them for only a minute. He'd stepped behind a clump of alder scrub to pee, and when he got back, they were gone. He'd been standing on the rock, annoyed with the kids, looking for them. They knew better than to go so far away;

19

they were supposed to stay in earshot. Luke knew that anyway, and he was pretty sure that Maggie knew by now that wandering off was a *very bad thing*. Richard had gone back uphill toward the heli pad, climbed the little swell behind it. "Luke!" he'd shouted. "Maggie! Come on! Lunch is ready!" They hadn't answered. He remembered being annoyed with them, wondering why couldn't they just be where they were supposed to be.

He'd looked around. There were big boulders up there, certainly big enough for a child to hide behind, and scattered clumps of hemlock, lodgepole pine. It was the granite, though, that you noticed first, blinding white, scraped bare by long-gone glaciers, crumbling in places where the feldspar was breaking down. It was this austerity they'd been seeking, the skeleton of the Sierra laid open across the spine of California. He and Anne had talked about it last night after the children were asleep. She'd been describing the new series of paintings she was planning—big open landscapes, abstract, transparent forms of color and light. He was glad she was moving toward abstraction; he, for one, wouldn't mind not showing up in her paintings anymore. He was thrilled for her recent success, and he'd never knowingly thwart her work, but he had to admit that seeing his family exposed like that, flattened into odd medieval forms, made him deeply uncomfortable. Sitting together listening to the water lap at the sandy beach, they'd gazed up toward the granite gleaming in the light of the nearly full moon. Listening to her, Richard had had one of those moments where he couldn't imagine living with anyone else, where he honestly couldn't imagine his life any differently from what it had become.

Luke trips and falls hard onto the palms of his hands.

Richard pulls him up, and Luke is crying in big gulping sobs.

"Shh," he says to the boy. Richard pulls Luke into his arms while perching on a rock.

"I'm okay," Luke objects, pulling back. It's another thing that's happened this year: Luke's started acting tough on them, squirming out of hugs, hanging out with the other third-grade jock boys. He shrugs to wipe his nose on the sleeve of his T-shirt and Richard sees his palms are skinned, have little bits of gravel embedded in them.

"Let me see," he says, catching Luke's hands in his. Luke sees the wounds and tears well up again. He stands there biting his lower lip to hide the quiver as Richard brushes the loose dirt off his son's hands, trying to see how bad the damage really is.

IT'S LATE when Anne, standing high on the shoulder of the cirque, watches the last violent streak of gold narrow against the western horizon. Stars begin to flicker in the purple night sky and a three-quarter moon douses the granite landscape with cold white light. It all looks like a charcoal drawing, she thinks. Like an illustration out of some gothic novel. She is still trying to search by this pale light, still calling Maggie's name into the chill silence.

Something rises up on the air. Voices? Anne strains to hear. Disoriented from having searched thousands of rockpiles and treeclumps and little flat sandy terraces between them, thousands of places where a small child could hide, or lie injured, Anne looks out over the valley, doesn't recognize the line of yellow lights bobbing up the trail. It looks like some articulated creature, she thinks, like those dragon dancers in Chinatown. Firecrackers. Maggie shrieking and clinging to her—throttling her, nearly—with her unpredictable terror.

As Anne watches them, she feels unbearable shame settling into her bones. They have come. She has not found her daughter. Maggie is truly lost and it will take all those strangers to find her. Anne has lost her child on an afternoon hike. It is dark and she has had to put on a sweater and a hat and her daughter is out there in a T-shirt and shorts. She watches the bobbing light creature moving toward her, hears voices floating across the still, cold air.

She knows she has to go down there, but she feels an odd urge to run, to hide up in the rocks with Maggie. Slowly, quietly she moves between the scattered hunks of granite, passes manzanita spreading like dark pools over the pale earth, walks through the armlike moonshadow of trees toward these people who move toward her up the trail, these people she hates needing.

Day One

For a moment after opening his eyes, Richard can't figure out why he's in someone else's sleeping bag. Sitting up, he bends forward to stretch out the sore muscles in his calves and back, then kicks his way out of the bag. He can hear Anne's shouts ringing through the morning quiet. His brain creaks into life like an old truck on a cold morning, stiff gears catching against the sputtering cough of the ignition. Last night. Headlamps. Shouts in the night. Temperatures dropping. No Maggie.

Startled by a static squawk, by the sound of a voice calling his name, Richard scrambles to locate the radio, finds it beside the day pack that has slumped over during the night.

"Yes? Yes?" Richard shouts into the radio, his voice panicky, like when one answers the phone out of a deep sleep, insisting, "No, no, I wasn't sleeping."

"Mr. Baker?"

"Richard," he says, rubbing the sleep out of his eyes, leaning against a waist-high bench of stone. "Please, call me Richard."

"How're you doing up there this morning?" It's Steve, the search team's leader. He's a wiry man, ten or fifteen years older than Richard. He has a calm, almost understated manner of directing the crowds of searchers, a quality that Richard found deeply reassuring last night.

"Fine," Richard replies, climbing onto the bench and looking for Anne. He can hear her calling to Maggie, but he can't see her. She must be over by the twin of Twin Lakes. The last thing he wants is for this search guy to realize he doesn't know where his wife is, where his children are, that he's a man whose life has spun entirely out of control.

"We've got a team on its way up," Steve continues. Walkie-talkie, Richard thinks, his brain still making those creaky leaps of early morning. That's what we would have called it as kids.

Gazing toward Anne's cries in the high end of the cirque, Richard listens absently as Steve tells him to check in before hiking out, reminds him about the stove and food they left him with last night.

"Get something to eat," Steve says, mothering him. "You'll need it—we could be in for a long day."

Richard stares into space, the radio at one ear, and nods assent before signing off. Behind him, he can hear Anne hurling Maggie's name into the new day, he can hear the hope and fear mingled in her tone, and he worries for her. He wants to protect her, even as he knows she hates that instinct in him. Maggie didn't learn her independence from the neighbors, he thinks.

Richard hardly dares to contemplate what might happen if Maggie is really gone, if they can't find her in time. In some profound way, Richard knows that Maggie is his wife's one true love. It doesn't bother him as much as he thinks it probably should; he's always held that everyone gets one big love in life, and that we have startlingly little control over choosing that love. Richard's is Anne, and has been since the night he first saw her across a smoky college beer party. It was the look of displacement about her, as if she'd gone to the party because she'd heard that was what one was supposed to do in college, hang out in old houses, drink beer, smoke pot. He'd watched her a long time before talking to her, watched the way her shiny hair swung back from her face, watched the way she stood on the periphery of conversations, smoking a cigarette and occasionally nodding at something that was said. Finally, she'd noticed him watching her, had smiled, a little quizzical look on her face, as if to ask, What?

Now, all these years later, he hears Anne's voice fruitlessly cajoling their child out from whatever place she has hidden, and he worries for her. Richard knows the lonely panic at the heart of that shouting, knows how he felt walking lines with the search teams last night, hurling Maggie's name into that rock-strewn and empty space. For the first time in his life, he was terrified by the indifference of the natural world, an absolute lack of response that emerged like fog out of the volume of night air and luminescent granite. As a climber, Richard was familiar with this implacability; indeed, it was what he'd loved about climbing—the rock was just the rock, no matter what funky head trips you brought to it. It was clear on the rock that it was *your* problem, whether you were scared, or pissed off, or having a great day, it was your baggage, and your responsibility to deal with it—to assess the risks you were willing to take, to be honest about your ability to take care of your partner, to place your own protection as well as you could, and then climb well enough so you'd never have to test it.

25

There was a self-sufficient thrill in it that largely came from the fact that whether you climbed well or peeled off, the rock remained unmoved. Totally indifferent.

But last night, it wasn't his life at stake; it was Maggie's. And she hadn't made any decisions about taking risk; *they* had. And clearly they'd fucked up somehow and the apathetic universe had managed to swallow their child. Richard's Catholic childhood welled up in him as he crossed the dark granite, shouting Maggie's name into the velvet darkness, and he found himself, despite all his better instincts, muttering Hail Marys while making deals with God, promising to go to Mass every week, if only that solid unresponsiveness might lift, if only the emptiness might be torn open to reveal his daughter, peaceful and safe, like a child in some Victorian illustration, watched over by a benign angel, all golden hair and protective wings.

Instead, he found himself deep in the night, up to his ankles in muck at the heart of a tangled willow thicket, calling Maggie's name. Like an Old Testament prophet, he heard his own voice crying in the wilderness, his voice cracking as he shouted her name over and over, his cries muffled by the deliquescing vegetation. Richard had never felt such terror as at that moment, when the absence of reply seemed to ring in the air like a bell, when his cries met only a silent wave of indifference, a wave that welled up out of the valley in an inky fog and submerged him in its darkness.

ANNE HAS climbed on a tall boulder overlooking the faded cross where the kids were playing helicopters. The place last seen, she thinks. That's what the search and rescue guys called it, "the PLS." She stands, all long legs and arms silhouetted against the sun, which has only just climbed over the high ridge behind her. She's looking for a sign, for something she couldn't see yesterday.

Anne knows that what we see is largely determined by what we are looking for in any given scene. It was the trick to learning to draw, learning to see not the *objects* in front of one, but the *shapes*. Learning to see negative space, to see absence as a series of curves and edges, to see transparency as presence. She knows that if she can only figure out the right way to *see* this landscape, to decipher the design of positive and negative space, she will find not the overall design of a picture, that falling-together of lines into a whole, but her daughter. Maggie, who has somehow become invisible but who must, who *is* still here somewhere. If only Anne can learn to see her.

She knows Richard is upset with her. They wanted her to hike out last night, to leave Maggie up here and go down to the base camp. She won't leave without Maggie. She is sure in her bones that she is the only one who can possibly see the crucial difference in form and curve and line that delineates her living child from the jumble of dead stone shapes that dominate this landscape. She'd never seen Richard look so bleak as after searching, and she knew she shouldn't have quarreled with the search teams. She could see how it upset him, her Richard, who had faith in getting along with people. But she couldn't believe they were quitting, even if, as they kept telling her, it was only for a few hours. Once the searchers had left, before they were even over the ridge, Richard fell into the dead sleep of the exhausted. She was too keyed up to sleep. Maybe if they'd let her search, but no—they'd made her sit, asked her one question after another, each more terrifying than the last. Did Maggie have any identifying scars? What was she wearing? What kind of underpants did she have on?

Anne rubs her hands over her eyes and tells herself that doesn't matter; what matters is finding Maggie. It's morning, and she knows that in the daylight everything will be different. She suspects that Maggie's on the move, wandering, then sleeping, then more lost. This is what she hopes, anyhow, because the alternative, that Maggie is hurt so badly that she's unable to call out, unconscious . . . Anne deliberately tells herself not to think about that; it won't help any to make up more terrifying scenarios than the one she's already facing.

Looking down off the flat-topped boulder, Anne decides that Maggie probably went along the trajectory that Luke insisted on yesterday afternoon. The search leader told her that small children tend to walk uphill, not down, and when she asked why, he said they didn't know, but it was what all the statistics showed. Statistics. Anne has spent a lifetime ignoring what the statistics tell her Maggie will and won't do—won't speak, won't grow, won't learn. She did, though; she speaks in sentences, simple ones, but they're sentences. She grew and learned to do all the ordinary landmarks of childhood: ride a bike, swim, ice-skate—wobbly and clumsy, but skating. She learned to read when they said she couldn't, learned her colors and shapes, although telling the time has been a persistent problem. Anne has always been convinced that if she follows her intuition, follows her belief in Maggie, they can defy those limiting statistics.

She surveys the light coming over the high ridge. Maggie should be waking up about now. She'll be coming out of wherever it is she's hiding. Anne can nearly see her: She looks confused. Hair sticks to her face and her pants are wet and cold because she still can't get through the night, especially in a strange place. She cries in confusion and frustration. Hungry, she's standing now, rising out of the rubble of talus, looking around in a panic. She seems so close that Anne can nearly feel Maggie in her arms, her weight, the long limbs wrapping around her shoulders and waist. The hot, teary face jammed into her neck.

She'll go up the far shore, cross over, and get up off the lake, where you can't see anything. She'll get up where she can see. Maggie will come out if she hears her mother's voice. Anne knows she can find her. The searchers are strangers, and Maggie's not good with strangers, but for Anne, for her mother, she'll come out. Anne jumps off the boulder, nearly runs across the bare rock, convinced that it isn't too late, that in the light of this new day she can find Maggie as she couldn't find her yesterday when her panic got between her and her ability, her mother sense, her convictions.

Her heart is nearly singing, so sure is she that she's figured out where Maggie has gone, so sure it is only a matter of minutes before her sleepy child calls out to her, emerges from the boulder fields groggy and hungry and glad to hear her mother's voice.

STEVE OUTLINES search quadrants on a topographical map that has been marked with concentric circles at half-mile intervals. The kid disappeared in the cirque, and there's a pretty good chance she's still up there. The area's nicely contained, a shallow hanging valley holding three little blue lakes. A low ridge delineates the end of the hanging valley, and from there the terrain drops in a series of terraces, mostly bare granite until it falls into forest just above Wright's Lake and the campground.

It's a good thing it's contained, Steve thinks while outlining and numbering in order of probability the major search areas, because it's complicated terrain. This exposed granite at the top of the Sierra is deceptive; it looks open and bare, but it's fissured and cracked, strewn with glacial debris, boulders, small hunks of broken granite. There's an old saying, The map is not the territory, and Steve knows that although the map tells him many things about the general contour and elevation of the area's largest and most obvious features, because the map cannot literally *be* the territory, because it does not have a one-to-one scale, an inch to an inch, a foot to a foot, a mile to a mile, because a map that is the territory would by definition be unworkable as a map, since you would have to be standing on or in it, the map necessarily contains gaps where cartographers decided that certain details of the landscape were insignificant. It is these gaps he's searching for—because these gaps are where people get lost.

Years ago, Steve had brought his own daughter up here, when she was about eight or nine. One of the first real backpacking trips they'd taken together. They'd hiked up to the lakes, then decided to head north to Gertrude and Tyler lakes, two small blue holes in the map. There were two routes. One went up and over the saddle that separates the two basins; the other option was to climb up and go around the end of the ridge. Steve and Jennie had decided to go around. It wasn't as much climbing, and it looked like there was some interesting route finding involved. Steve remembers boosting her up onto the ledge they were going to follow. She was so little then, those twiggy arms and legs, the pigtails. And so excited to be on a "real" backpacking trip, carrying her own pack and sleeping bag, some of the food. Steve hadn't been sure the ledge went all the way around—from the topo, it looked like there could have been a dead-end cliff—another one of those necessary cartographic omissions. Since he hadn't wanted to use up all Jennie's energy on a disappointment, he'd left her there on the ledge, making dams in the little creek that trickled out of a July snowfield, while he went to check it out. He'd had to walk nearly a mile down the small interior gully. Every few dozen feet, he'd turn around to check on her, and there she'd be, still playing by the creek. It had made him nervous to leave her, and he'd thought how strange it seemed, this landscape, so bare and open that he could watch his daughter even as he went farther and farther away from her. It had seemed so clear and harmless, but he'd known that could all change in a moment, that the vision of his daughter playing could vanish without a trace, and that he, too, could become one of those frantic, terrified parents.

He turns just as Jane climbs the bus steps. "I drove up as soon as I got off shift."

"Thanks," Steve says. Then, looking closer at his wife, he asks, "You okay?"

"Yeah."

"What?"

"Joey . . . early this morning."

"Oh no," Steve says. "I'm sorry."

"Well," she says, rubbing her eyes a little. "We've known most of this week that he probably wouldn't make it."

Steve pours coffee into a heavy white mug and hands it to her.

"Thanks." She wraps her hands around the warm ceramic. Jane's a nurse, pediatric oncology, and while Steve's relieved she could come up—he relies on her for secondary interviews, for keeping track of the first-aid supplies and training, and, most of all, for her calm good sense—he knows how hard it is on her when they lose one. Especially one like this; Joey had come in as a baby and fought off the cancer the first time, then gone into remission for nearly five years. He showed up again right before his ninth birthday. Jane came home in tears that day. He'd been so close to the magic five-year mark.

"You sure you want to be here?" he asks.

"Yeah," she says, swirling her coffee. "How's the search?"

LUKE WAKES up and has to pee. It is barely light inside the canvas tent, and he can see his breath outside the scratchy green

31

blankets. In the other cot, a lumpy form sleeps quietly, and for a moment he can't remember who it is.

Then it comes back. He lost Maggie, and they had to call the police, and they're up there looking for her.

Luke slides out of the bed, wiggles into his jacket, and creeps to the door of the tent. He doesn't want the ranger, the one who took care of him last night, to wake up. Her name is Susan, and he doesn't want to tell her that he has to go to the bathroom. He doesn't want her looking all concerned and asking him a bunch of questions. He wants to pee and to find his parents. He wants them to be at the campsite with Maggie. He wants it to be okay.

Outside the tent, it's warmer, and a thick lozenge of mist hangs over the lake. Luke runs down the path toward the outhouses, and as he pulls open the heavy steel door, he doesn't know what's worse, the outhouse smell or the freezing, dirty concrete floor.

Luke sits on the step outside the bathroom and looks around. He feels really dumb in his cowboy pajamas and his jacket. He decides to find his clothes. The campsite. His parents are probably there. They probably came back late in the night and didn't want to wake him up. They're probably in the tent, zipped up, and Maggie's asleep between them. Her face is dirty from wherever it was she was hiding, and her white-blond hair is sticking up in weird directions, and her mouth is open and she's snoring. Maggie snores really loud.

Walking through the campground, there are few people awake, and he's glad that none of them pay the slightest attention to him. He likes to look at other people's campsites. In some, the big RVs hum and rumble, their engines running to heat up their insides. Luke imagines gray-haired people sitting in their bathrobes drinking coffee, like they're at home in their kitchens, but they're not. That's what he thinks is so neat about RVs. His dad hates them, and they had to move tent sites once the night they got up here because a big one pulled in next to them. Luke's dad grumbled that he hadn't driven all the way up here to wake up in a pool of motor exhaust.

Luke walks softly toward the zipped-up tent. He doesn't want to wake them up, because they're probably tired after searching all night. He crouches by the door and slowly, so it doesn't make that loud zipper noise, edges the door open.

Luke stares at the sleeping bags, hollow carcasses stretched across foam pads. Rocking back on his heels, Luke gazes into the yellow nylon space. He's not a baby. He won't cry.

RICHARD THROWS a handful of coffee grounds into the pot and tops it off with a slug of cold water to settle them, then leaves it to sit while he finds Anne. He can't stand listening to her shout like that anymore, and they don't have much time before the search team arrives. He'd like a chance to talk to her, to figure out what they should do, how they should proceed.

He follows her voice uphill; she sounds like she's on the far side of the first lake. She was so rude to the searchers last night—he knows she's scared, but he hates it when she acts like that. She refused to leave. Three in the morning, every- one exhausted, Maggie still out there somewhere. The nearly full moon had set behind the ridge, taking what little light there was with it, and in this terrain, even with headlamps, it was impossible to search in the dark. Too many ledges where the granite breaks away, too many boulders and dark patches of manzanita brush. It was dangerous. Steve didn't want his searchers getting hurt, breaking an ankle or a leg falling into some crack that would have been clear in the daylight. They were all volunteers, and they'd gotten up that morning expecting a normal day at their jobs, then found themselves up here, after a full day of work, walking grid searches in the dark. They were tired, and God forbid it went on that long, but if it did, they'd need them the next couple of days. Steve explained they were just going to take a couple of hours, let everyone get some sleep so no one got hurt, did something stupid.

"What do you mean you're quitting?" she asked in her most imperious rich-girl voice, the one Richard hates. Everyone dead tired but Anne: Anne stalking back and forth across the flat patch where they'd set up the coffee; Anne refusing to leave; Anne being difficult.

Steve explained in that low, gentling voice of his that not finding Maggie was a better sign than it looked; it meant she probably wasn't hurt. Meant she was probably holed up someplace, scared, could even be asleep, for all they knew; that was why she wasn't answering.

"You *can't* quit," Anne repeated. "My *daughter's* out there."

Steve looked to Richard, as if Richard could do anything about Anne. He remembers staring back at him, stupid with exhaustion and fear, overcome with shame that he'd gotten them into this mess. That big searcher, Ed, turned and walked off, muttering something that Richard didn't want to hear.

"Anne," he said quietly. "Be reasonable."

She backed off, glared at him. But he was tired and she was being rude. These were the search and rescue guys; they did this all the time. Richard figured they should let them do their job.

High on the ridge between the upper and lower lakes, Richard turns, looks back down into the valley. A shaft of sun lights the lake mist. It hovers there, a luminous gray-gold disk, and Richard watches the colors change for a few minutes before turning to go after his wife.

"IT'S NOT going so great," Steve tells Jane. He's learned over the years not to press her when she loses a patient, to give her some space. She'll talk about it when she's ready. "We ran eight sweeps last night and no sign of her. I've got calls out for K9 teams and helis."

"How's Ed?" she asks. He's Steve's oldest friend, and even at the best of times, there's no way that you could say Ed isn't odd. The qualities that make him a great searcher aren't exactly traits that make for social ease. Ed's most at home outdoors, preferably close to the ground, and he's sensitive to birds and animals and trees in a way that makes living among people difficult. They get on his nerves, he says. They're so noisy and careless.

Ed and Steve met in college. They'd both chosen to major in geology because it would get them outside a lot, and they'd spent two summers in the Sierra backcountry, living out of packs while mapping the surface for evidence of long-gone three-dimensional features. "It was like mapping ghosts," Ed had told Jane once. "All those missing mountains worn down to a single outcrop, the unconformities—gaps of tens of thousands of years between two bands of stone. It made you wonder," he said. "What happened during those ten thousand years?"

Ed's young wife, Amy, had left him nearly three months ago, and he'd crashed at their house most nights since. She'd taken their five-year-old, and Jane figures he can't stand the empty house, would rather spend the night on the lumpy couch in their old rec room.

"He's hanging in," Steve says. "This victim's about Aaron's age, though, and you know how Ed can be about kid searches."

35

"He's been ranting about 'Yuppie idiots'?"

"Yeah," Steve says, leaning against the counter. "But he's still this one's best hope." Jane yawns. "Do you want to climb in the back and get some sleep?"

"In a little while," she says. "Can I do something? Interview the parents?"

"Can't do that."

"Why?"

"We couldn't get them off the PLS," Steve says. "The mom said she wouldn't leave the little girl up there."

"What did you do?"

"I left them a radio," he answers. "And told the father to check in this morning."

"What are they like, the parents?"

"Nice enough," he says, reaching for the coffeepot. "Youngish, educated, they've both had guide experience, seem pretty competent outdoors."

"Well," Jane says, sipping the hot coffee. "What *can* I do?"

Steve pauses for a moment. "You could go find the little boy."

"Little boy?"

Steve checks his notes. "His name's Luke. He's eight years old. He spent the night in the ranger tent. . . . "

"Is he still there?"

"I hope so," Steve answers as the radio transmitter squawks. "I told the ranger to keep an eye on him. Here're my notes. See what info you can get out of him—see what he remembers," Steve says, handing her a clipboard as she descends the bus steps.

Steve flips his notebook to the stats on Wright's Lake. Eighty percent of children lost here in the last ten years were found within twenty-four hours and in a two-mile radius of the place last seen. Sixty-five percent of kids lost here were found along the

36

creekbed between the campground and Twin Lakes. There have been only two fatalities in twenty years—one a drug-related suicide, and one a hunter who had a heart attack. Any missing child throws a search into emergency mode, but if the statistics hold, they should find her pretty quickly.

Steve picks up the radio and scans the map as he tells Margaret's team to fan out along the road, run big open sweeps into the forest. He's got teams spread out below the ridge that demarks the cirque. They did a pretty good job up in the basin last night—but he's running two secondary teams up there this morning. One team's starting on the ridgeline south of the PLS and moving downhill, and he's got four other teams stretched out in a sort of belt below, ready to start low and move uphill. Ed's up there floating among teams, getting the sense of the landscape that he seems to need. It always startles Steve, the way Ed can sense the life of a whole area, animals, plants. He learned long ago not to interfere with him, that Ed might look like he's aimlessly wandering around, might look like he's not doing anything, while inside that head of his he's drinking in the story of the landscape and the forces, wild and tame, that have been moving across its surface.

Looking out the window, Steve thinks of that Arizona kid again. Every searcher's got one who haunts him, and Steve's is that little girl in Arizona. It was one of his first searches; he wasn't more than twenty or twenty-one years old when a five-year-old girl disappeared out of the campground in Organ Pipe. They searched hard for a week and never found her. Seven years later, a camper found the bones—150 feet from the campsite. Despite using this story a hundred times in training, as an example of how important it is to get dogs into a search site early, how crucial scent evidence can be, it hasn't lost its power over Steve.

If they'd had dogs on that search, they probably wouldn't have lost her, not so close to camp, anyway.

ANNE KNOWS she's getting close. If she can just figure this out before they come back, before all those self-assured men start telling her what to do, start telling her they know more about Maggie than she does. Anne is Maggie's *mother*. She'll find her. If she can only keep them from getting in her way, she knows she can find Maggie. High in the back of the cirque, she's certain Maggie is holed up nearby.

With every call that goes unanswered, however, she gets a little more shrill, a little more frantic. She knows Maggie's up here; she saw her so clearly. Waking among the talus, cold and wet and hungry. Crying for Anne. It's the first time since Maggie disappeared that Anne's been able to picture her in this lost landscape. If she can just keep that vision in front of her, if she can just trust it, she can follow it.

Calm down, she tells herself. Think. Maggie has to be out here somewhere. It's morning now. She'll come out from wherever it is she's hiding. Anne crouches between two boulders, her hands over her eyes. She doesn't realize it, but she looks very like Luke did when Maggie ran off. Anne's convinced that if she can think hard enough, feel deeply enough, she will be able to sense Maggie's location. She feels her own ragged breath, sees the blackness inside her eyelids as she sinks, concentrates; slowly, quietly, she feels herself honing in . . . can nearly see Maggie sitting among boulders . . . if she can just get the image to clear . . . she can see boulders . . . sunlight. She tries to see the angle the sunlight is coming from. . . . Is Maggie in the high talus fields to the east? They're still in shadow this early. . . . Or is she below? Anne's working to focus in on the periphery of her vision of Maggie. . . .

She sees boulders ... no trees ... and sunlight. Maggie's not crying. ... she looks confused ... dazed. ... She's just woken up. ... There are marks on her cheek from sleeping. ...

"Anne!"

She jumps, heart racing. "Jesus! You scared me." She stands, barely containing her fury at Richard. If they'd leave her alone, she could *do* this. She knows she could find Maggie if they would only give her the chance.

"Are you okay?"

"I'm fine."

The rage in her voice belies her words. She knows she should explain, but she isn't going to. He ruined everything. She was nearly there; she nearly had her. It's all Richard's goddamn fault. Now Maggie has slipped once more through her fingers. She looks at her husband and knows she should do something, say something, but she doesn't want to.

"I made some coffee," he says very quietly.

She hates it when he's nice to her when she's angry. "Fine," she says, clipped, bitter. "Let's go have some coffee and discuss our lost retarded daughter." She hurls this sentence at him, then turns and stalks across the cold granite, back to the place where they woke up, the place where they last saw Maggie.

LUKE'S FOUND some clothes in the car. He feels better now that he's got jeans and a shirt and warm socks on, and he sits in the open hatchback and wonders where everyone went. He's hungry.

Stupid Maggie, he thinks, why couldn't she play by the rules? It's not like she doesn't know how to play hide-and-seek. She did this on purpose. He hops off the car to see if there's any food in the bear box. Just like that time she ran off in the airport. She's only trying to scare everyone and make a big scene. He goes over

39

it again in his head. He explained everything to her. You have to explain the rules every single time you play a game with Maggie.

"Okay, Maggie," he said. "Remember, I cover my eyes and count and you hide." Luke saw that she wasn't listening to him. "Maggie!" he snapped.

"Wha—"

"You have to listen to me. What are the rules?"

"Hide."

"Right. How far away?"

"Far!" she shouted, flinging her arms wide.

"No, Maggie, not far," Luke said very seriously. "Where?"

"Close," she said with that "if you insist" tone in her voice.

"Where?" Luke asked again, testing to see if she was going to be good or not.

"Hide!" She stamped her foot.

"How far?"

"There," she said, pointing at the willows. She was getting mad.

"Okay," he said. She grinned at him. "Now I'll count to twenty and then I'll come look for you."

He crouched and covered his eyes, started to count. Maggie bent down to make sure his eyes were really covered. She patted his hands and breathed her hot breath all over his face.

"Maggie!" he snapped. "Cut it out!"

Then she stood up. Luke remembers being surprised that he could feel the reverberations of her feet as she ran across the granite.

"Are you Luke?"

Luke jumps.

"Yeah," he answers. It's a lady.

"I'm Jane," she says. "Steve sent me. . . . You remember Steve?"

"The search guy."

"Have you had any breakfast?"

"I was just looking for some in here," he says. "There's gra-nola."

"Is there any milk?"

"I think so," Luke says. "In the cooler."

She goes to the cooler and smells the milk while Luke finds the cereal.

"It smells okay."

"Do you want some?"

"No," she says, and smiles at him. "Thank you. I already ate."

They sit at the picnic table and the lady watches him pour the cereal. Luke wants to ask where his parents are. He wants to ask if they found Maggie. But he doesn't want to sound scared, so he just waits, wondering what this lady wants, wondering if she's going to tell him what's going on.

RICHARD HOLDS his breath, counts to ten backward as he watches his wife storm away. He and Anne are not one of those couples who find screaming matches refreshing—they negotiate serious disagreements with circumspection and as many good manners as they can muster. She did this in the hospital, too, so sure she was the only one who knew what was right for Maggie, acting as if he weren't also Maggie's parent. He knows she understands Maggie in a way he doesn't, but that doesn't mean . . . Richard exhales suddenly. Stewing over old wounds isn't going to help any, he thinks, trailing Anne across the granite. I just wish I didn't want to kill her sometimes.

Once, he and Anne had been locked in some battle over Maggie—he can't remember which one, whether it was Anne's determination to mainstream Maggie, or if it was Maggie hitting the other kids at preschool—some instance of Anne going to war with the authorities, who claimed to know what was right for Maggie, while Anne was equally sure that she, as Maggie's mother, was the ultimate authority. Richard had asked his mom if she and his dad had fought much. Richard didn't remember them fighting, but now that he was a parent, he knew that what he remembered might not have been what was going on. Richard thought of his parents' marriage as a particularly good one, full of genuine love and affection. He'd tried to emulate them, tried to be polite and loving, tried his best to take care of Anne and his children. But he couldn't remember either of his parents ever being stubborn like Anne could be; he couldn't remember either of them refusing to discuss something, storming off in panicked anger.

"No," his mother had answered on her end of the phone. "Maybe it was because there was so much space," she'd mused, her voice going soft with nostalgia. "We'd each go off to some corner of the ranch and try to figure out a compromise. There was plenty of heavy work around to burn off all that energy." She'd laughed a little. "Thank God there's always plenty of weeds in a big garden. There were a couple of times I thought I'd run out of weeds before I got over being mad. Then we'd sit down after you kids were asleep and we were tired, and we'd figure out what we wanted to do." Thinking about it, Richard remembered long days setting fence—his father pounding posts with an energy he hadn't understood at the time.

He had never figured out how to put this knowledge to practical use in his own marriage, except to give Anne her head, let her run herself out, and wait for her to return to him, worn-out and ready to talk. Sometimes it took days. Meanwhile, he'd go trail running. His instinct was to go climbing—lose himself in the total concentration climbing requires, but he'd given it up when, shortly after Luke was born, one of his old college roommates, the most gifted climber he knew, inexplicably fell while leading an easy climb, a climb he shouldn't have had to think twice about. Craig's protection failed, and he went fifty feet to the deck. His wife was pregnant at the time with their first baby, and looking at Rosie at the funeral, it just didn't seem fun anymore. He misses it, though, misses the focus. So now he runs up in the coast hills near their house, and when Anne's in one of her quiet rages, he ups his miles, spending as much time as he can on those ridge tops in the wind, watching the red-tails ride thermals, spiraling high into the blue above the tawny hills, feeling the air rip raw and fast through his lungs, waiting for his anger and frustration to burn itself out through his legs.

We don't have days this time, he tells himself.

As Richard watches Anne's angry strides across the granite, he feels fear engulf him like black water. As a boy, he'd gone through the ice one winter, horsing around with his cousins on the pond at the far corner of the pasture. It was that fast—one minute he was running through the dry cold air, trying to tackle his blocky cousin Mike, and the next minute everything was black. Maggie's absence hits him sharp and cold like that oily pond water sucking the air out of his lungs, bubbles flying past his face toward the light, where Mike was reaching for him, and he knows, as he knew that frozen day when he was eight, that he'd better kick against this or he's going to drown.

"YOUR FOLKS are up top," Jane says, waving toward the high country.

"Did they find Maggie?" Luke asks, looking studiously into the bowl of cereal.

43

"Not yet."

Luke scoops another spoonful of granola. It crunches so loud inside his head, he can hardly hear. He sort of likes this. They haven't found Maggie. She's still out there.

"She's not answering when the searchers call," Jane says. "Not even answering when your folks call for her."

Luke chews faster. It's pretty loud, but he can still hear.

"Can you think of any reason your sister wouldn't answer when they called for her?"

Luke thinks for a minute, chewing. He knows better than to talk with his mouth full.

"She might have fallen asleep," he says, swallowing. He's been thinking about this. "Maggie falls asleep if you don't find her right away," he adds. "Usually you can hear her snoring—she likes the laundry hamper at home."

Jane writes something down on a clipboard and Luke eats his cereal. He's hungry; all he had for dinner last night were some SpaghettiOs before his dad left him with the ranger and went back up to search. They were gross.

"Your dad says you were gone for a while looking for her," Jane says, glancing at the notes on the clipboard. "He said they were starting to worry. Can you tell me where you went?"

"I followed the creek."

"How far?"

"Pretty far," Luke says. "I went through a big flat wet place. There were fish there." His voice goes a little dreamy.

"Then what?"

"Then it got narrow again, like a real creek."

"And you kept following it?"

"Yeah," Luke says, remembering how the creek fell away. It slipped into a rectangular slot, wide enough for Luke to climb into. It was wet at the top and sort of slimy with algae. There was a dead brown algae, and a bright green algae that waved in long, hairy strands. He lowered himself onto the ledge, careful not to slip, and braced against the sides. The rock was black and smooth to the touch, not like the rough white granite above. He inched toward the edge and, clinging to a big knob on the side, leaned over. The cliff dropped a long way. Luke thought it was at least as far as falling off the roof of the house. They climbed on the roof sometimes when his mom wasn't looking. Luke and his friends went out through his bedroom window, but he wouldn't let Maggie, because she wasn't careful and she'd fall.

At the bottom of the waterfall was a steep canyon, flat on the bottom and dense with manzanita bushes, the kind you couldn't walk through because they're so thick and springy. It was hot out there in the sunshine, and he half-expected to see Maggie sprawled in the manzanita bushes like the cartoon coyote after he goes off the cliff. Luke watched for a long time. It was hot and quiet, and it suddenly came to him that Maggie wasn't hiding, that he couldn't find Maggie, that she was gone.

Turning, Luke scrambled back onto flat ground and ran, ran as hard as he could, up the creekbed, ran for his parents.

"Luke?" Jane asks quietly. "What did you see?"

"Nothing," Luke says into his cereal bowl. "I didn't see anything."

"HERE," RICHARD says, handing her a tin cup full of boiled coffee. His voice is tight with restraint. "Sit down and drink this. We need to figure out what we're going to do next."

"What do you mean?" she asks icily. Part of her wants to make him mad, wants to hurt him, even though she knows this is childish.

"We need to hike down to the campground. We need to find Luke and make sure he's okay. We need to check in with Steve and see what's going on with the search," Richard says slowly, with deliberate calm.

"I'm not leaving without Maggie."

"We have to, Anne."

"Have to what?" Anne snaps. "Leave our daughter here like what? Like some goddamn lost mitten?" She slams the tin cup on the granite and coffee sloshes over the side. "I'm not going anywhere until I find Maggie."

"Jesus, Anne!" Richard says. He stands there, silent, for a very long moment. Anne sees his nails dig into his palms. "What the hell is wrong with you?" he says, his voice cracking. "Don't you get it? *We can't find her by ourselves.*"

Anne stares at him, her face impassive.

"*You're in their way.*"

ED STANDS high on the small ridge that overlooks the cirque. He watches two teams, twenty-five people each, file past on the trail below. He can see the parents standing at the PLS. She's a piece of work, that mother, Ed thinks. "You can't quit," she'd said, like she was the queen of the universe or something. "My daughter's out there." Parents, in Ed's book, are to be carefully managed, handed off to someone sensitive and kind, like Jane. Someone who can keep them out of his way, where they can't wreck things any more than they already have, so he doesn't lose it and give them a piece of his mind when he's tired and worn-out and they're bitching at him for not finding the kid they so unforgivably lost.

He shakes his head as if to shake them out of his consciousness. He can't waste time being annoyed with the parents. Not if he's

46

going to find this one. Ed squats on his heels, looks out over the cirque. He needs to get quiet, needs to pay attention to the site, needs to start hearing what it has to say to him.

Slowly, Ed descends to that place inside himself where he can read a landscape. It's like learning to read water, learning to see not a jumbled heap of foaming white, but features: currents and eddies, the hydraulic holes that will hold and spin a boat or a body, harmless standing waves. Landscapes, Ed tells his trainees, are much the same. Pay attention and you can begin to see how the different animals are moving: where a deer bedded for the night, the piles of cut grass mice use for nesting, how the shadow of a hawk overhead will freeze all movement on the ground.

Ed watches the landscape below him, a landscape now full of the busy movements of panicked human beings, and waits for the stories of the last day or so to begin to reveal themselves to him. If he can begin to piece together the traces of movement across this place, then he figures he can see where the animals' patterns go awry, where they're avoiding the intrusive presence of a little girl. It's these disturbances he's hoping to track, disturbances this lost child has left behind her like a wake.

"I NEARLY HAD her," Anne shouts, her eyes filling with tears. "I could *see* her, up in the talus. I just couldn't find the spot yet. . . . "

"Oh, Anne," Richard says. His hands hang by his sides. "We're not going to find her that way." They stand looking at each other for a long moment. A jay squawks and lands on the rock near them, cocks his head, looking to see if they've dropped anything edible.

Anne looks across the granite. It rolls out in front of her, drops into the valley below.

"We're running out of time, Anne."

"I can't leave her."

"We're not *leaving*," Richard answers. "We're going down to the campground. We're getting out of the way of the people who are here to help. For all we know," he adds, trying to keep the bitter tone out of his voice, "she's wandered down there by herself."

Richard moves toward her slowly, then takes her coffee cup and tosses the cold remains into the bushes. "Let's clean up here and start down, okay?"

Anne doesn't answer. She senses movement above them, on the low ridge. "Look," she says, pointing to the line of people trooping into the cirque. "It's too late."

She can feel Richard's puzzled look and knows he doesn't understand. To him, those people look like help, like Maggie's saviors. Anne, however, is convinced all those people and searchers and strangers are the ones preventing her from piercing this veil of rock, from finding Maggie behind whatever curtain has separated them.

Anne blinks hard as she reaches for her day pack and mechanically begins stuffing it with the debris her family has left behind. She knows Richard is wrong, knows she should fight this, fight all steps that lead to giving up on Maggie. But she's frozen somehow, and she'll go down to the campground; she'll leave Maggie up here despite all her most deeply felt instincts . . . because she has to, because there are too many of them. She won't believe, though—she can't concede that the dogs, the helicopters, the search teams can succeed where she has failed. If she can't find Maggie, then how are these strangers going to find her complicated, stubborn, utterly different child?

From the bottom of the pack, she fishes up the apple she was

48

cutting yesterday when Luke came running, panicked, to tell her that Maggie was gone. Half-wrapped in the greasy plastic that came off the cheese, it's gone all brown. Anne flings the pieces suddenly, frantically, into a nearby bush.

Jonathan strides across the search area. *Finally,* he thinks, trying not to bounce with excitement, a live search. He called his boss and got a couple of days off, then drove up, flying through the bright moonlight, telling himself to slow down, to be careful. They'd warned him in training that the biggest danger to searcher safety is traveling to and from a search. No search is so important, they'd said, that you should cause a wreck getting there. It's why he'd taken this job, because his boss had been a volunteer fireman when he was younger, said he'd do his best to let Jonathan off for searches. He was so excited he hardly slept in the back of his truck, was one of the first people to sign in at six when the search resumed. Pay attention, he tells himself as he zigzags across the landscape. This is it, the real thing, a real search, not practice where Steve's hidden the clues. He's wound as tight as a kid outside on a summer night playing one of those deadly neighborhood games of kick the can. "Search is an emergency," they'd told him in training. Especially when it's a little one like this.

Jonathan checks every rockpile, manzanita bush, tree clump as they pass it. This must have been a bitch last night. He thinks of darkness pooling in the bowl of this high alpine cirque, cloaking boulders, talus fields, fissures in the granite. They're searching the area right below the PLS, the terrain that was too steep, too broken to search in the dark.

Where is she? The question echoes in the thin mountain sunshine. He's seen the pictures—they passed them around this morning at the briefing—she's a cute little girl, mugging for the camera, running down the driveway in big fluorescent sunglasses and an old pink feather boa. She reminds him of his youngest sister, who was always goofing off, trying to make them laugh. You could hardly tell from the pictures that she's Down syndrome— she looks pretty normal.

Jonathan checks to his right, his left, making sure he's keeping even with the search. It's a big group, and the area is so complicated, steep, and boulder-strewn that they can't exactly hike it, but, rather, must scramble over boulder groups, dropping into the small terraces between them. Jonathan nods to the searchers on either side of him and hops down into a small sandy flat spot. He signed up for search and rescue because he wanted the chance to do something good, the chance to help someone. His buddy Rob went off to be an EMT, but Jonathan couldn't stomach all that blood. Rob used to show him the gruesome photos in the training manual, gray bones sticking through the bloody flesh. Gave Jonathan the creeps.

Having checked beneath the manzanita shrubs in the little clearing, Jonathan continues downhill, following the closest thing

51

to a straight line that he can find. He waves that he's ready to move forward, jumps down into the next little terrace, and as he lands, something gives beneath his foot.

It's a small white shoe.

He reacts as if it's alive. Jonathan dances around the shoe, trying to get off it, afraid.

"Hey!" he yells. "Hey—I found something! Come here!"

Jonathan remembers about scent, K9 teams, the possibility that he's ruined the clue. He freezes, stands still, the shoe at his feet. He's afraid to move, can't believe this—he found something!

"Hey!" he shouts again, waving his arms at the other searchers. "Look! A shoe!"

"WHAT DO you mean there aren't any dog teams in Sacramento?" Steve says into the phone. He looks at his watch as Kevin from the Office of Emergency Services tells him that half the teams have gone to Peru for that big earthquake last week, and the others are up in Humboldt on another search. It's 9:00 A.M. He's got to get dogs in here before it gets too hot. . . .

"What about the Monterey teams?" he asks. It'll take them at least six hours to drive up from Monterey. When that granite heats up, it sends scent straight up into the air, where the dogs can't find it. He should have called them out last night, but so often little kids will pop up when it gets light and answer the searchers.

"Well, call around," he says, impatient. "We've got a retarded girl up here, six years old, and she's already spent one night out. There's got to be somebody left in Sac." He listens as Kevin explains that there're a couple of green teams in Sacramento, and he'll call down to Yosemite and see who's down there.

"Call Nevada," Steve says. "There're some good teams I've

worked with out of Carson City, and they're close. Look, get teams from the Rockies, for all I care. I need dogs, and I need them as soon as I can get them."

He hangs up, and there're five people waiting to talk to him. Terry says the TV crews are on their way up and asks where Steve wants to put them. The county sheriff wants to consult about closing the campground and tell him that he's got deputies interviewing everyone who's been camped here for the past three nights. So far, they haven't had reports of a "suspicious car seen leaving the scene," but they will—there's always a suspicious car that needs to be tracked down. Maryellen's sent word from the sign-in tent that she needs relief and they need to come up with a game plan for the onslaught of untrained volunteers who'll show up as soon as this hits the TV. They can't turn them away; since search and rescue is run entirely by volunteers, they like to use the opportunity to recruit new people, but then again, they can't just let people run amok across the site. Two of the hasty teams are back from Rockbound Pass and need to debrief before being reassigned. Steve starts with Terry and works his way through, one thing at a time, and just hopes that Kevin will scare up some dog teams and get them up here ASAP. Ed's a good tracker, but as much as Steve wants him to, he just doesn't have a dog's nose. And the way this one seems to be hiding, he thinks dogs are probably their best shot at finding her.

RICHARD HADN'T counted on the searchers not knowing who they were. Hiking back to the campground, they were stopped again and again by search-team leaders. Each time they were asked if they'd seen a little girl, Richard saw Anne wince and retreat a little deeper inside herself. Again and again, he explained that they were Maggie's parents, and he watched the searchers' eyes go flat, watched that "managing the victims" look come over their faces as each one apologized, then said not to worry, they'd find her.

"You okay?" he asks Anne after the fifth search team stops them.

"I'm fine," she replies. *Fine* is never a good adjective in Anne's vocabulary.

"They're just trying to help," Richard says, realizing even as he says it that this comment isn't going to help matters any.

Anne doesn't reply, just keeps hiking, doggedly watching the trail in front of her feet.

When they reach the trailhead, even Richard is surprised by the number of people milling around, and he realizes that he doesn't have any idea where Steve is, where to find the center of this swirling mass of people and police cars and horses unloading from trailers and the healthy, vigorous-looking people carrying packs and ropes. He and Anne look at each other, and he can see how appalled she is. Richard knows there are few things Anne hates more than a scene, and this is very much a scene.

"Hey," he says, approaching the nearest person, a gray-haired man who looks to be ten or fifteen years older than Richard. "We need to find Steve. . . . "

The man takes an evaluative look at Richard, then at Anne, who hangs behind a little, who is looking at the chaos with panic and fear in her face. "Incident Command is set up near the information kiosk at the entrance to the campground. You want to go down this road." He points through the crowd of search personnel. "Keep going straight—it's about a ten-minute walk."

"Thanks," Richard says, grateful that he hasn't had to explain once more who they are, what they have done. Turning back to Anne, he sees that she's close to tears. "It's this way," he says very gently as he takes her by the hand. He knows the last thing Anne wants is to cry in public, so he leads her through the worst of the crowds before asking quietly, under his breath, if she's okay.

Anne nods her head silently, struggling to maintain her composure.

JONATHAN STANDS stock-still, afraid to move, afraid he'll destroy the one clue that will lead them to the little girl. Dennis, the team leader, hops down through the boulder field. "I stepped on it." Jonathan's pulse pounds in his ears. "I didn't mean to—I was looking for the line."

"Back out this way," Dennis says. He pulls the radio out of its chest harness. "There don't seem to be any prints back here." While Jonathan gingerly backs away from the shoe, he hears Dennis calling on the radio for Ed. Jonathan's face flames. Everyone is looking at him, the bonehead who stepped on the clue.

Dennis pulls a roll of surveyor's tape out of his pack, then tears off long strips and hands them to two of the other team members. "Start flagging the area—watch for footprints." Jonathan stands, watching them pace off—they're about ten yards away from the shoe, and they tie the bright flags of surveyor's tape to the ends of bushes, to the scrubby manzanita. Downhill, Jonathan sees that older searcher, the one with gray hair, using rocks to anchor the fluttering tape across a bare patch of granite. Michelle, Jonathan thinks. Her name is Michelle.

"That's to keep people out of the area, so they don't contaminate the scent," Dennis says when he sees Jonathan watching. "Now we wait for the K9 team."

"How long will that be?" Jonathan asks.

"Don't know," he says, pulling a Polaroid camera out of his pack. He begins shooting pictures of the shoe. At one point, he gets down really close, shoots a photo of the shoe's sole. Jonathan remembers from the training lectures that it's important to know what the sole pattern is, so you can be sure you're tracking the right person. He's still standing there, wondering if he should do something. Everyone else seems to have a job, to be doing something useful.

Dennis hands Jonathan the Polaroids as they emerge from the camera, and he's glad to have some purpose, even if it's just to hold the pictures. Jonathan watches the shoe emerge from the gray-green murk. He always tries to guess what's going to emerge first in a Polaroid, and he's nearly always wrong. He waits as the shapes emerge, distinguishing themselves one from the other. He thought it'd be the white shoe, but it's not; it's the red manzanita twig in the upper-left-hand corner—Jonathan watches it change from an outline to a solid shape, then to a fully formed image of the manzanita twig, then shoe, then pebbly background.

Ed suddenly appears, jumping down into the gravel area. Jonathan hands him the photos, hoping no one will tell Ed he's the one who stepped on the shoe. Jonathan's a little afraid of Ed: All through training, Ed stood in the corner of the classroom, arms folded, while Steve gave the lectures. Once, when they practiced knots and bandages and stuff, he complimented Jonathan on the way he secured a "victim" to the backboard. Jonathan said he'd done a lot of that stuff when he was in the Scouts. Ed had nodded but didn't say anything.

Ed is on the radio, talking to Steve at the base camp, when he holds his hand out for the Polaroids. Jonathan hears him describing them to Steve. The group of searchers has gathered around, waiting to hear what they'll do next.

"What the fuck?" he hears Ed say into the radio. "What do you mean all the dogs have gone to Peru?"

LUKE'S SHOUTING, "*Mom, Mom,*" as he runs across the gravel parking lot and jumps into her arms. Anne's not prepared, and the lanky nearly nine-year-old almost knocks her over. He is heavy. She staggers. Limbs twined around her, he throttles her, head jammed in the curve of her neck.

"Hey, Spider," she says, surprising herself. She hasn't called him that in years. She crouches so his feet touch the ground. "You're getting too big for me." She knows he doesn't want to get down, and while part of her longs to hang on to him, revels in his weight, she's exhausted, and afraid she'll fall, even as she gently untangles his arms from behind her head.

"Hey, buddy," Richard says, hand on his shoulder. Luke hangs his head, trying to hide his tears. Anne pulls him into her, cradles the head he buries in her side. He's getting so tall, she thinks, relieved to have Luke back in her arms.

"Scary?" she asks, and Luke nods yes without lifting his face from where he's buried it. "It's okay," she whispers, rubbing circles between his shoulder blades. "We're here now." For all the good that's going to do, she thinks, still stunned by the search scene they've just walked through. She had no idea there would be so many people. She's horrified by what they've wrought.

"There's news," Steve calls from the bus door.

Richard and Anne exchange a look over Luke's head and Anne tries to untangle herself enough to get to the bus.

"What?" she says climbing into the bus, Luke hanging off her hand. "Have they found her? Where is she?"

"No, no," Steve says, waving them into a seat. "But we've found a shoe," he says.

A shoe? Anne slides into the seat and Luke leans into her side.

He's crowding her, but she stifles the urge to scooch him over. Just a shoe? There's a map on the table, covered with a sheet of plastic, marked thickly with red and black grease-pencil lines, arrows, circles radiating out from the spot where they last saw Maggie. The tangle of red and black marks, like a nest of snakes found underneath a porch plank, alarms and frightens Anne, indicates nothing but danger and death to her. She struggles to maintain her composure, to appear interested, calm, appropriate.

"Denny's team found it," Steve says. "Right here, just below the ridge, just below the sections we searched last night. We've had a little trouble scaring up K9 support, but there're a couple of teams driving over from near Reno—with any luck, we'll be able to run a scent track out." Steve traces a green line on the map transparency with his finger. Anne stretches to see, but Luke's got her pinned in place.

"Let Mommy see," she says, quietly disentangling him.

Luke flops back into the bench, sulking. Anne tries to concentrate on Steve's map. A shoe. Maggie's shoe. Maggie is out there. She can make nice with Luke later.

"Why is it way down there?" Anne asks. That's not right. Anne was sure Maggie was up high, in the talus field. "You said kids went uphill."

"We're not sure," Steve answers after a moment's hesitation. "We'll have a better idea once we get the K9 teams up there. What we've done this morning is set a perimeter." He traces the thickest black line with his finger. "That is, we've calculated the probability of detection area by area, then taken natural barriers like this ridgeline"—now he traces the thread of brown lines that marks the ridge that separates this basin from the Lake Aloha basin—"into account. We've sent teams out to check the entire perimeter, looking for any sign that she might have crossed it. The theory is . . . " he continues.

Anne's trying to follow him, but she's getting claustrophobic in the bus; all the air is rushing out of the long, narrow space. She struggles to listen.

" . . that we'll search from the perimeter in. That way, if she's spooked, if she's running away from the searchers, we'll flush her back up into the cirque where it's contained, and open, rather than chasing her down into all these trees."

She fights to breathe as this man describes hunting her daughter like a woodcock. She's got to get out of the bus. Luke's leaning all his weight on her, pinning her to the window. She nudges him, then shoves him a little as she scrambles to get out into the aisle, to stand up. The tin walls.

"I . . ."

They are looking at her. That concerned look she hates.

"I need air," she says.

Steve and Richard start to say, "Are you—"

"You can explain it to me later," she says as she backs out of the narrow aluminum tube that is the bus.

"Mom?" Luke shouts. "Wait!"

"MOTHER?" RICHARD says into the phone. "Well, no . . . It's Maggie. . . . " Richard rests his head on the wall next to the pay phone.

"I only left the trail for a second—you know, I had to take a leak, and she's . . . We can't find her. . . . Yeah, all night . . . Yesterday afternoon . . . The search and rescue team is here. . . ."

Eyes closed, Richard rests his forehead against the faux logs of the cabin and listens to his mother's voice on the phone. The reality of Maggie's absence begins to sink in. She's gone. He may have permanently lost his retarded daughter on a day hike. He was not raised to make this sort of mistake. He has spent much of his adult life in sports that require him to judge and accept risk—backcountry skiing, kayaking, backpacking—he's counted from high peaks as thunderheads boil across the summer sky, gauging how far off the lightning is; he's perched on rocks above difficult rapids, checking out the crucial move, deciding whether it's really runnable, or if it should be put off for another day; he's climbed all day in winter mountains, only to dig a snow pit, decide the avalanche danger's too high, turn, and hike back out. He's never fucked up like this before. Head against wood, Richard listens gratefully as his mother asks which airport should she fly into.

"Reno probably . . . we're just off Highway Fifty, past Strawberry. . . . Wright's Lake—it's on the maps. They gave me a phone number you can call when you know. . . . " He gives her the number. She says she'll be there as quickly as she can. "Thanks, Mom. . . . Okay, I'll tell her. . . . Thanks again. . . . Bye."

Richard hangs up the phone and remains for a long moment with his head resting against the wall of the ranger station.

"Sandy get that Xerox going again?" Steve asks Jane as she mounts the bus steps. He's marking the hasty perimeter searches on the map transparency. All three teams reported that it was a solid perimeter, no sign of tracks or any crossing. Of course, on that high ridge to Aloha, it would be nearly impossible to tell if anyone had been up there, but with talus that steep, unless they hear otherwise, they'll just have to assume she hasn't gone over the top.

"Yeah, it was just the electrical connection," Jane answers, and pours herself another cup of coffee. "A fuse blew in the cabin."

Steve stares out the window.

"What?"

"I don't know," he says. "There's something funny with this mother."

"How do you mean?" Jane asks.

"Maybe she's just flighty," he says. "She got all strange on us when I was debriefing them." Steve's examining the map again. Where is this girl? It's got to be here, the hole in the lines, the missing piece of topography, the thing he's not seeing. "Ran out of the bus in a panic. And then last night, when I was interviewing her . . . she kept staring off into the dark."

"Come on," Jane says. "You know how weird people get when they're scared."

"Yeah," Steve says. "She was a tough interview, though."

Jane crosses to the table, checks out the "To do" list. Steve had gotten so frustrated with Anne's silences that he'd finally come straight out and asked her what she thought had happened that afternoon. Sometimes, the direct approach can be the most effective. Put away the prepared lists of questions and simply ask.

"I don't have the foggiest idea," she'd answered. "We were on a day hike. We've been on hundreds of day hikes with the kids. When they were babies, we took them out in backpacks. It was like every other hike, except . . . " Her voice had cracked as she looked out into the night, toward the sound of people shouting her daughter's name.

Steve could envision them, two good-looking people making the effort to get outside. Making the best of the little one's handicap, not letting it stop them. Trying to give her every opportunity, always putting a positive light on it. Better than in the old days, he thinks. When they never let them out of the house.

"There was another thing," he says, turning to Jane. She looks up from the list she's making. "When we got to the site, she wasn't there."

61

"What do you mean she wasn't there?"

"She wasn't there," he repeats. "We were on the site five, ten minutes maybe before she stepped out of the darkness. It was so strange." He looks out the window into the calm sunshine filtering through the pines, illuminating the ordinary chaos of volunteers, sheriff's deputies, and police cars that marks any search scene. "When she did appear, everyone froze. She just stood there blinking in the light." He looks out the window into the deceptive sunshine. "Finally, the husband walked across, took her in his arms . . . like he wanted to shield her. . . . " His voice trails off.

"She's probably shy," Jane says. "It's hard, all those people staring at you."

"Yeah," Steve says, glancing down at his clipboard. He needs to call the Civil Air Patrol again about the helicopters. "Maybe."

JESUS, ED thinks as he slips the black radio back into the holster on his belt. His best clue's just been walked all over, and now there aren't any dog teams. What's Sally Mansfield doing in Peru, for Chrissakes? She's got the best team in the West, keeps winding up on TV during things like that Oklahoma bombing. Ed told Steve they should call K9 teams out last night. Retarded kid—I mean, you just don't know what they're going to do. Retarded kids and the Alzeheimer's folks, you can't predict them very well, and they're hard to track. And now this new searcher spacing out and stepping all over the only sign of her they've had . . .

Ed takes a breath to calm himself. He hears Dennis talking to the crew. "We're in for a wait people," he says as a general groan goes up from the group. It's the first day; they're pumped; they want to keep going. "We're having trouble getting dog teams up here. Looks like we've got a training team out of Sac and two teams coming up from Reno—we're looking at a couple of hours at least. So try to stay out of the immediate area; we don't want to muck up the scent lines any more than we already have."

As the searchers break up into groups of two and three, slip off to find someplace to get a little sleep, Ed waves Michelle over. "What'd you find?" he asks.

"Not much," Michelle says. "Good news is, there's no sign that she's bleeding. Bad news is, there's not much sign." Ed scrambles behind Michelle to a spot about fifteen feet downhill. The shoe lies as they found it, tipped on its side, empty.

"Look here," Michelle says. "See these broken pussytoes? Now, if she's going this direction," she continues, following the trajectory between the shoe and the clump of plants, "I'd expect to find more sign in here." Ed notices that the new guy is trailing along behind them. Won't hurt him to learn a little tracking, Ed thinks.

"I mean, see these asters?" she asks, pointing to a low clump of late summer purple. "If she came this way, we should see something here. These are real dry and brittle this time of year." Michelle sits back on her heels and looks uphill.

Ed looks at his watch. Nearly nineteen hours. He runs some quick calculations—water's the biggest variable. Since she doesn't seem to have hurt herself, or at least isn't bleeding, they have to hope she'll find water. Dehydration and hunger are her biggest enemies—if she hasn't eaten, when the temperature drops at night, she won't have any calories to fight off hypothermia. Ed leaves Jonathan with Michelle; he's glad to see him asking Michelle to explain what she's seeing. Tracking's mostly learning to see, Ed thinks as he heads back up toward the shoe, turns to scan the area. It'd be good for him to learn to see a little better; then maybe he won't walk on the clues next time.

LUKE LEANS into Anne as they cross the campground to the shower building. He hasn't let her get more than two feet away from his own hot little flesh since she returned to the campground, and she fights the urge to shake him off. It's been nearly twenty hours since Maggie disappeared, and Anne feels each moment ticking away, intimate and inescapable as her pulse.

At the shower house, she turns to hand Luke his towel. He makes no move to take it, so she drapes it around him, "Go on, Luke—the boys' side is around the corner." He doesn't move, just stands there looking at his toes with the big beach towel draped over him. She can't do this right now. "Go on," she says, and turns to the women's door.

She hears him sniffle behind her. "Luke," she says more sharply than she should. "What?"

He stands, rooted, staring at his toes and sniffling back the tears.

I don't have time for this, Anne thinks. I need to get a shower. I need to get back to finding Maggie. She watches her son's shoulders shake and knows she should take him in her arms. She should be the mom. Slowly, she counts to ten, stifling the urge to shake him until his ears rattle. "Do you want to wait for your dad, then?" she asks with deliberate calm in her voice.

Luke shakes his head, tears dripping into the dust.

"Come here," she says quietly, sinking onto the bench, her anger exhausted, along with everything else. Luke butts his head into the crook of her shoulder and sobs, shuddering and gasping for air while she wraps him in his towel. "Hey, sweetie," she says, rocking him a little bit. He's been so independent lately, she's a little surprised by his tears, and she hates herself for being the ogre mother with him.

"What's all this?" Anne snugs her firstborn in her arms, takes a big hit off his limbs, the sheer comfort of his body. She doesn't mean to be awful to him, her bright and shining boy. How amazed she'd been, those first years when it was just the two of them, astonished that this funny creature had come from her body, stunned by how much she loved him. She hadn't known it was possible to love anyone like that. He'd toddle across the honey-colored boards of their living room and look up at her with that blazing love face, and she'd nearly die with the joy of it. She lets him cry for a few minutes, feels him start to calm down, then, patting his back, pulls him away from her.

"How about this?" she says, wiping his face with a corner of the towel. He's a very grungy bunny, and his tears have left long, clean streaks where they've rolled across his cheeks, down his chin. "I'll go in and make sure there aren't any other ladies in there, and you can have the shower next to mine. Would that make you feel better?"

He nods, looking at his feet, big enough to think that maybe he shouldn't be crying. "It's okay," she whispers, his temple against her cheek. "We're all scared." She wraps him a little tighter in his towel, steers him onto the bench. "Stay here for a minute, while I go check out the bathroom, okay?" He nods, and huddled there on the bench, wrapped in his beach towel, he looks suddenly tiny, and lost. They think of him as so grown-up, the capable one; she forgets that he's just a little boy. "I'll only be a second." He nods, shaking with those hiccups kids get when they're trying to stop crying.

Walking into the women's shower, Anne's nearly in tears herself. This is so fucked up, she thinks as she calls into the shower stalls.

Suddenly, a wave of panic and nausea nearly sinks her. She gasps, then stands for a long moment, her head resting against the cool metal of the shower stall.

Maggie isn't gone, she tells herself, repeating it over and over, choking back the panic that rises in her throat. Maggie isn't gone.

"WHAT DO you see?" Michelle asks Jonathan. They are crouched in the spot where Ed left them.

Jonathan looks around the area. The same rocks, low vegetation, and more rocks that they've been looking at all morning. "Nothing that looks like a sign," he says to her.

"Forget looking for signs," she tells him. "Just tell me what you see."

"Where do you want me to start?"

"Anywhere," Michelle answers.

This wasn't really what Jonathan had in mind. He was hoping for more specific instruction.

"Tracking's all about learning to see," she says quietly. "So just tell me what you're seeing."

"A lot of bare granite," Jonathan says slowly, "and loose rock. . . . There're those biggish rocks, the ones that will twist your ankle if you're not looking, and then there's some smaller, pebbly stuff, gravel."

"Good," she says, encouraging him. "What else?"

"A bunch of different plants. I don't know the names of all of them," Jonathan says apologetically. "There's pussytoes, like these." He points to the crushed plant they'd been examining. "And some little asters, and a few penstemon left—but not very many; it's kind of late in the season. Then there's bigger plants—those manzanita over there. . . . "

"So now," she says. "What kinds of things would you look for if you were tracking?"

"Anything that looked disturbed," Jonathan says. "A plant that's been mashed, or a scuff in the gravel . . ."

66

"Right," Michelle says. "Now, we know she's only got one shoe on, right?"

"Mmhmm," Jonathan says.

"So how's that likely to affect the sort of terrain she seeks out?"

"She won't want to walk on sharp stuff," Jonathan says. He's starting to get this.

"Good," Michelle says. "We've got some time here, so let's divide up the terrain. Say there's an imaginary line between here and"—she holds one arm out in front of her, sights down her forearm—"and that little drainage notch down there. See the one I mean?"

"Yeah," Jonathan says.

"You take the left side of that line, and I'll take the right. Starting here, I want you to go over the area as slowly as you can, and see what you can find. Stay low to the ground; try to see the terrain from her angle of vision." She looks at her watch. "Let's say an hour. . . . Meet back here and tell me what you've found."

Jonathan nods, excited. This is fun—it's like being a kid again and getting to play outside. Then he remembers they're looking for the little girl. He should be serious. He watches Michelle, who doesn't move. She's still sitting on her haunches, looking at the area she's going to search. Jonathan watches her, then does the same with his space. He looks over every inch of it, slowly, as though he is trying to memorize this particular configuration of rocks and manzanita and wildflowers.

STEVE WALKS through the milling crowds of people toward the parking lot to meet the K9 trainee out of Sacramento. Glancing at his watch, he figures he'll have to let the trainee go in despite the fact that his dog's never been out on a search without a more experienced dog to follow. The Reno teams called twenty

67

minutes ago to say they were on their way, and he can't afford the three hours it'll take them to get to the site. You have to expect these kind of problems when all your crews are volunteers, though. Couple of years ago, there was a big search up north, and Steve's best dog team was tied up because George is a trial lawyer and was in the middle of a big case. You've just got to try to go with the things you can't control, and sometimes getting the teams you want is a factor you can't control.

Besides, they're all cross-trained to run on both track and air scents, so it'd be hard for this one dog to wreck it for the others. As long as this breeze holds up, he thinks, the dogs should be able to follow whatever scent's coming off her. Tracking guy explained it to him once: A victim will give off a plume of little scent particles that travel through the air, ride the currents. It's a sight Steve's never quite gotten used to, watching a dog run those big zee sweeps, then pick up that invisible line of scent, and take off. Some of them go off like a shot—straight through brush, over ledges, trainers running behind, awkward and noisy. If he wasn't already so busy as the incident commander, he'd take up training a dog, but there just isn't the time or consistency in either of their lives right now. He figures he can debrief the tracker and get him up to the site in about an hour, hour and a half. That'll be nearly twenty-four hours from the time this kid ran off. He wishes he could heli them up; it'd save nearly forty minutes, but the Civil Air Patrol can't get him helis until later. They'll have to hike in. It should be okay; the dog is still fresh, and he should be able to fly in the Reno teams when they get here.

That conversation with Jane is stuck in the back of his head, and he reminds himself to ask her about Down's kids and heart surgery. Scars. That was it—he'd been asking the mother about scars. She'd stared at him, face blank. It's always a tough moment, and he'd waited until he saw the despair crossing her face, until he saw it dawn on her that they might have to identify her daughter by her scars. Then he'd repeated the question.

It was the hand gesture, though. For some reason, it had startled him. She'd run a hand between her breasts then across her diaphragm line to demonstrate Maggie's scars. Heart surgery, she'd said. When Maggie was nearly two. She'd said it was pretty common for Downs kids, one of the side effects of the chromosomal abnormality, but that it wasn't a problem anymore, that they'd fixed it. It's one of the reasons Down's children live longer than they used to, she'd said.

As he enters the parking lot, three more vehicles drive in, kicking up a cloud of dust behind them. Well, he thinks as he looks for the K9 team. She's very beautiful; maybe I'm not as old as I think I am.

Then the thought is lost in the chaos of filling the dog trainer in on the progress of the search effort. He's got a nice little bitch, a red heeler who sits quietly, drinks the water her trainer puts out for her. She might be a trainee, but it turns out this guy—Jon Scanlon's his name—has been training dogs for some fifteen years. Steve remembers him; he used to have a shepherd. It's unusual for a trainer to switch breeds, but Steve doesn't have time to ask him about it. The runner Ed sent down with the sole-print photos finds Steve and hands them over, and Steve tells him to lead Scanlon and the dogs back up to the site. Maybe now, he thinks, watching them disappear into the pines. Maybe now we can find this kid.

SITTING AT the picnic table with his pad of paper and colored pencils, Luke thinks how much he hates this. He hates Maggie being lost and his mother running off and his being so scared that he does stupid things like cries about having to go into the boys' shower all alone. That was dumb. He hates the public showers, though; it's cold and horrible. Someone you don't know could come in, and the water taps are too high on the wall. Then some guy came into the campsite and said Steve wanted to see his mom, and she just ran off.

Luke is drawing a map of the ranch. All the other times something's gone wrong, like when Maggie was in the hospital, either his grandmother came to stay with them or he was sent to the ranch. He likes Gramma. She wears blue jeans and drives a truck and makes pies—real pies, not like the gummy ones you buy at the store.

If he was at the ranch, he'd be drawing at the kitchen table, waiting for her to take him out to the barn. They'd take two horses out of the stalls and lead them outside into the sun and the wind, then tie them to the board fence. They'd take Diesel, who is old and slow and nice and is the horse Luke rides, and Gramma's horse, whose name is Spy and who has socks on his feet. Spy is not so old, and too much for Luke. They'd currycomb them and brush them and pick their hooves, and then they'd saddle the horses, and Gramma would make him hold the bit and stick his thumb in the corner of Diesel's mouth so he'd open it and they could get the bridle on. Then Luke would climb the fence to mount, and he'd kick Diesel and turn his head with the reins and he and Gramma would walk the horses out of the yard and down the gravel road along the hay field. It would be hot and still and the blackbirds would be calling from the tall cat-tails along the irrigation ditches, and it would smell like dust and hot sunshiny horse and leather. They'd walk down the gravel road in the sunshine and Diesel would take big swiping bites of the tall grass that grows along the roadside and would chew with loud tearing noises that went with the creaking saddle noise and he and Gramma wouldn't really talk; they'd just ride together down the hot road.

Stupid Maggie, he thinks, looking at the drawing. It's a stupid drawing and it doesn't even look like the ranch at all. Stomping out of the campground, Luke runs down the beach. He hates Maggie for getting lost and ruining everything. She's so stupid, he thinks as his heels dig into the soft sand. Why couldn't he have a normal sister like everyone else?

RICHARD SURVEYS the campsite. Clothes spill out of the hatchback of the Subaru; there is a scattering of colored pencils on the picnic table and Luke's tablet of paper has blown up against the trunk of a Jeff pine. He hates untidiness. He starts folding clothes where they spill from stuff sacks, Anne's T-shirts, Luke's grungy pajamas. Quickly, he piles them into the big duffel bag, zips it up. The car's still a mess, but at least it's contained, and he should find Luke. Picking the tablet off the ground, he shakes the dirt and pine needles out of its pages, then anchors it on the picnic table with a grapefruit-sized hunk of granite and goes looking for his son.

Richard strides out onto the spit of rock, scans the shore in both directions. This spit was the reason the kids wanted this campsite, because they had their own private pier. "Just like at Granny's," Luke said. Richard was surprised that Luke had remembered that visit. Three years ago. They'd gone out in the summer to visit Anne's mother and stepfather at their summer place in northern Michigan. Luke was afraid of the lake weeds, would only leave the pier reluctantly and in the arms of one of his parents. It had been an awful visit, in the usual way visits to Anne's family were awful. Her mother was one of those cheerful, vague alcoholic women

71

you see at country clubs, and her friends were much the same. They either made too much of Maggie or seemed afraid to touch her, as if Down's were contagious.

Richard looks up and down the lake, but there's no sign of Luke. He couldn't have gone far, Richard thinks. He's not Maggie, he tells himself, suppressing the small wave of panic that rises within him. But then, Richard thinks, the only time the boy's been lost this trip is when I left him behind. He squirms at the memory of Luke, crying, limping down the trail to where Richard stood describing his "lost" child Maggie. It was terrible. Richard had completely forgotten Luke, had gotten in the truck with the ranger and driven off in search of a phone to call for help. Luke had followed them, desolate and weeping, his foot bleeding from the blister he'd gotten hiking out. Richard and the ranger had patched together Luke's foot, and eventually he'd stopped crying. That was when the ranger had suggested leaving Luke with her for the night, so he wouldn't have to worry about him. The whole thing was so awful and embarrassing. Richard hasn't even told Anne about it yet, although he knows he'll have to eventually.

Walking along the shore, Richard sees Luke's prints, deep welts in the sand heading east, toward the point of land that blocks their view of the swampy bog where they'd seen the steers. See, he thinks, this is Luke; he left prints. He's not lost; he went for a walk, that's all.

Richard follows the footprints across the sand and tells himself that Maggie, too, will be found, that this is terrifying but that it will be okay. This is a manageable situation, not something like his father's heart attack, so quick and final that it was over before anyone could do anything. This is more like that awful moment just before Craig was killed—for a long moment, his belay had held—long enough for them to start laughing a little with relief, for him to say, "That was close." Before the cam popped and he dropped like a stone onto the rock ledge at the base of the cliff. He'd lived through the fall, lived three or four days in the hospital. Maggie's being lost feels a little like that situation—all these places where Craig could have been saved, if only he hadn't relaxed when the cam held, if only he'd gotten back on the rock, placed another piece for good measure, hadn't taken that moment. If only they'd been able to get him down faster, to the hospital sooner. There were a lot of *if onlys*—and Richard tells himself that this time, they'll use one of them. They'll get to her while there's still a chance.

"DID YOU find her?" she asks, breathless from running across the campground. "What is it? What—" She looks from Steve to the woman standing behind him. Anne hasn't seen her before. She's got short dark hair and wears jeans and a T-shirt, running shoes.

"No," the woman says. "Sorry."

"It's the shoe," Steve says. He waves a small pack of Polaroids. "We need you to identify the shoe."

"The shoe?" Anne looks at them.

"Can I get you anything?" the woman says again. "Coffee?"

"No," Anne says puzzled. "Thank you."

"This is Jane," Steve says, handing her the photos. "My wife." Anne flips through the photos. Maggie's shoe from above. Maggie's shoe from the side. Maggie's shoe.

"Take your time," Steve says. "Be sure it's Maggie's shoe and not someone else's."

"It's Maggie's," she says. She traces the shoe in the photo with her index finger. Maggie's shoe. Maggie's foot. Maggie.

"Are you sure?" Steve asks. "Sometimes things look like what we want them to be."

"This isn't what I *want* it to be," Anne says, surprised at the fury in her voice. "What I *want* is my daughter back. This," she says, pointing to the picture, "is Maggie's shoe. It's not Maggie." She looks at the photo again; the shoe is on its side. Like any ordinary time Maggie kicked off her shoe, impatient, confined. But it's in this unimaginable place, and Maggie is not with it.

Steve gently takes the photos from her and hands them to Jane. "Take these to Mary," Steve says quietly.

"Sole pattern?" Jane asks.

"Yeah," Steve says. Anne sees them exchange a glance in her direction. "We'll need it for the two o'clock debriefing."

Anne watches the photos go. She wants them. She doesn't want Jane to take them away from her. Those photos mean Maggie is still out there somewhere. She hasn't disappeared altogether. She's really out there.

RICHARD AND his mother hadn't talked about the heart attack much at the time. There had seemed so little to say. His father was there, and then he was gone. But one night, right after Maggie was born, he and his mother had stayed up late into the night talking. "I know there's nothing I could have done," she said. "But he shouldn't have had to go all alone."

Dad had been out checking irrigation lines when it hit, but he'd managed to get to the truck and call the house. Richard's mother came in from the garden and saw the message light blinking on the machine, heard her husband's voice calling for her. By the time she called 911 and got out to the far pasture, he was gone. He was still holding the car phone, and she did CPR on him for an hour and a half until the paramedics got there.

Richard can envision his tough little mother, bouncing on the heels of her hands, counting one and two and three and four and five, blowing two breaths to inflate that barrel chest while the red-winged blackbirds trilled in the cattails beside the ditch.

She was so angry with herself. All through the wake and the funeral, when people tried to comfort her, she shook them off, kept repeating that she should have done *something*. Everyone told her it wasn't her fault—how could it have been? But she didn't hear them, stood stony and dry-eyed through the services. Richard wasn't sure she'd ever quite forgiven herself for missing that phone call. He hadn't understood any of it until Maggie was born, when he found himself wondering whether Maggie's extra chromosome wasn't somehow his, hadn't somehow stuck to her through an invisible working out of his own personal faults.

But this event—Maggie being lost—still seems rational. There are explanations, plans, things they can do. It's daylight now, and the K9 teams will be here soon. It's not that large an area, he thinks, looking up toward the high country. There are pretty good natural barriers, and with more people, dogs, helicopters . . . He's seen search and rescue operations before, even went out on one years ago, the summer he worked up in Estes Park. It was a little girl that time. She wandered off from a trail ride, and they found her the next morning, only five hundred yards from the campfire circle. They'll find Maggie, too. She's out there somewhere.

Rounding the end of the point, he sees Luke down the shore, throwing rocks in the lake, and he shouts. He is surprised by the wave of relief that overcomes him at the sight of Luke, and he fights the urge to sprint down the beach, scoop his son into his arms, hold him tight, revel in his squirms, his shouts of "*Dad! Let go. . . .*"

W hy can't you put me on a search team?" Richard asks as he paces the length of the bus, stooping a little to accommodate the low ceiling. "I've done grid searches before—I won't be in the way." Richard can hear the echo of Luke's voice in his own, pleading for some forbidden treat, and he hates it.

"I know," Steve says, continuing to pore over the map. "But I explained to you why we don't allow parents on search teams— it's just not efficient and it upsets the search crews."

"But last night—"

"Last night, we thought she might respond to your voice," Steve says. The radio squawks. Richard freezes. Radio communication is nearly constant, different teams calling in from up top, reporting each time they finish a sweep, each time they begin to search a new area, but even so, each time the black box coughs to life, his heart crashes to a stop.

And then it starts up again as Steve nods, asks a question, makes more marks with grease pencil on the transparent plastic that covers the map. Richard studies the map. The map is the key, he thinks. Just as Anne insists she'll be able to sense Maggie, that she can find her on intuition alone, Richard is equally sure that the map will lead them to her. He's an architect; he trusts the ability of lines on paper to represent three-dimensional objects in space. Steve signs off the radio and turns back to Richard.

"We're running open grids up here," Steve says, pointing to the pale blue of the linked lakes in the high valley. "While trying not to get too many people down in this area." His finger traces the thin blue vein of the outlet creek. "We've got one team of dogs on their way up, and several more on their way in."

"But what if she's down in that lower section?" Richard asks. "Aren't we losing time?"

"If she's in there, the dogs will find her. And since they left the parking lot approximately"—Steve flips his left wrist, checks his watch—"seventeen minutes ago, we didn't lose much time by waiting on them." The radio screeches again and Steve picks it up. Richard catches his breath, unconsciously holding it until Steve begins marking another search pass that has not turned up Maggie.

Richard looks back at the map. She has to be there somewhere. It's just a matter of finding the right combination of lines and angles. Just like a blueprint, he thinks. Like when he's trying to figure out how to cantilever a house out over one of those California hillsides. If we can just get the angles right.

IT'S ABOUT fucking time, Ed thinks as the K9 team arrives. He looks at his watch, twenty-three hours since the child disappeared. The trail's getting cold and they've just been sitting on their asses up here for an hour and a half. Teams C and D have run three passes and come up with nothing. Ed's got them running two more, longitudinally this time, as high up into the talus fields as they can manage.

The trainer introduces himself. Scanlon. John Scanlon's his name. Ed's never heard of him. Nonetheless, he points out the PLS, the trajectory they presume she's traveling, as he explains that Down's victims tend to go in a straight line, that it's been twenty-three hours now and they're worried about dehydration. Scanlon nods, points out a couple of gullies on the topo map that he wants to check out. His dog slurps water out of a bowl Scanlon poured for him when they arrived, then plops on the warm granite, pants a little.

"There's the shoe." Ed points to the spot. "Did they give you a scent article?"

"Yeah," he answers, pulling a Ziploc bag out of his pack. It's the feather boa the kid had on in the photos. "You ready to get started?"

Ed nods. Ready. They've been doing nothing but being ready for most of the morning now. He still can't figure out why Steve didn't make the calls last night; they could have had dogs first thing instead of halfway through the day.

Scanlon holds the Ziploc bag open and the dog stuffs its nose inside, takes a good sniff. He points to the shoe, and putting its nose to the ground, the dog worries the area for a few minutes, then swings in semicircles from the spot where Jonathan

78

stepped on the shoe. Should be okay, Ed thinks. Looks like she plopped herself down, pulled it off. There should be plenty of scent. They've been careful to keep everyone out of the immediate area.

Seems like the whole group holds its breath as the dog works to pick up a track. Circling back and forth, its stubby tail moves like a metronome. Ed looks at his watch. Four minutes stretch into hours. The dog sits and whines. Scanlon holds the bag open for her again, encourages her. Where did Steve find this guy? Ed's wondering as the dog takes off, heads up and over the edge of the drop, weaving between boulder piles.

Jonathan and Michelle follow Ed and Scanlon, who follow the dog. They've got a scent trail. Ed knows better than to get his hopes up, but he can't help it. We've got her, he thinks. We're right behind her now. After all, how fast can a little retarded girl travel? Especially in this terrain? These are the moments he loves in searching, the moments when the pulse quickens and you can nearly see the trail, like a dotted line, leading to the victim. But for Ed, the most exquisite joy of searching is the moment just before you find the victim, that rush when you know you were right, that your hunches paid off, the close observation, the scrutiny of maps, the bright flags of the dogs tails. You found the lost child, the one with the Yuppie parents who, despite their fancy training, despite the high-tech fabrics of their jackets and tents, despite their plans and schedules and organization and smug self-satisfaction, couldn't even keep an eye on their small retarded child, the one who got lost, the one he's now about to find and return to them.

RICHARD WASN'T raised to make this kind of mistake, and he's as mortified as Anne is that all these people have had to come pull his ass out of the fire. He was raised to know things: to know you don't put a horse away wet; to know that you've got to watch irrigation systems or they'll blow a gasket, flood out your fields; to know that you watch the sky so weather doesn't surprise you; that you never leave a gate open behind you on a dirt county road; to know that with careful maintenance, machinery might last longer than the loan you took out to pay for it. His father would never have let something like this happen.

Turning a corner in the trail, he sees Anne sitting at the picnic table in their campsite. His heart's in his mouth at the sight of her. When he'd fallen in love with her all those years ago, it had taken him a long time to patch together the events of her childhood— the ugly divorce, the alcoholic mother, the father who'd taken her away, and the years and years of not knowing what was going on and being unable to ask anyone, because in Anne's family, the things one does not discuss are made clear without anyone ever mentioning them. He'd thought he could make it all up to her. He'd promised her as much when he'd gone down on one knee, and she'd just smiled, said he couldn't promise the future. He'd taken her home and offered her his family like a treasure, his parents—long-married, reliable, and kind—his tribe of older sisters, who doted on him because he'd been their baby, the eight years between him and Sherrie making Richard their toy. He'd held it all out to her like a promise: See, we can have this; we can be this, happy and settled and safe among kin. It took years for her to settle in, years for his sisters to learn she wasn't a snob, to learn that they scared her witless, that all the family happiness looked like danger to her, dangerous because it could be taken away. Somewhere in his heart, Richard held that teaching her to trust in happiness was his purpose, and he'd been pretty successful so far. They'd had scares, sure, bad ones—Maggie being born

80

Down's, or when she had heart surgery, but despite knowing that he'd made the sorts of foolish promises that only someone as young as he'd been when they'd gotten married could make, some part of him felt that protecting Anne was his true duty in life. And he is sick with failing her up there yesterday afternoon.

"Any news?" Anne asks, looking up from her sketch pad. He can see that the fight over hiking out has long since blown over, and that his wife's eyes are dark with fear and despair.

"Not yet," he answers. "The K9 teams are on their way— Steve said the dogs are our best hope, that they have real good luck with dog teams and children." Absently, Richard kneads Anne's shoulders from behind. She leans her head forward a little, stretching the tight muscles. "He says it's because kids are so low to the ground, they leave a lot of scent."

"Did he say when—"

"He said they'd send someone down here as soon as they know anything." He leans over her shoulder. "What are you drawing?"

"Nothing much," she says, moving an arm so he can see the sheet covered with abstract geometric designs. "Just scribbling, really."

He smooths the hair across the top of her head. "Where's Luke?"

"Down by the lake," she says. "Building something in the sand."

"I'll go check on him," Richard says. He squeezes her shoulders slightly as he turns away.

Richard finds Luke dragging a huge limb back toward the campsite. Richard had really thought they were okay for those few minutes yesterday afternoon. He'd looked over at Luke and Maggie playing, Anne a few feet away, tucking in a moment for a quick sketch, and he'd thought they'd made it. For a while now, it had seemed that Maggie was big enough, trustworthy enough that they didn't have to watch her every minute. He'd been thinking that they'd come through the worst of it, and that even though it wasn't the family he'd imagined, he was a happy man.

Then he'd climbed up the little embankment to get behind the alder scrub, out of view, staying far enough from the lakes so as not to foul the water, which he was certain wasn't safe to drink— he'd been worrying over how they were going to keep Maggie out of that water; they didn't need another bout of giardia like the one they'd gone through last year.

"Luke!" he'd hollered. "Keep an eye on your sister for a minute."

"Okay, Dad," Luke had called back, only half paying attention. He'd been stalking a lizard that had scuttled under a manzanita bush.

"Luke!" Richard had called, wanting his attention, wanting Luke to look at him so he could be sure he'd heard. "I'll be right up here, okay?"

"Yeah," Luke had replied, still watching the bush.

Richard had looked at his son for a moment, hesitating. It seemed they were always pulling Luke away from his own life, just to watch after Maggie. She'd been a few feet behind him, building a cairn of rocks. Richard had paused, then climbed up the granite swell. Luke was a responsible boy. He was only going to be a minute.

STEVE NEEDS to get those three cars out of the parking lot, but no one seems to know who they belong to. The helicopters are on the way, and they need the space for a landing pad. There are a couple of rangers out checking the campsites, but they could easily belong to backcountry hikers. He's got someone checking the wheel wells and undercarriages for spare keys, but if they can't find keys, he may have to let the guy with the big four-by-four drag them off. He claims he can do it without wrecking the transmissions or emergency brakes. Steve told him to find the sheriff's deputy, get the doors jimmied open, take them out of gear, and then he can go for it.

Steve heads back to the bus, worrying about the K9 teams. The Nevada teams haven't turned up yet, and he hasn't heard back from Emergency Services. He checks his watch. Three o'clock. Helis should be here by four. He needs to write up a media statement, and he reminds himself to send a runner down to warn the Bakers about the news people. And he should call his office, check that the roofers got on that Norton house this morning, and let them know this looks like it might take at least a day, maybe more.

Steve goes over the map in his head. The creek's the key. When children do go downhill, they usually follow water, and the stats for the area bear that out: All the kids who'd been lost here were found along the creekbed. Now if I could only get this real little girl to pay attention to the stats, he thinks as the searcher he left in charge of the heli pad/parking lot comes running up, says they found keys to two of the cars and should he *really* let the guy with the monster truck tow that last car away?

"WHAT'RE YOU building?" Luke's dad asks.

"Did they find Maggie?"

"No," his dad says. "Not yet."

"Oh." Luke looks at his fort.

"Can I see?"

"Later," Luke answers. His dad builds real buildings, and sometimes Luke doesn't like to show him stuff because he wants to add things, or change it, or make it something else. "It's not done."

83

"Oh," his dad says and stands there for a minute. "I'll be up there if you want any help."

"Okay," Luke says, breaking pieces off the big branch he hauled down the beach; it's still a little green, and he has to twist the twigs until they break off. He doesn't like the frayed way the twisted ends look, but he doesn't have a knife, so they'll have to do.

Luke concentrates on stacking the twigs, concentrates on the structural integrity of his fort. It has to be strong. It can't fall down. He doesn't want to think about the waterfall canyon, doesn't want to think about the clammy black walls, the electric green slime growing over the wet rock, worse even than the fake stuff that comes in the jar, because this isn't fake; it grows there. It's growing there now. He doesn't want to think about the way the water slides over the edge, not all at once in a beautiful white veil like waterfalls are supposed to, but slowly, dribbling over the edge, slick down the rock face into the tangled manzanita.

Mostly, though, he doesn't want to think that Maggie is somehow in that waterfall canyon, that Maggie somehow has that algae on her.

WEEKEND TRAFFIC is heavy and Jane has to wait before pulling onto Highway 50. It feels like one of the last fine weekends before winter; although warm, there's that unmistakable slant to the light, that sense that a cold wind is just around the corner, waiting to come rushing down before the winter coats are quite out of the closets, before the camphor smell has evacuated the sweaters.

Hopping out into the first break in the line of cars, Jane turns downhill, toward Placerville, headed for the store. There's a list of things people need, and since she's the person with the fewest official duties, or, actually, since she's the person whose official duty is to be available to run these sorts of errands, to pick up the slack where no one else really has the time, she's collected all their wants into the long, narrow list that lies on the seat beside her. Jane would love to take a more active role on the squad, but her schedule's too inflexible, so she comes up when she can, tries to make herself useful. Mary needs more of those little sticky notes and some staples. Steve wants extra sunscreen, a box of pens, and a bag of those little Snickers bars. It's close to Halloween, and every year, he gets addicted to mini-Snickers bars for several weeks. Penny's low on chili powder, and she thinks maybe an extra couple of boxes of oatmeal and some packets of that chopped-up dried fruit wouldn't hurt for tomorrow morning, and more fresh vegetables. They never want to buy vegetables too far in advance, since they can't store them if the search ends suddenly.

The funeral is Tuesday. Probably, this will be over by then—Steve seemed pretty confident about the K9 teams. She doesn't usually go to her patients' services, but she loved Joey. Jane lets her eyes well up. Sometimes you get kids like that, and Jane's never wanted to learn how not to love them. If anything's going to save them, she trusts, it's the power of being loved.

Coming around a corner, Jane's momentarily blinded by the afternoon sun shining straight up the road, cutting between the trees and into her swimmy eyes. She blinks quickly, jogs the steering wheel to correct herself. She forgets how tricky this road can be. She lowers the visor to correct the glare.

Joey and his stupid basketball quizzes, she thinks, blinking through tears. Making her learn all the players, one team at a time. He wouldn't let her take blood, wouldn't let her put in a new IV until she'd given him three centers and two forwards. "Trading," he called it. Steve had gotten in on the act, happy to have her join him on the couch all winter and spring, throwing out random names at the breakfast table, challenging her to name their teams, positions.

Twelve years old, Jane thinks, tears coursing down her cheeks. Late one night, when he couldn't sleep, he said he wished he'd gotten to kiss a girl. And his funny parents, who were so quick with a joke, quick to make fun of the ugliness of it all, turn it around by laughing at the blackness of the drugs and the puking and the baldness. She'll miss Jim and Sheila, too, knows better than to think she'll see them again.

The road curves and there's the turnoff into Placerville. Jane wipes her eyes. Well, she thinks as she pulls into the Safeway, now I've had my cry. Sitting in the parked car, Jane wipes her face, then checks the rearview mirror and carefully reapplies her lipstick before getting out of the car.

RICHARD BACKS out of the hatchback, stands up, stuffing a sleeping bag back into its sack. Luke still seems occupied down by the lakeshore; he'll leave him for a bit. Richard notices again that Hail Marys are running through the back of his mind—for all intents and purposes, he'd left the church years ago, about the time he discovered the mountains that had loomed like a backdrop from the back porch of the ranch his whole life. It was there, in the serpentine patterns of a mogul field, or the follow-the-dots pattern of a series of holds on a rock face that Richard had found the sort of meaning his mother found in the church. It was a kind of faith, a belief that if you were careful, took precautions, and paid very close attention, you could live at a higher pitch of awareness, you could get to that place where time slows down and you're fully in your body and absolutely focused on the experience of the moment. And it would shimmer afterward, shine in your memory as a perfect moment, a place where everything fit and was whole and *worked*. Of course, he couldn't really talk about it, just like his mother could never really explain her deep and true love of God. They had an understanding—they each respected the other's mode of approaching the big mystery, and they shared the quest like a secret between them.

Tucking the stuff sack in the car, Richard crosses to the bear box. "Think I should pack up the food?"

"What?" Anne looks up from her sketch pad. She's got that glassy-eyed look she gets when she's working.

"The food—should I pack it up?"

"I guess so."

They gaze at each other for a long moment before Anne slowly turns back to her pad. The ranger who took care of Luke last night said she could get them a cabin for the duration of the search. Packing the food into the cardboard box they brought it up in, Richard finds himself frozen, holding the blue box of pancake mix.

Breakfast. Yesterday. Maggie'd pitched a fit over the pancakes. Cheerios. She'd wanted Cheerios, wouldn't believe that there weren't any hidden somewhere. They'd opened all the boxes and coolers for her, showed her. "Look, Maggie—no Cheerios." She'd shaken her head, made that sad-clown face.

"Cheerios," she'd shouted, stamping a foot.

They'd put pancakes in front of her, but she'd clenched her jaw and put her face in her hands, big tears rolling down her face. They'd tried to joke her out of it; Maggie's sense of drama over these events always annoyed Richard. He had to remind himself that for her, it really was a tragedy.

But hell, if he'd known, he would have gotten her the goddamn Cheerios. They tried not to spoil her, not to overcompensate for her disabilities, but maybe they were too strict with her. Maybe if she hadn't been cranky, if she'd had a good breakfast, if all had been well, she wouldn't have run off, wouldn't have hidden from them. If they'd just brought some goddamn Cheerios, maybe Maggie would still be with them.

Richard pulls himself together and with shaking hands packs the stove. As he's carrying it to the car, he thinks, A cabin. We'll be in a cabin, and she's still out there somewhere.

He is suddenly angry. *Goddamn it, Maggie. Where the hell are you?*

THIS IS the third time they've followed this dog over the rock ledge and through the maze of boulders, manzanita, bare granite. Each time, she picks up the scent near the shoe, then runs it downhill for several hundred yards before losing it on a large curved shield of bare granite.

"We could cross over and try the other side," Scanlon suggests. "It's tough to hold a scent on this bare rock, particularly this time of day." He looks up toward the afternoon sky. Despite the fall colors starting to show, patches of scrub oak turning orange up on the high slopes, the day is warm, probably close to eighty, and Ed knows that heat burns off scent. It's the big problem with trying to search with dogs this late.

One more time, the trainer holds open the bag with the feather boa. Once more, the dog sniffs, then begins to crisscross the area. This dog's barely more than a puppy, Ed thinks as he radios to Steve to find out where the hell the other dog teams are. Steve calls back that they've just checked in by phone, says they've been stuck in traffic between Carson City and South Lake and they should be here in about an hour. The searchers watch as the little heeler works the edge of the terrace where they found the shoe. She goes uphill about twenty feet, then scrambles back down before taking off downhill, nose following invisible trails of scent. Ed checks his watch—nearly eight minutes, and they haven't picked anything up. You can't run them at a dead scent too long or they get discouraged, give up. It breaks them, especially these young ones. Scanlon whistles, and the dog runs to him. He holds the plastic bag open once more. She sticks her nose in it, then gets back to work.

Ed's trying to keep a lid on it, but the dog isn't the only one getting frustrated. This kid has to be out here somewhere. Ed wonders if they shouldn't try to get one of the parents back up here to call for her. Maybe she'd respond to her mom or dad. It's sort of a long shot, since all their experience shows that after the first night out, most victims, even adults, will get scared and hole up, won't answer searchers' calls. Their panic at being lost gets them in such a state that they fear everything, including rescuers. More than once, Ed's come across a conscious victim who didn't call out, even as they must have been able to hear the searchers coming. The isolation and fear freak them out.

With children, though, sometimes it's a little different. Like those two little girls last summer, the ones whose parents had taught them never, *never,* to talk to strangers. They were afraid of dogs, too, so for three days they hid, and kept moving. Those kids went nearly ten miles across country, and crossed a river. Ed knew they weren't in the area—he kept arguing they needed to widen out the search, but everyone said they'd never have gotten across the river. He just knew, though, that they weren't there. He could feel it the way you know a house is empty when you walk into it. But the river was high—it was a miracle really that they got across without drowning—and no one would take the chance that they'd gotten past it. Lucky for everyone a fisherman spotted them, caught them hiding, and managed to talk them out.

It kills Ed, these people who lose their children. And a retarded one no less. What were they thinking? Ed *never* let Aaron out of his sight. It isn't that he thinks taking kids out in the mountains is a bad idea—he and Amy had taken Aaron camping with them plenty of times. But they didn't let him wander around. When he'd been really little and they'd been doing a lot of horse packing, Amy worried that he'd get kicked. Not that they didn't trust the horses, but he was so little and so fast, and she was afraid he'd get behind one of them and startle it. So she found this big dog collar with jingle bells all over it and put it around his waist. A couple of times, they'd heard his little jingle bells trotting off into the woods, up the hill behind the campsite. They'd go after him, hollering and following the jingle-bell sound until Aaron would turn around and, running downhill too fast for his toddler legs, hurl himself into his father's arms. Ed would carry him downhill and he'd jingle around the campsite, and the horses could tell that he was coming up behind them.

Amy had said she was only taking Aaron down to see her folks in Florida; it was only supposed to be a three-week visit. She's been gone almost three months now, and when he calls, her parents almost always say she's "out." They usually let him talk to Aaron, but he can feel their presence, can feel the little boy hesitate before speaking.

Last night, he'd stood on the granite outcrop, listening as Richard shouted into the night for his missing daughter. They all stood silently in the dark, listening to the man plead with his daughter to answer him. The only sound was the steady breeze blowing through the night hemlocks. Standing on the exposed white rock, Ed again hears nothing but a noisy jay scolding them from a lodge-pole pine and the crashing noise of the rescuers following the dogs.

ANNE GAZES up into the open granite cirque. She's gone numb, feels guilty for not carrying on in the manner she thinks they expect her to. But that's never been the way she's met catastrophe. Anne's mother, a demonstrative person, once accused her only child of being cold, of having no feelings.

She'd sat up there last night on a granite boulder much like this one, struggling to give this stranger some clue to the unpredictable behavior of her absolutely different child, a child whose behavior often remains, even to her mother, utterly incomprehensible.

"Does Maggie know what she's supposed to do if she gets lost?" Steve had asked.

"We taught her to stand still and wait for us," Anne replied. Steve's list of questions struck Anne as weirdly endearing, as if by this litany of reason, they could find Maggie, who so rarely reacts to anything in a predictable manner.

"Has she ever been lost before?" he asked.

"Once," Anne answered. "In the Denver airport."

Anne could still feel it—Maggie's slippery wrist wriggling out of Anne's grasp; Maggie's blond flag of hair, gone.

"What happened?" Steve asked.

"She took off into a crowd," Anne said. "We were frantic. Security nearly shut the place down. About twenty minutes later, the Delta counter called—she'd tried to ride the conveyer belt with the baggage."

"Was she scared?"

"No," Anne said "She thought it was funny. They'd given her a lollipop and she was quite pleased with her little adventure."

Anne didn't tell Steve about the shock on Maggie's face when Anne yanked her off the counter and spanked her. All those people watching, as if Anne were Medusa herself, snake-haired angry mother. *Hitting the poor retarded child.* Sometimes, though, it was the only way to make sure Maggie knew she'd been bad.

"Could she be doing that now?" he asked.

"I don't think so," Anne said. "Maybe for a little while this afternoon, but she's afraid of the dark. We've been trying to teach her . . . " Anne paused, stared out into the night. She could nearly see Maggie in her white shirt and pink shorts, wedged up under some manzanita bush. A cold wind blew down out of the cirque and Anne shrugged the collar on her jacket up around her neck.

After a long silent moment, Steve said quietly, "You know, this happens to all sorts of people. . . . "

But we're not all sorts of people, Anne thought. She had stared into the dark, listening as Maggie's name moved slowly away from them down the mountainside. It dawned on Anne as they sat quietly beside each other on the rock that she liked him because he reminded her of her uncle—her mother's brother, the one who taught her to fish. Childless himself, he took Anne out summer weekends at the cabin up north, taught her to bait and remove fish from the hook without flinching, to scale and gut and fillet the catch, tossing the skeletons into the water. The shallows around his boathouse were eerie with the bleached skeletons of fish.

STEVE'S LISTS are filling up from the bottom as he crosses things off from the top. These lists, written on long, thin pads of paper that he buys specifically for this purpose, then slides in on top of the wad of maps and crew and information sheets on his clipboard, are, for Steve, the visible reminder of the race against time, the ticking clock against which any search must compete.

Scratching off the dive teams, he picks up the ringing telephone. It's the Monterey dog team. Should they pack up? Will he need them? Yes, he says. He's having trouble finding teams—everyone's out of town or working. How soon can they get here? Hanging up, he checks the list again. The dive teams are checking out the lakes; shouldn't take long—the water's so clear up there. Kid's parents said she hates cold water. They don't think she's in there, but you never know.

He checks his watch; it's been forty minutes since Ed checked in, and Steve wonders how that young dog is doing. In the bus last night, Ed went off about these parents, how could they be so dumb, how could they let a retarded kid wander off like that. "Goddamn Yuppies," he'd muttered. "Think they can just buy a lot of gear and . . . "

Steve let him run on for a while, before telling him to can it. These folks knew what they were doing—they'd been serious climbers, had both guided rafts on the Arkansas, were experienced backcountry hikers and skiers. They weren't idiots. They knew the outdoors. Like most people Steve and Ed are called out to help, they'd been caught in a series of bad luck moments, each of which contributed, like chemicals in a solution, to that moment of supersaturation when the mix either crystallizes out or goes explosive on you.

"I'm giving you the dad," Steve had said later that first night as he was dividing up those first search crews to run loose grids over the area. As he spoke, Steve had smoothed a transparent sheet of plastic across the map. There were concentric circles at one-half mile intervals printed on the transparency. He'd felt their raised edges as he pressed the thin film over the map; it looked like a target, with the PLS as its center.

"Parents don't belong on searches," Ed had replied.

"Well," Steve answered. "This one does." He'd looked straight at his friend. "He's competent, she might answer him, and he's going out with you. I need you to keep an eye on him—and Ed, try to be kind."

A moment passed.

"What section do you want me to take," Ed had asked, looking at the map.

"This north side of the creek . . . " Steve began, outlining the quadrant. They'd retreated into technical vocabulary, vectors, scent trails, clue awareness.

LUKE'S BUILDING a place he can put Maggie in so she can never get out, never wander away. She'll be safe in this fort, and he's trying to think of cool stuff to fill it with so she'll like being in there. He's building a jungle gym for her to climb on, and a set of swings. Maggie loves the swings. When she was still really little, before she knew how to pump, he'd have to push her and push her. When he'd quit to take a turn himself, she'd cry and hit him so he had to keep pushing her. Now she pumps really well by herself, and she'll stay on the swings sometimes until Mom has to come pull her off—she'll hang on the chains and Luke's mom has to pick her up and drag her away. Luke thinks she does it just so the other people will stare, because she almost always clings to the equipment in really crowded places, but if it's just Luke and Mom and her, she won't.

Luke digs a moat around his fort. He's built a climbing gym made of sticks inside, and a swingset. He used the long dry grass that grows on the edge of the woods to tie the gym together, to

94

hang the swings off the crossbars. Maggie will like this fort, he thinks.

The blister on his heel hurts when he crouches to dig out the moat. The Forest Service people had been there when they got to the bottom, they'd been checking the trail register or something. Luke sat on a log listening to his foot throb and thinking about Maggie. Why would she hide from him? What if he'd been wrong? What if she didn't go down the creek? What if she'd snuck around behind Mom and went to the lakes? They thought she was in there—when Dad dove. His parents didn't want to tell him they thought Maggie had drowned, but that's what they were doing—looking for Maggie in the lake.

One of the Forest Service guys had called from the phone in his truck. There would be people soon to look for Maggie. They'd get that ooh-the-poor-retarded-girl look like that guy at Sea World. Maggie wouldn't get out of the pit of balls. She knew about taking turns, knew she was supposed to get out with the other kids. But she wouldn't. Mom told the guy she'd go in and get her, and he was all grumpy and said that he couldn't let her go in there. Mom laughed and said, "Well, good luck." Then Luke and his mom had to go sit on a bench and wait because Maggie was being so bad, twining her fingers in the rope netting, letting her tongue hang out and drooling, and they were giggling so hard that they had to hide so Maggie wouldn't think she should act that way. The guy was big, and he didn't want to touch Maggie, and she knew it.

Then a jay had flapped down in front of Luke and squawked at him and he'd looked up and the Forest Service truck was gone. Luke had jumped off the log and walked further out into the road. It was gone. He was all alone.

"Dad!" he'd shouted. "Dad?"

There hadn't been any answer. The jay had flown up and sat in a tree branch, squawking at him. He'd been all by himself on the long gravel road that led back to the campground and he had a blister on his heel and his dad had left him behind.

Luke digs deeper into the sand, trying not to think about that long road, and how much his foot had hurt, and how he couldn't believe his dad had left without him. He'd been really sorry when Luke finally found him. Luke knows that. Luke has a rough rock he's using to sharpen the sticks to put in the bottom of the moat. He rubs the edge of the stick back and forth across the stone until it gets sharp and pointy, and then he carefully places it in the bottom of the moat, sticking up, where it is very dangerous.

JONATHAN HIDES beneath a manzanita shrub, waiting for the red heeler to find him. After they ran the scent out the fourth time, Scanlon got worried about his dog.

"She's only a puppy," he explained. "I'm still training her."

When he asked for a volunteer to play victim, Jonathan jumped at the chance. Giving Scanlon the bandanna that had been tied around his neck all day, he climbed over a bunch of boulders until he found a scrubby manzanita with enough room beneath it for him to hide under.

From underneath the bush, Jonathan thinks about the little girl. Is this what she's seeing? he wonders, looking up through the branches at the blue sky. She must be hungry, and scared. Jonathan had gotten lost once as a boy, at a street fair. He'd been watching one of those sketch artists, the ones who do caricatures, and when he'd looked up, his mom was gone. He knew he was supposed to stay put if he got lost, so he had, but he couldn't help crying when every time he looked up, all those grown-ups were not his parents. A lady had found him and taken him to the police who were manning the barricades where the street was blocked off. He'd been so scared, he didn't even want the ice cream the big policemen offered him; he'd stood by the blue barricade, crying and watching the crowd for his parents. He hadn't been there long when he saw his mother emerge from the crowd, one hand shading her eyes, looking for him. Jonathan had taken off, screaming for her, while the cop had yelled, "Wait," but he hadn't waited. He'd wanted his mom and he didn't stop until he had her, arms around both legs, face buried in her skirt. Above his head, he'd heard the cop's amused tone: "Just had to be sure, ma'am."

He hears panting and lies very still until the dog finds him, and then there's a frenzied few minutes of play. This is his job—to play false victim. To let the dog find him. To reward her with kisses and pats and cries of "Good dog" so that they can go back to that feather boa, go back to the site of the shoe, and try once again to find Maggie.

IT WAS that headache, Anne thinks as she turns and looks back into the campsite. Luke is still busy with his fort, and she can't see Richard, but she assumes he is still organizing and reorganizing the contents of their car. He always organizes during a crisis. When Maggie had heart surgery, every drawer in the house had balls of socks neatly lined up, color-coded. If only she didn't get these headaches, if only she didn't sometimes feel suffocated by the children, by family life. Both times she was pregnant, she'd had dreams that she had left the baby somewhere—in the bank, the grocery store, somewhere unspecified. Panicked, she'd retrace her steps, run from blank face to blank face: *Have you seen my baby? Where is my baby?* People had assured her that all women have those dreams. They'd kept telling her not to worry, said it was perfectly normal. Anne wonders sometimes if she's really that important, that central to them all, but Maggie's absence would certainly seem to argue that she'd done *something* terribly wrong, had certainly failed in the most basic task of motherhood—not to misplace one's children.

She'd felt the headache coming on, knew what it meant, that the too-familiar blue pain was back, sitting at the base of her skull. She'd only gone on a little way down the trail, hoping to get her wits about her again, hoping not to ruin their day. The breeze was soft and the sun was warm on the white granite. Unpacking the lunch, she'd taken a deep breath—they were in one place for the whole afternoon, no more shoes to tie, no more cajoling to get the children up the trail, keep them walking. She had felt the pressure lifting off the top of her head and had imagined that the vise behind her eyes was loosening its grip. They had made it to the top, to the lovely blue lakes under the late summer sun, and the afternoon stretched out before them. She'd checked the sky to the west—no storm clouds, no lightning to watch out for.

Then Maggie had skidded down the gravel path, yelling something.

"What?" Anne had said, startled and a little annoyed because Maggie had crashed her one moment of quiet. "Slow down," she'd reprimanded. "Finish one word first, then the next."

"Hide . . . and . . . seek?" Maggie'd said, deliberately forming the words, one at a time. "Luke? Okay?"

"Sure," she'd answered. As Maggie had turned to run back, Anne had called after her. Maggie'd spun midstride in that funny way she had, which looked like her body was going in two directions at once.

"Not too far—stay close—okay?"

"Ok-ay," Maggie had roared in her growly Cookie Monster voice. It was the voice she used when she thought her mother was being silly. Anne had smiled and rooted a hat out of the pack, hoping to stave off the flashing lights in her head.

Had she been too cranky with her? Had Maggie run off because she knew Anne was annoyed, knew Anne was having one of those moments where she thought her kids were a pain? Anne watches Luke dig in the sand and tells herself this is crazy, that every parent feels that way sometimes. Then she looks up toward the mountainside where Maggie is still hiding. I didn't mean it, she thinks. Come back.

RICHARD CAN'T help thinking that because he let Anne waste so much time, Maggie slipped through their grasp. If I had stopped her, he thinks, insisted we *do* something. It was one of those times when Anne had some improbable idea lodged in her head, the kind of thing that just *might* work. But it didn't work, he thinks as he surveys the inside of the car. Everything is stowed where it belongs, the pots nested in their stuff sacks, the tent and coolers secured with bungee cords. He worries about bungee cords; he's told the kids a thousand times to be careful, not to fiddle with them, because they could come loose and someone could lose an eye. If only he'd insisted, put his foot down, they wouldn't have lost so much time.

And it was so unfair to Luke. Richard looks toward the shore where his towheaded son is constructing his fort. I have to talk to him, Richard thinks. He's going to think this is all his fault, that *he* lost his sister. Anne is back at the picnic table, back at her sketch pad. She sits there staring into the trees. Finally, sensing his gaze, she turns to him. Her face is blank with despair. They hold each other's eyes for a long moment before Anne turns back to her pad. He wishes he could say something to her; he wishes there was something *to* say. I can't blame her, he thinks. It's not her fault, it's not my fault, and it's not Luke's fault. This is an accident.

"You know," Anne had explained to Luke. "Like when you lose your keys and you try to retrace your steps . . ."

"Anne," Richard had said. Luke was shifting nervously from one foot to the other.

"What do you think, sweetie?" Anne had said, striding back to them after making Luke crouch, cover his eyes, and count while she pretended to be Maggie, ran off at an odd, oblique angle, which, Richard had to admit, looked exactly like the sort of thing Maggie might have done.

"I don't know," Luke had said, still holding his hands over his face.

They'd repeated the experiment three, four times. Each time, Anne had nearly bounced back out of the trees, asked Luke what he thought, stood expectant and bristling with nervous energy while Luke sank lower and lower into his crouch.

Richard had tried to warn her, to stop her. It was getting out of hand. "We should start looking—"

"Think, Luke," Anne had said, and glared at Richard, refusing to answer the suggestion she didn't want to hear. "Just think about it for a minute. I'm going to go in another direction, and you see if that one sounds right."

She'd tramped off down the nearly bare granite, across the faded orange and black cross, and had taken the little trail to the dam. Richard had tried not to lose his temper as he watched Luke hunch in concentration and misery on the granite. I should have lost my temper, he thinks as he slams the hatchback on the car.

Maybe if I'd been a little more willing to lose my temper, we wouldn't have lost so much time.

"What do you think?" Richard had finally said, running his hand across his son's smooth head. He had to put a stop to this.

"I don't know," Luke replied, still hiding in his hands. "It sounds the same as the last one."

"You can open your eyes if you want," Richard said, trying to get the boy to unhunch. He'd crouched to look his son in the eyes, but he didn't take him by the shoulders. It was making him crazy—they needed to stop all this foolishness and start walking grids, calling, shouting. They needed action, not all this pretending. And they needed to stop torturing Luke.

"Luke," he said quietly, inches from his son's face, but still not touching the tense and unhappy child. "This isn't your fault. Nobody is blaming you."

"Yeah, I know," he mumbled, looking at Richard's feet.

"Did that sound like the right direction?" Anne called as she rounded the corner, returning to them.

Luke looked at Richard, who put a hand on his shoulder. They stood up together, turned to face Anne.

"He's not sure," Richard told her. "Why don't we split up and each take one of the last two directions you tried?"

"Let's try it once more. . . . "

"No, Anne," Richard said. This time, Luke didn't shrug his father's hand off. Struggling to keep his voice calm, he'd insisted. "We need to start searching. We know the general direction. It's been twenty minutes already."

"Fine," Anne said, her whole body going stiff. "You guys search down toward the dam. I'll take this side of the creek." Spinning on her heel, she'd turned and walked into the alder brush, shouting Maggie's name.

101

Luke wouldn't look at Richard. "It's okay," Richard said. "She's scared, that's all. She's not mad at you."

"Which way should we go?" Luke had asked. Once we find Maggie, Richard thought. I'll deal with it after we find Maggie.

STEVE HAS the helicopter circle down below the area where the young dog keeps running blank. He's got the Nevada teams with him and he wants to give them a look at the terrain before they get up there. With each phone call this afternoon, he could hear Ed getting more frustrated, more tense. Ed's got the best intuition of any searcher he's ever known, but sometimes it seems to get in his way, as though whatever it is that's trying to bubble up in him is pushing so hard that he can't see the terrain. Steve has never had the sort of hunches Ed does; he goes strictly by the maps, the statistics, the numbers. It's the only way he knows how to search, but Ed's hunches have saved his ass so many times that he knows to trust them, to listen when Ed has some oddball idea.

Steve stares out the window, looking for a narrow canyon, some chunk of topography that doesn't show on the map, a cranny where this girl could be lodged. Near the campground, and off to the south, there are conifers, lodgepole mostly, fairly thick forest, and nothing weird that he can see from up here anyway. It all looks like rolling forest, which means the hiding places can only be found from the ground. Forests mean downed trees, logs, sometimes hollow, that little kids can climb inside. Makes sense to them, anyway, keeps them warm, but makes them a son of a bitch to find. All the signs so far, though, seem to indicate she's still out in the rocks. Let's hope so, he thinks. The infrared's not going to find her in those trees.

He motions to the pilot to swing around, take him to the site. He's got a pile of maps rolled up and propped between his feet.

He needs to get Ed on the maps with him. Together, Steve thinks, he and Ed can probably figure out what's tripping up the dog. It's got to be topography; there's no other explanation for it. There's got to be some little gully they're missing, someplace tight she's wedged herself into, if they can only figure out where. . . . Steve braces the roll of maps as the helicopter banks to the right, swings down toward the orange cross painted on the granite that marks the old high-country heli pad, the place last seen.

So," Jane says, climbing into the bus. "What's the plan?" Steve sees that tight look around her eyes. She's got to be tired. He'd like to get her alone for a minute, but it's been so busy all day that he hasn't had the chance. She catches his glance, smiles slightly, as if to say, Stop worrying. I'm fine.

"Check this out," Steve tells her, pointing to the map. He's got to stay focused, at least for now. "The dogs found a track, and they did pretty well with it until here." He points to a convergence of thin brown topo lines.

"It's really steep right in there," Ed says. "I can't believe she went over. I had Team C sweep the area below the cliff three or four times, but they didn't find anything."

"Let's hope she didn't fall," Jane says.

"The bottom of this cliff is deep in scrub oak," Ed says. "But

I think we'd probably have found her if she'd fallen. I think that either she went around the cliff—which means over here into this swampy stuff, or out here toward the forest—or she turned around and somehow got past us, is heading back uphill."

"Down's children behave a lot like the Alzheimer's folks," Steve says. "They just keep going straight until something stops them."

They stand looking at the map for a few silent minutes. Ed reaches across for the clipboard. "What's on deck for tonight?"

"The helis are flying infrared scans," Steve says.

"That'll find her if she's out on the rock," Jane adds.

"Yeah," Ed says. "But it won't do us much good if she's up in the trees, or down in that swamp."

Steve looks out the bus window at the falling twilight. The temperature's supposed to drop down into the low forties.

"DO YOU see?" Richard asks. He has spread the map across the table and has been showing Luke the details of the search. Anne watches the two of them, heads bent over the table as though this were any ordinary project. They've always tried to explain even the scariest things to Luke, figuring whatever he makes up will probably be more frightening than the truth. Thanks to Maggie's surgery, Luke was the only child in his kindergarten class who could name all the ventricles and arteries of the heart.

"Are they going to keep looking all night?" he asks.

"Yes," Anne says. "Of course."

She's sitting on the far side the table, trying not to get too close to the map. It frightens her. She doesn't want Luke to know, because she doesn't want to scare him. She figures she did enough of that already, bolting from the bus—but that map terrified her, those lines twisting like live creatures. Anne is trying very hard to rouse herself out of the strange lethargy that came over her this afternoon, the numb sense that everything was happening behind a pane of glass that slightly muffled everyone's voices.

"Remember I told you they'll have a meeting tonight?" Richard says.

"Yeah."

"I think they'll tell us then. Last night, it got too dark; they had to stop for a little while." Anne feels Richard's glance. She stares into space, pretending not to have heard that part. They *have* to keep searching all night. It's Maggie's second night out, and it's getting too cold. Anne knows from her guide years that it doesn't take much for a child to slip into hypothermia. They always took extra gear if there was a kid on the trip—children don't have the body fat to keep warm. Ten minutes wet and in the shade and their lips would go blue and they'd start shivering in their T-shirts. Someone would pull out a polypro sweater, and they'd scrunch the kid into it, life jacket and all.

"What about the helicopters?"

"They're flying them now," Richard says. "Remember? We heard them go over a little while ago."

"Will the helicopters still be here tomorrow?" he asks. Anne watches him. He's got that intense look on his face that she recognizes. Her firstborn is often more like her than she'd care to admit; sometimes she wishes for his sake that he'd inherited his father's easy personality.

"Why?" she asks.

"I want to see one," Luke says. "I want to see what it looks like inside."

"Okay," Anne says. "We'll ask Steve in the morning."

"But now," Richard says, scooping Luke out of his chair, "it's time for you to get ready for bed."

"Wait," he says as his father deposits him at the foot of the loft stairs. "What's that thing called again?"

"What thing?" Anne and Richard ask in unison.

"The thing the helicopters use to find Maggie."

"Infrared," Richard answers. "It's sort of like radar, except it picks up heat, not motion."

Luke pauses a couple of steps up the ladder. "And that's what they're doing now, right?" he asks. "Looking for Maggie with that thing?"

"Yes, Luke," Anne says softly. "That's what they're doing."

"WHAT DO the numbers look like?" Ed asks.

"We've still got to run close grids up in the basin tomorrow to be sure," Steve says, looking at the calculations that cover his clipboard. "But the possibility of absence is ninety percent up there."

"She's not in any of the usual kid spots," Ed says. "We've been all up and down the creekbed."

Jane watches the two men calculate and assess. The statistical side of searching fascinates the scientist in her—that you can run the numbers, come up with figures that reliably reflect the likelihood of the victim's presence, or absence, in any particular sector of the search area. She likes listening to the jargon, listening to the two men weigh their assets, listening to them allocate their resources so that they have the best chance of finding the missing person.

"What are you going to tell the parents?" Jane asks. This is the part they sometimes forget—soft skills, dealing with the families, bystanders.

"Tell them they should have been more careful," Ed says.

"Oh, Ed," Jane says. She knows this is just reflex with him, but it gets tiresome. He can't be trusted around parents, particularly not if he's tired. If he wasn't so good at finding their children, he would have been thrown off the squad years ago.

"We'll fill them in on the plan," Steve says. "I suppose we should start trying to apprise them of the possible outcomes."

"How much time do we have?" Jane asks. She's thinking about hypothermia. "As far as we know, the child hasn't eaten anything in almost thirty-six hours, and it's going to be cold tonight."

"If the weather holds," Ed says, peering out the window, "we could have as long as another three to five days."

"There's weather coming in from the coast," Steve says. "It was on the radio this afternoon—and you've seen the cloud cover."

They all know that in bad weather, the death rate for children rises to 66 percent.

"So we've got about twenty-four to seventy-two hours," Steve says.

"Do you want me to talk to the parents?" Jane asks.

"No," Steve says, rubbing one hand across his eyes. "I'll do it. At least the first round."

LYING IN his bed, Luke is thinking about helicopters. He imagines the infrared as a sort of television screen, a screen that can see Maggie, waving like someone on a desert island. Here I am. Come get me.

"Mom?" Luke asks as Anne comes up the stairs with the nearly forgotten Mr. Bear.

"Mmhm," Anne murmurs, sitting on the bed's edge, next to Luke's knees, tucking Mr. Bear in beneath the covers.

"Is Maggie—" He stops, looks away from his mom.

"Is Maggie what?" his mother asks quietly, smoothing the hair off his forehead.

"Nothing."

"Maybe," his mom says, still fiddling with his bangs, "if we think good thoughts for her, if we think of her warm and safe and tucked in under a nice cozy bush . . . "

Anne leans over to give him a kiss on the forehead; then the bed bounces a little as she stands up; he can feel her footsteps moving across the loft.

"Mom!"

"I'm right here," she says, standing at the head of the ladder.

They look across the dim loft at each other.

"Sleep tight," Anne says, backing down the ladder.

"I'M GOING to call it off until six," Steve says. They're gathering the materials for the debriefing. He sees Jane pause, turn from the cabinet where she's gathering yellow pads, debriefing supplies, and stand, leaning against the counter.

"What's your thinking on that?" Ed asks. Steve can hear him working to keep his voice steady.

"The dog teams came up empty" Steve says. "And we won't have fresh teams until morning. The sky's getting overcast, there's only spotty moonlight, and it's really tricky terrain."

"It's not that bad," Ed interjects. "Everyone's got headlamps."

"I'm not willing to endanger the searchers. Especially since we think she's probably holed up underneath something."

"What about endangering the child, Steve?" Ed says. "You said yourself there's weather moving in. We might not have much more time."

Jane's standing by the cabinet, a stack of legal pads in her arms, watching. Steve knows she'll try not to take sides; he's just hoping that with her there, Ed will stay calm.

"You heard the heli guys," Steve says. "If there'd been any sign of her, I'd have teams up there now—but they didn't find anything out on the granite. And if she's in the trees, we're sure as hell not going to find her in the dark."

"Fine," Ed says. "We'll just sit around on our asses a little more and chat about it. Maybe she'll wander in to camp on her own. . . ."

"What's the problem here?"

"This is totally fucked up," he yells, slamming the map tube on the table. Steve looks to Jane. She's holding her ground by the supply cabinet. "We should have had dogs first thing. We should have had experienced dogs and not some idiot puppy mucking up the scent evidence, and we should have gotten those goddamn parents out of there last night. . . ."

"Steve?" Jonathan's voice says from the stairwell. "They're ready for the debriefing."

"Thank you, Jonathan," Steve says. "Tell them we'll get started in a minute."

"Are you ready?" Steve asks Ed.

"Shit," Ed says, looking down at the tube of maps in his hands. "I hate kid searches."

"I know you do," Steve says.

"I still think we should run grids all night," Ed says. "We could move folks down into the trees."

"Objection noted," Steve says. "Let's go."

ANNE IS walking the empty road through the campground in the dark. The woods smell damp and piney; someone has a campfire and a faint wood smoke hangs in the air. Since childhood, these have been the most comforting scents she can think of, but after tonight, she wonders if she'll ever be able to bear them again. "Longing"—she remembers the line but can't remember the poem—"because desire is full of endless distances." She can feel Maggie's weight as she thinks of it, and yet there is no Maggie.

She has been thinking, until now, that this situation is somehow similar to Maggie's surgery. It's the only other time when Maggie has been away from her—they wheeled her down that bright hallway, strapped to a gurney, drugged, unconscious. Anne remembers her terror, seeing Maggie gone like that. Knowing they planned to open her chest, winch her ribs apart like the hood of a car. The ribs, the doctor had told her, are a little tricky on children this young, because they're still so flexible—not like the fifty-year-old men with their solid, stiff ribcages. However, it's better for the child, he'd told her over his glasses—because they heal so quickly. Anne remembers her horror when they explained the operation, how they planned to stop Maggie's heart by pouring ice water on it, a stream of cold slowing, then stopping the pumping muscle inside her chest, while they diverted her blood through a machine. They didn't really have a choice; the abnormality had to be fixed, another manifestation of Maggie's chromosomal difference. It was the cold that bothered Anne the most; she couldn't believe that somewhere, underneath the anesthesia, Maggie wouldn't know that her mother had sanctioned this false death.

Is this what I get for it? Anne wonders, pulling the sweater around her more closely.

Where is she, where is she, where is she—the phrase has been running through Anne's mind so quickly, so relentlessly that it no longer seems like a phrase, but like her pulse, the sound of her blood running through her very being. The silence is breaking her; she cannot understand why Maggie does not answer, and nothing anyone is saying makes any sense at all. Maggie's silence goes against everything she knows deep in the core of her being, that place where she *knows* Maggie. Maggie has always responded—from the very first, from before the doctors said it was possible. She knows them, has always known them. She recognized her family long before the doctors and experts said it was possible, and recognized them with a joy that infused her whole being, awkward and uncontrolled as that response might have been. So why won't she respond now? Why this silence?

As Anne stands surrounded by the tiny lapping waves of a still night, the moon breaks through the intermittent clouds. It drenches the mountains and granite and trees with a pale, clear light. A ghost glacier of silence pours out of that high basin, rushes over her, engulfing her in the pounding quiet of a landscape into which one has called one's child's name over and over and over, and from which one has heard no response.

"DAD?" LUKE calls out from the loft.

"What?" Richard answers. He's rinsing off the last of the plates from their camping set. Everything got so sandy.

"Come here."

"Hang on a second," Richard calls as he shakes the excess water off the soft aluminum pot, then climbs into the loft to see what Luke wants.

"Where's Mom?"

Richard answers with deliberate calm. "She went for a walk." Air, she said she needed some air, some quiet before having to face all those people.

"She's mad at me," Luke says.

"No," Richard says. He crosses the loft, stooping a little so as not to hit his head on the low rafters, then sits on the edge of

Luke's bed. He can see that Luke's close to tears. "Why do you think she's mad, sport?"

"She's acting like she's mad," he answers quietly, tracing something on the bedspread with his finger.

Richard straightens the covers a little while he thinks about this. The thought had crossed his mind, earlier in the day, that Anne just might, in some not entirely conscious way, blame Luke for losing Maggie. "She is kind of acting like she's mad, isn't she?" he answers. Luke nods yes, and Richard wonders at how much he picks up. Does he forget only because Maggie is oblivious? He knows that Anne's head knows Luke didn't lose his sister, but she's not entirely rational about Maggie, and it's her heart he worries about. Nonetheless, he tucks the blankets around Luke and says, "But she's not mad at you."

"Who's she mad at then?" he asks.

"I don't know, honey," Richard says. "I think she's just mad because she can't find Maggie. . . . You know how it is when something goes really wrong and you can't seem to fix it?" Richard's scared of how close he's coming to admitting that they may not be able to fix this, that they may not, in fact, find Maggie.

"Come on," Richard says. "It's late. Time for you to get some sleep, okay?"

"Okay, Dad," Luke says, burrowing into the covers. Richard leans down and kisses him. "I love you, Luke."

"Love you, too, Dad," Luke answers, his voice muffled beneath the blankets.

ANNE SITS on the picnic table, trying to look as though she can hear the debriefing through the roaring in her ears. Steve seems to be saying something about Maggie's shoe, and how they couldn't pick up a scent afterward. Actually, they picked up three or four

113

scents, none of which panned out. One trail, however, went farther before they lost it, and this, it appears, is the trail they now consider the most viable. Anne sits on the table, her feet rest on the bench, and she carefully clasps her hands in her lap. It is important, she knows, to appear calm, rational, orderly. It is important to appear reliable, despite the undeniable fact that she has lost her child, a child who is now spending her second night outdoors, dressed only in a T-shirt and shorts. Reliable. Calm. Rational.

"Hey," Richard whispers, hand on her back as he sits beside her. Richard, she thinks to herself. My husband. Maggie's father. She smiles in what she hopes is an appropriate manner. She realizes he probably knows that she's cracking up, but she'd rather pretend for now that she has everything under control.

"How's Luke?" she asks quietly, straining to be normal, concerned, motherly.

"He's okay," Richard answers. "You need to talk to him. He thinks you're angry at him. He thinks it's his fault."

It *is* his fault, she thinks before she can stop herself.

"No!" Anne says a little too loudly. Heads turn and she lowers her voice. Steve continues to talk in the background about the helicopters and infrared detection. "No." She looks at Richard in appeal.

"I told him you were just mad at—" His voice breaks slightly as his hands gesture toward the scene around them. "But you should talk to him. He's scared."

Anne nods. She'll talk to him in the morning. She doesn't really think it's his fault. He's only a boy. It was only a game. See, she thinks, look at these people. They'll find Maggie and then we can all go home. Anne ignores the howling inside her head, her deafening fear that Maggie is gone, gone forever, vanished. It can't be true. She can't let it be true. Tomorrow, she tells herself, I'll talk

114

to Luke; they'll find Maggie. We'll say thank you; we'll go home.

Side by side, Anne and her husband listen to Steve relate how, one after another, the search teams found nothing today. They listen to the plans for the next day's search.

"I'm sorry," Steve says. "I'd love to send people up there all night, but it's simply too dangerous."

"Actually," Richard replies, "I expected it. I tried to prepare Anne. . . ."

"How's she holding up?"

"About as well as can be expected," Richard replies. Steve sees, all at once, how exhausted Richard is—happens like that with some people. One minute, they look perfectly normal; next minute, they look like they're going to fall over.

"Which is?" Steve probes.

"Which is not so great," Richard snaps. "How *should* we be handling it?"

Steve sits on the table beside him. "When's your mother getting here?"

"Tomorrow," Richard answers. "Her plane got into Reno late, so she was going to spend the night, drive up in the morning."

"What about Anne's family? Would that help?" Steve asks.

"Hardly." Richard laughs. "Anne's mother is a very sweet old lush. Her father's dead." He pauses, looking at his hands. "Anne's a little short on family."

"Is there anything I can do?" Steve asks.

Richard stands abruptly, wearily. "You could try to convince Anne to come back to the cabin and get some sleep. She's gone back out to the lake."

"You sure you want *me* to do that?" Steve asks.

"Yeah," Richard says, turning away. "Seems like she responds better to strangers at times like these." He turns to Steve with a wry, pained grin on his face. "She was raised to be polite."

Steve watches him head back down the dark road to the cabin. Last thing he wants to do at this point is track down that strange, intense woman. He's wiped out already, and the thought of having to justify himself one more time tonight is almost more than he can handle.

Steve takes a deep breath, slides off the table, and follows the narrow trail to the lakeshore.

FLAT ON her back, Anne feels the cold seep up into her bones from the dark rock. She feels it seeping through her clothes, into the blades of her shoulders where they touch the rock, the back of her head, her buttocks, calves. Anne's hoping that somehow the cold she absorbs will, by some magic, protect her daughter; that the cold flowing into her body is the same cold that is flowing out of Maggie, leaving only pink, warm, blond girl-child up there, surrounded by an aura that can protect her until morning, until the sun comes back up, until the searchers go back out.

"I'm sorry folks," Steve had said. "But it's just too dark; the terrain is too unstable. I'm going to have to keep you all here until morning."

Anne heard the groans. They would have gone back out. He stopped them; he left her daughter out there alone, in the night, refused to let willing people look for her.

Anne concentrates once more on her vision of Maggie. The anger is distracting her from her real job, which is to keep Maggie safe, to keep her from freezing to death out there.

STEVE PICKS his way through the dark. Every so often, the clouds part and white moonlight pours like water through the trees, leaving bright strips along the forest floor. He thinks of the little girl up there. Where is she? Under a bush someplace? Dug in under a hollow tree? Is she smart enough to take care of herself like that?

Steve steps down onto the beach, then stops and sits heavily on the embankment. He sees Anne out there, flat on her back. He can't seem to get a bead on this mother, doesn't have any idea how she'll react. Most times, Steve can predict people, but he can't predict Anne, and it spooks him. He listens to the faint clanking of people getting settled for the night while he collects himself.

What if it were Jane? he thinks. What if it were Jennie lost out there—what if that day in the high gully above Twin Lakes he'd turned and Jennie hadn't still been playing there by the creek?

It's a tricky question. He'd like to think that with all their training, he and Jane would be model parents, but he knows it's not true. They'd be any search leader's worst nightmare—parents who know enough to second-guess every move. It's the lack of control that would make him wild. Having no control at all over the situation, stranger making these essential decisions, taking factors other than one's child into account. Steve knows if it were him and Jennie were out there somewhere, he'd be hiking it alone up there, headlamp illuminating one rock at a time, one clump of flowers, one bush.

He stands, pushing slightly on his bad knee. It was his decision; he'll take the heat. Besides, the last thing he needs is to lose a mother to hypothermia.

ANNE HEARS but chooses to ignore the footsteps ringing through the stone.

"Anne?"

117

"Yes," she answers, not moving. She can't move; if she moves, the cold will flow back into Maggie and she will die.

"Are you all right?"

Opening her eyes, Anne sees Steve leaning over her.

"Yes, I'm just fine, thank you," she answers in her most polite voice before closing her eyes in order to concentrate once more on the pink glow she is willing to surround Maggie. She doesn't want to deal with him. She can't; she won't let her anger distract her.

"What are you doing?" he asks.

After a pause, she answers, "I'm resting."

He crouches near her head. "It's pretty cold to be resting here."

Anne opens her eyes to reply. "I'm quite fine. Really. I like it here." Go away, she thinks. She can't let the vision of the pink glow fade. She feels the importance of this with every fiber in her body.

"Mind if I join you?"

"No," Anne replies. "Go right ahead. Be my guest." It's too hard to make him go away—she doesn't have the energy to spare right now, not when she's got Maggie in her sights, not when she's got Maggie in that pink glow.

She feels him sit awkwardly beside her. Despite all the time outdoors, he doesn't seem comfortable sitting on the bare rock. His presence is too much. She doesn't want him there. She's angry at him, but anger will distract her from the Maggie vision. His legs uncomfortably crossed, his hands with their wide knuckles, the faint campfire scent of his clothing.

"What's the most frightening thing that happened to you as a child?" she asks. If she can keep him busy, she thinks, get him to tell stories, then she can concentrate on keeping Maggie warm. She knows he's come to take her inside, come to collect her like a wayward child.

"Me?" Steve asks, startled.

"Mmhmm."

He's silent for a minute, then says a little wryly, "I got lost."

"Where?"

"Hunting," he begins, pulling his knees in, wrapping his arms around them. "My dad and I, on my grandfather's ranch up in Oregon."

"What happened?"

"We were up in the foothills, in the scrub oak, and I got separated from my dad somehow. It was just like in one of my Irish gram's fairy stories," he muses. "One minute I was walking along with him, and the next minute I was alone in the forest with my gun."

"How old were you?" Maggie's coming into focus now, pink, warm, safe.

"About eight, I guess," he said. "I shouted and shouted, but nobody answered. I couldn't figure out how we got so far apart so quickly. . . ." His voice trails off.

"Then what?" Anne asks, trying to keep him going. It's working. His presence is fading back into the sound of a voice. She's breathing in the cold, feels it flow into her through the points of her shoulder blades where they jut into the rock, and the light around Maggie's curled-up body is pulsing now, a pulsing red glow. She can't, won't disturb this, the first clear image she's had of Maggie since she vanished.

"I wandered around for a little bit, then decided to go downhill. I knew the ranch was below us, and there was a big marsh in the valley. I figured if I kept going downhill, I'd run into water, and I could follow it home. When I got there, I had to fight my way along the edge; it was mucky and I had to go through the hemlock thickets, then cut downhill every so often to make sure my line was straight. Finally, I flushed out at the

119

bottom edge of the marsh, about a mile uphill from the ranch house, and walked home along the road."

"Weren't they looking for you?" Anne asks. Her vision of Maggie is beginning to waver. It's not working. He's still distracting her.

"Yeah, they were. My grandad had figured something was wrong when we didn't come home for supper, and when I got to the house, he'd taken the hands and gone up to find us. My gram took one look at me all torn up and muddy and then went out and started ringing the big dinner bell. She rang and rang until we heard my dad shoot into the air; then she took me inside and put me in a hot tub, trying to get all the burrs and thistles out of my hair. Boy, I'll tell you"—Steve laughs a little at the memory—"was I nervous when they got back to the house—I was sure I was going to get my hide tanned for wandering off. My dad, though"—he pauses a moment—"he just stood there. He was a big tall man, nearly six four, and he had tears in his eyes. He put his hand on my wet head and told me I'd done right, that he was proud of me for getting home by myself."

Anne is losing the Maggie vision. It's fading from red to pink to yellow.

"Your turn," Steve says to her. She feels a warmth radiating off him, like waves, and fights it. It is his warmth that's chasing off her vision of Maggie. "What's the scariest thing that happened to you as a kid?"

"Me?" Anne answers vaguely. She's trying to hold on to Maggie, who is slipping away from her, like a dream figure who is longed for but can't be touched. "When I was ten, my father picked me up after school and took me to Singapore for three years." She says this nonchalantly, still thinking of Maggie, then feels the shock in Steve's gaze as he swings toward her. "He didn't tell my mother where we'd gone."

THE CABIN is freezing. Richard stokes the fire, then sits at the table to make a list. He needs to call his office, the children's schools, check with Anne to see if there's anyone else. Oh God, his office. He hasn't been there very long, and this is going to sound terrible. Really, I'm a responsible guy, he thinks, imagining the conversation. But I won't be in today because I just lost my retarded daughter on a day hike. He's glad his mother will be here; she's capable, good at things like this.

Richard smooths the topo across the table. He bought it at the ranger's station on the way up, hoping to start teaching Luke to use a map and compass. With a pencil, Richard sketches out the actions they've taken so far, the PLS, the place where they found the shoe, the dead-end trails the dogs found. He runs light hash marks through those areas that have been searched twice, those places that don't seem to be in her line of travel, or what they think was her line of travel. If she kept moving in the same direction as the line between the place last seen and the shoe, she could be anywhere in the forested area to the east of the lake.

He hears Luke roll over in bed up in the loft, sigh. He listens for a moment. Is he awake? Maggie's the thrasher; she kicks and punches in her sleep, fighting for the whole bed, snores, too. Quiet descends out of the loft once more, and Richard turns back to the map.

Gazing at it, he realizes that despite the lines, the hash marks, the little *x*'s marking Maggie's debris, this piece of paper tells him nothing about the location of his child. It is not a blueprint, not a treasure map; it's just a piece of paper he's scribbled on.

121

Please, Richard prays. Sitting at that strange kitchen table, head in his hands, every prayer Richard learned in twelve years of Catholic school wells up from some forgotten place inside his soul and, despite his doubt, he prays, hoping somehow to reclaim his lost daughter, hoping to calm the panicked bird that slams around inside his rib cage.

For a very long time, Richard remains still at the table, before rising and slowly, like a man sleepwalking, closing down the dampers on the woodstove, preparing the cabin for sleep.

Where is Anne? He looks at his watch. It's nearly 1:30 and she's still out there. She's so far away from them. He lets the thought trail off. This is an old argument. She can't help it. But she's got to talk to Luke.

Leaving the small light over the kitchen sink on for her, Richard stumbles toward the bedroom, so tired that he can hardly unlace his boots.

"I LEFT SCHOOL one afternoon," Anne says dreamily from her position on the cold rock surface. "But instead of the house-keeper, my dad was there to pick me up."

Steve had thought he'd humor her with a story, get her to open up a little, get to the point where he could talk her inside. He wasn't counting on something like this.

"I thought it was a little weird," she said. "But I was an obedient child. . . . " Steve really wants to get her off the cold rock. Singapore. He'd been there a long time ago, when he was in the service. "I got in the car, and twenty hours later, I was there."

"Why Singapore?" Steve asks. The thing he remembers most was the flowers, flowers everywhere, and women dressed in bright saris and pajama outfits. It rained buckets on them every afternoon at three, like clockwork. Steve listens to Anne and hopes that if he can keep her talking, he may be able to get her up and off this rock.

"Oh, I don't know," she says in that strange, bright voice. "I know he had business there. I never asked. I got up in the morning, put on my uniform, and went off to school. In some ways, it wasn't that different—at a certain point, a private school is a private school." She pauses and Steve can see she's lost in whatever dreaminess has her out here, flat on her back on a cold, damp stone. He's got to keep her talking or he'll never get her up, on her feet, back to the cabin.

"Didn't you ever ask where your mother was?"

"No." She pauses for a moment. "Daddy never mentioned her and I was too scared to ask. I knew they were getting a divorce, and that she'd been behaving badly—staying out all night, drinking too much at parties. We'd have dinner every night in the dining room—it was beautiful, silver and china and candles. I don't know what I thought was going on. I wrote her letters—God, I must have written her a hundred letters during those years. I'd come home every day and check the hall stand, then go upstairs and cry because she hadn't written me back."

"What happened?" Steve asks.

"I finally sent a letter on my own. I didn't even know where the post office was, but I saw it one day when I was being driven back from a friend's house. I had to sneak out to get there without the servants knowing. That was how she found me."

She falls silent, and Steve waits. "So she came for you?" he asks. He's losing her again. The clouds part for a moment and he watches moonlight pass across the planes of her cheekbones, sees her skin glow white as stone.

"They showed up at my school," she pauses. "Mother and Arthur, my stepfather. I got completely hysterical and they had to

123

give me half of one of Mother's tranquilizers to get me to stop screaming at her and hitting her. Everyone was shocked—I'd always been so good. On the plane, they explained that Daddy had taken me the day Mother asked for the divorce, and she and Arthur had been in court ever since, trying to get me back. Then they told me that Daddy knew I was with them, that when he'd kissed me good-bye that morning, he'd already handed my passport over to the embassy."

"Where is he now?"

"Dead," Anne answers. "He died right before I graduated from college. I never saw him again. I went back to Michigan and lived with my mother and Arthur, and once a week a letter would arrive from Daddy, typed by his secretary. When I came out, we invited him, but he said he couldn't come and would appreciate it if Arthur would do the honors."

"Came out?" Steve asked.

At this, Anne sits up. Steve does not know that she has lost her inner sight of Maggie, has lost even her sense of Maggie's shape. "Debutante. White dress, long gloves, summer of parties. Arthur trotting through the cotillion with me like the good sport he is. Daddy sent pearls from the Far East; then, two years later, he was gone." She leans forward, puts her face in her hands.

Steve stands. The bad knee really sticks on him; he leans on it, pressing the leg straight. "Come on," Steve says, taking her by the elbow. "It's time to go inside."

Anne follows him through the darkened campground. She can no longer see Maggie. She's no longer sure Maggie is alive out there; she fears she will never see Maggie again. Anne wonders for a moment if this was how her mother felt when she didn't come home from school that day. The sick fear that she might never get Maggie back, that Maggie might not live to be found, blinds her and she stumbles over a fallen tree limb, braces herself against Steve.

"This way," Steve says. Hands on her shoulders, he steers her in front of him on the path. Her dark hair swings across her face as she turns.

"Careful."

At the cabin steps, he leaves her.

"We'll find her, Anne," he says, despite himself. He knows he's being foolish. "She's not gone. We'll find her, you'll see."

Halfway up the steps, she stops and looks back at him. She says nothing, just turns and walks into the cabin. He waits until the one light inside goes off before he walks on down the path, returns to the command bus.

Day Two

In the blue light before dawn, Ed crouches in the sandy terrace where they found Maggie's shoe and listens. The birds have been calling for an hour already: chickadees and brown creepers circling up and down tree trunks, searching for insects and tiny seeds, setting up their winter hoards. Ed sits entirely still, watching to see what happens. It's something he's always done—go outside and wait until the birds and animals forget he's human and go back about their business. The problem, he thinks, is that people have all these *ideas* about what they think they're supposed to be seeing. They think it's all just landscape, that it just hangs there like some inert curtain behind the real action. He tries to work with new searchers on this, to get them to stop thinking that things have to be a certain way, and get them to start looking at what's right there in front of their faces. There's so much people don't see, all sorts of evidence about the life that goes on when human beings aren't around, animals tracks and plant patterns and whole webs of relationships that don't have anything to do with people at all. It's a little woo-woo for Ed ever to have talked about much, but he knows that the only way to find something is, in some sense, to stop looking with your brain and start *seeing*.

From the big lodgepole thicket to his left, Ed hears a great horned owl boom out an all clear, a bouncing five-note signal that she's done hunting for the night. He's watching to see what the patterns are in this place. Ed has a theory that just as you can tell a hawk's come into an area by the flight squadrons of little birds attacking it, shrieking out warning, fighting off the predatory shadow, so, too, can an observant searcher find a lost person by paying attention to what the place is saying. Problem was that yesterday, Ed got so caught up with the dogs, he forgot to listen, forgot to pay attention. He'd missed what this place might have said to him before it was tramped over by team after team of people, before they made this big mess chasing the dogs through the brush.

The sky is pinking up behind him, lighting the great canyon of air that hangs above the Central Valley. Standing on a rock, Ed notes that the sky is clear except for a bank of clouds over the coast hills; it's too far away to tell if it's weather or just morning fog creeping up from the Delta.

A Swainson's thrush starts up in the willow thickets. Its fluty call, spiraling upward, always reminds him of the opening notes to *Peter and the Wolf*. Ed's surprised; it's late for a thrush still to be hanging around, probably only a week or two till the snows come.

Ed can hear the helicopters revving up down at the campground and he tries to shut them out. The site's a mess, broken plants all over the place, tracks everywhere—even though they tried to be careful, it's clear that several dozen ordinary human beings spent hours milling about on this site. Put it away, Ed tells himself, working to hear through the din of the helis, through his annoyance that people are so messy. He feels himself sinking into the rock, letting his eyes go into soft focus, waiting to see what happens in his peripheral vision, trying to take the scene as a whole, not as the summation of little parts our tricky brains tell us it is. If he were this girl, and lost a shoe here, what would he do? The mother says she hates shoes, and the Velcro was worn on the one they found; it had been coming loose all morning. So, she gets rid of the hateful shoe, and she's heading downhill, toward the sound of running water that hums like a bass note beneath the sounds of wind and birdsong and scolding chickaree. Ed resists the impulse to jump up, race off downhill toward the creek—a trickle, really, this late in the season, snowmelt gone, nothing but an occasional summer thunderstorm to feed it. Forcing himself to stay put, he feels himself sinking into the landscape, and it's as close as the tips of his fingers, the sense of how this lost girl might be thinking, where she went.

MARTHA DRIVES across the spine of the Sierra, passes the faux alpine facades of Strawberry, and begins to watch for her turnoff. "Wright's Lake," Richard told her on the phone, *it's marked*. It's the roadblock that tips her off, nothing fancy, just one sheriff's deputy parked at the end of the road, checking who comes in and out, advising people to stay elsewhere, that the campground's crowded with search and rescue personnel. Martha tells him who she is, and he touches his hat, says he'll radio up and let them know she's on her way. Then he pats the side of her open window twice with his big flat-knuckled hand and says he hopes they find her little girl real soon.

"So do I," Martha says as she puts the white rental car in gear and begins the ten-mile drive to the campground. A couple of miles up, the road leaves the forest and traverses high above the valley. The landscape seems defined entirely by granite and air. Boulders the size of small houses litter the mountainside as far to the west as she can see; they look suspended somehow in an enormous volume of mountain air that is very clear and yet gives off a substantial sense of presence. She is high above the highway, and the valley is wider than she had thought. Martha pulls the car over for a moment. Suddenly, she needs to get out. She's a little dizzy from the exposure.

It's broken, she thinks. Then, shaking her head, she tells herself she's being silly. How can a landscape be broken?

Martha stands for a long while gazing out across the valley of fractured rock that yawns below her. She shakes her head. I'm turning into a foolish old woman. Compared to the rolling expanse of grassland that stretches east from her front porch, even the Front Range looks broken. Somehow, though, these thousands of terraces, these enormous boulders separated by small clumps of trees unsettle her deeply and in a way she can't explain to herself.

Martha drives a little too fast after that, as if trying to outrun the spooked feeling that overtook her back there. When the car fishtails on the washboard, she countersteers, tells herself to be careful. The spring grading is long gone.

Passing through a big burned-over area, she surveys the scorched trunks of pine trees buried waist-deep in blackberry canes, the profusion of purple-and-yellow late-season asters. Maggie will be difficult to find in this sort of undergrowth, she thinks. A little girl could hide in there for a long time without being seen.

What are they going to do? How is she going to help them through this? Martha has been thinking about little else in the twenty-four hours since she got Richard's phone call. She's a practical woman, sees no point in getting upset about worst-case scenarios, which may not, after all, come to pass. But Maggie's been missing for nearly two days now.

It's Anne that she's most worried about. Richard has a sturdy sensibility much like her late husband's—but Anne is different. The first time Richard brought that beautiful, quiet girl home with him, well, they all recognized that she was the one. Her aloof wariness fit in with the reticence of ranch people. Richard, her huggy youngest child, went out and found himself a girl who temperamentally fit into the family almost better than he did. And the story of Anne's early years, that strange episode between her parents—she never speaks of it and yet it's always there, like a shadow behind her eyes. Every time Martha's flown out to help when Maggie was in trouble, she's watched Anne fight that fear she carries around with her, her conviction that no matter how safe things might seem, everything could be gone tomorrow, wrenched away from her without warning.

Martha's been reading about medieval women mystics lately, and it strikes her that Anne shares their sense that the world is but a veil, that death is always with us. Of course, she muses, the difference is that the saints had faith. They sustained themselves on a sort of faith that she knows Anne lacks. Martha doesn't blame Anne for this; she believes that faith is a gift, and if there's a reason that it's been withheld from Anne, it's part of that bigger mystery, the one Martha knows it's not her job to solve. But she worries for this near daughter, wishes she could give her something to cling to, some talisman of belief.

Driving through the open high-altitude forest, Martha sees

glades of bright grass shining in the morning sun slanting through the trees. Then, rounding a corner, she brakes for a line of what must be searchers—men and women spread out along the edge of the road, heading up into the forest. They're sweeping at the long grass, dry now with the onset of fall. She hears them calling Maggie's name.

Maggie, she thinks. Sunshine child, where have you gone? The rental car slips into the curve, rattling in its plastic insubstantiality, so different from the blue truck she usually drives. Maggie the brave, who will jump off the highest stack of bales in the barn, run straight at the geese as though they are long-lost friends, tease the Border collie who hides from her, afraid of her oddness. Look at that happy child, Martha remembers thinking when they visited earlier this summer. Anne's done a good job. Finally old enough to be well most of the time, healthy and running.

Martha had been teaching her to ride, walking her around the yard on big Diesel. Maggie, who exaggerates everything. Martha'd warned her to be gentle around the big horse, not to startle him or he might kick, buck at her. She'd explained that horses do that when they're scared. Patting Diesel, Maggie had tiptoed around the big gelding, whispering "Good horse. Good." Then, astride, her short legs sticking out nearly perpendicular; she'd been so proud, up high like that. Waving at Luke, Anne over on the screen porch. "Just like the homecoming queen," Martha had called out to them, and everyone had laughed as Maggie vamped it up, so excited to be up there alone, high on the big horse's back.

As Martha drives through a level forest of widely spaced ponderosa pine, a helicopter passes, flying low. Turbulence rattles the car and she grips the steering wheel tightly until it passes, roaring on ahead of her.

THE PERCUSSION of helicopter rotor blades tattooes across Luke's chest and he bolts from bed, stumbles, nearly falls down the loft ladder. Dashing through the cabin and out into the gravel driveway, he chases the clamor, hoping to catch a glimpse through a gap in the trees. The helicopters are hidden, but he can still feel the beat of the blades against his ribcage. Standing in the thin sunshine, Luke listens to the drone fade up the mountain, then turns, picks his way across the sharp stones, tiptoes back to the cabin.

His mother is asleep at the table. Luke is surprised he didn't wake her up when he ran outside. She's in a chair, with her head on the wood. Luke watches her for a minute. She looks uncomfortable, but he tiptoes to the bathroom, reluctant to wake her. At least this morning, his parents are here, he thinks, and the bathroom isn't an outhouse, and he isn't in a tent. He decides flushing will be too noisy, so he leaves it and creeps back into the kitchen.

His stomach grumbles, but he doesn't know if there's any food; last night, they ate with the searchers. They stood in line and the lady gave them some stew and noodles and salad and they sat at one of the picnic tables. One of the searchers pulled a quarter out of Luke's ear and then told him really dumb knock-knock jokes, like he was a little kid or something. He smiled to be nice, then nudged at his dad to leave as soon as they finished eating. He doesn't like the way all those people look at him, with those fake smiles grown-ups get when they don't like something. They do it all the time to Maggie, just because she's Down syndrome and she drools.

His mom is not waking up, so he heads outside to wait. He'll watch for more helicopters. His dad said that heat thing works best in the morning, so maybe they'll find Maggie and they can all go home. Luke can't figure out what she's up to. This is worse than being bad; this doesn't make any sense. Maggie likes to be naughty, and she gets in trouble all the time—like when she wouldn't take the bus home from kindergarten and made the bus driver chase her around the building. Kids were watching out of all the windows and yelling "Go Maggie! Run!" even though the teacher said, "Hush. Don't encourage her. Sit down." The bus driver was old and sort of fat, and finally he had to tackle her and carry her, shouting and fighting, onto the bus.

The steps are cold and Luke scootches down a step or two into the warm sunshine. This is so weird, he thinks. There's nobody to see her being bad, and that's what she likes best, an audience. Maggie hates to be alone, and she's afraid of the dark. Luke could understand her being lost the first day—she probably fell asleep—but he can't figure out why she didn't start screaming that first night when she woke up and found herself alone in the dark. Or yesterday when all those people were looking for her. Maggie always makes a scene when she doesn't get what she wants. He half-expected someone to come back with her, saying she'd jumped out from behind a tree and yelled, "Boo!" But all they found was her shoe. That made sense—she hates shoes, and it was really hard teaching her that she had to keep them on at school.

He wonders if there're animals up there. His dad says that wild animals are more afraid of people than we are of them, and if you just leave them alone, they won't hurt you, but Maggie isn't always smart about that stuff. What if she found a bear or something? Maggie might think it was friendly, like on TV, and make it mad, and it could hurt her. Or snakes. Luke doesn't think she could have gotten bitten by a snake unless she surprised it. Maggie won't even go in the snake house at the zoo. But that's because she's afraid of the dark. She might poke at a snake with

133

a stick and get bitten. Or maybe she fell off of something and hurt herself. What he can't figure out is how, if any of these things happened, the search people didn't find her. There were thousands of them. They were everywhere.

Luke sighs and rubs the sleepy bits out of his eyes. He's getting really hungry and he wants someone to wake up.

ED AVOIDS the trail on his way down, cuts along the far side of the lake and comes up on Steve's bus from the back. He doesn't want to have to talk to anyone just yet, doesn't want to lose that focused quiet he's spent the last two hours building. All the action's on the other side of the lake, on the road that leads to the trailhead. Over here there're just a few folks in campsites, just beginning to wake up and get going. Ed walks through the quiet morning, thinking about the site. He's pretty sure she's moved down out of the rock, that she's in the trees below. It's a smart move on her part; it's always warmer in the forest than up high, but it's going to make finding her much harder. Once they go to ground like that, once they're under a log or holed up in a brush pile, it's a bitch to find them, especially if they won't answer when called. Approaching Incident Command, Ed sees that Steve's got a meeting going, so he quietly pries the door open and slips inside.

"I realize that, George," Steve says as Ed steps up into the bus. "But historical statistics for this area show that eighty-seven percent of lost children in the last ten years have been found in the area between the head of the creek and Wright's Lake. Therefore, we assigned the POAs accordingly."

"What are the POAs for the cirque?" Ed has to crane a little to see Melanie over in the corner. She's been on the team for ten years, and she is the sort of person you can always count on to stay calm when the hotheaded guys like himself start locking horns.

Steve checks his clipboard and points to the map mounted on a board behind him. "Yesterday, we calculated possibility of absence in those segments that border the lakes at fifty-eight, fifty-five and fifty-three percent, respectively. Now that we've searched them twice, the POAs are up to seventy-three, eighty-seven, and eighty-six percent."

"We put too many resources up there," George interrupts. Ed can see that he's frustrated. A ginger-haired man with a real Irish temper, George takes kid searches nearly as hard as Ed does. He's a good searcher, but Ed hasn't worked with him much because they both tend to be emotional and short-tempered, and together they're bad for group dynamics. "That's where we lost so much time. I mean," he continues, "it's all granite—you can *see* she's not there."

"That granite's deceptive," a voice says from the far corner of the bus. It's Tim. A big, quiet, transplanted Southerner, he doesn't usually talk much in team leader meetings. "It looks solid, but then as you walk across it, it's all cut with fissures. There's plenty of places she could have hidden in there."

"That's why we're planning to send one last crew across it," Steve says. "We'll use those green teams of new volunteers. It'll give them something to do, and they can't make much trouble up there."

"What about the talus slopes above the lakes?" Dennis asks.

"We've done loose grids across them twice," Steve says. "But with all these volunteers showing up, we've got the manpower to do tight grid searches up there. The POA is pretty high." He glances at the clipboard again. "But if she's up there, we could have missed her in any one of those holes."

"I think she's in the trees." Ed interrupts.

Everyone turns to look at him.

"I was up on the site this morning. I think she got turned by that cliffband that stopped the dogs yesterday and has headed down into the trees."

"But the stats don't say anything about the trees," George replies, looking at a sheaf of papers clipped to his board. "There's never been a kid search that wound up in the trees."

Ed shrugs and leans against the wall. "There's a first time for everything, George."

WHAT WAS that? Anne wakes to a quiet cabin. She hears Richard turn over in the next room. Her neck is stiff. I must have fallen asleep at the table, she thinks, twisting her head slowly, grimacing as she rolls it around on her shoulders. The pain is sharp at first, fades only gradually.

Rising from her seat, Anne walks to the gleam of light that shows through the cracked door. Luke is on the steps, barefoot, in his pajamas. It is not warm out here, she thinks as he turns and sees her.

"I didn't mean to wake you up, Mom," Luke says.

She sits on the step above him, rubs between his shoulder blades. "You didn't wake me up, buddy," she says, restraining herself from pulling him onto her lap. He doesn't like that anymore, but she is hungry for the feel of her child's body, his warm weight, the solid elbows and knees. "I woke up by myself," she says, settling for the lean of him against her legs, his head on her knee. She rubs his warm back through the pajama top.

"Why were you sleeping on the table?" he asks.

"I don't know," she says, yawning. "I guess that's just where I fell asleep."

"It looked uncomfortable."

"Yeah," she answers. "My neck is stiff." They sit, companionable for a few silent moments. Without thinking about it—indeed, almost without noticing—Anne smooths down the place where his hair sticks up in the morning. They can hear shouts down the road at the campground, and the sheer quiet of the morning seems strange to them. Mornings are characterized by Maggie's stomping grumpiness, her difficult wants, specific cereal in a specific bowl, certain school clothes, wanting morning to be somehow different than it is.

Anne and Luke sit on the steps of the strange cabin in unfamiliar silence, neither of them exactly sure what to do next. He needs something on his feet, Anne thinks groggily. It's cold out here. She looks at Luke's slender feet, bare and pink against the unfinished pine boards of the steps. They look as though they are separated from her by deep water, or air with a different specific density.

"I WANT a really small team," Ed's saying to Steve. He's pacing the length of the bus. "I want anyone with tracking experience. . . . "

"There aren't many in this group," Steve says. Ed's got that focused look he gets when he's onto something, and Steve's glad to see it. Ed's useless when he gets scattered like he did yesterday.

"I know," Ed agrees. "Can I get Michelle, and Sandy, and—"

"What about Roy?" Steve suggests.

"Oh God." Ed groans. "Just as long as he doesn't start yammering at me about all that 'inner vision' crap."

"He's good, though."

"Yeah, he is."

"What about that guy who was following Michelle yesterday?" Steve asks.

"Jonathan? He stepped on the only decent clue we've had."

"Give him a break, Ed," Steve says. "It's his first search. Michelle told me last night that she thought he might make a real good tracker, with a little practice."

"Whatever," Ed says. "Send him along. He's not a bad guy. The thing is, I want to get in there before the dog teams. . . . Can we have an hour or forty-five minute lead? Once the dogs and their handlers start running through the area, we can't track for shit."

Steve looks at his clipboard. The Nevada teams spent the night and are already back at the site of the shoe. The Monterey teams should be here within the hour. "Which section are you thinking of?"

They lean over the map. Ed points to the section south of the trail. "I think she's down in here," he says. Tracing a finger from the place last seen, he narrates: "We know where she started, and where she lost the shoe. Yesterday, the dogs tracked her to the top of this cliffband. . . . I think she got turned around by the cliff, edged her way across to here, and headed down into the woods."

Steve nods. "It's plausible," he says. "I can give you forty-five minutes ahead of the dogs. Then I'll send them in behind you. If you're right, that changes the possibility of detection for all these areas in here, and we'll have to reassign teams accordingly. But it's a good hypothesis." Steve hesitates while flipping through the notes on his clipboard. "You sure you want to pull Sandy off her team? She's a good team leader."

"If this works out," Ed says, "that won't really make a difference, will it?"

"Gramma!" Luke shouts as he rockets off the porch and wraps himself around her.

"Careful!" Anne calls after him.

"Hello, dear boy," Martha says, gently unwrapping his arms so she can close the car door.

"Mother?" Richard stands barefoot in the doorway, rubbing sleep out of his face. Jane closes the passenger door of the little rental car and stands waiting. Richard is surprised to see Jane with his mother.

"I found her at the command center," Jane says, waving toward Martha.

"Hi, sleepyhead," Martha says, face alight at the sight of him. They embrace and Luke nearly dances at the sight of his grandmother.

Anne is standing at the top of the stairs, hands crossed in front of her, grasping her elbows. "Is there any news?" she asks Jane.

"Up on the steps, you," Martha says, swatting Luke gently on his bottom. "Look, you don't have any shoes on."

"Nothing yet, I'm afraid," Jane replies. "But if you'd like to come down to the bus, Steve said he'd be happy to go over the plan for the day with you. The morning teams just went out, so he's got a little time."

"Let me get some clothes on," Richard says, ducking back into the cabin.

"When can we expect some news?" Martha asks.

"Hard to say," says Jane. "Ed's gone up with a group of mantrackers—he thinks she's headed down into the forest on the far side of the trail. They'll send dogs in after they're through, then run line searches after that."

A moment of silence descends over them.

"Well, young man," Martha says, steering Luke by one shoulder. "It looks like you need to get dressed." Martha rests a hand on Anne's shoulder as she climbs past her.

Richard holds the door for them, then emerges, pulling on a jacket. "Are you coming?" he asks Anne. She's still standing there, elbows in her hands.

She shakes her head no.

Richard pauses on the stairs.

"Please," she says. "I can't."

"WE DON'T have much time," Ed tells the little group assembled in the woods south of the cliffband. "So, everybody, spread out at a distance of fifteen paces, and let's see what we can find."

Jonathan can't believe they chose him to come along. But he really wants to make up for stepping on the shoe, and he's trying to pay attention.

"Jonathan, we're going to put you between Roy and Michelle. They'll keep an eye on you, and if you see *anything,* tell them so they can come check it out."

Jonathan nods. Single file, the group heads out across the segment, leaving fifteen paces between them. He drops to his hands and knees; then when the signal comes, he begins to crawl across the area, looking for anything that might be a sign of this little girl. She only had one shoe on. She was probably scared after that cliff; he knows he would have been. She's hungry, although if she crossed the creek, she's probably had something to drink. As long as she doesn't get giardia from the water, he thinks. That would dehydrate her faster than anything.

Learning to track reminds Jonathan of that field-biology class he took last spring. The TAs split them into small groups and took them out in the field. His TA was named Wendy, and the first thing she made them do was go sit in the woods alone and write down everything they saw in a little notebook. Jonathan remembers how quiet it was, how he just sat there doodling in his notebook and thinking it was the dumbest assignment he'd ever had. But then, as the semester went on and Wendy pointed out the birds, little ones, hiding in the branches and taught them to recognize the birdsongs, he began to notice things. What had sounded like background noise, what had sounded like nothing, really, became specific. He could hear the whistling of a pair of whitethroats calling to each other, the "loose trill" of the juncos he'd seen all his life but never noticed. It was the hermit thrush that he fell in love with, though. He thought there was nowhere he'd rather be than sitting in the woods at dusk, those spiral songs falling around him like streamers at a birthday party.

Tracking seems sort of the same, once you learn to see things that ordinary people never notice—the signs a person leaves behind, especially a frightened person who isn't being careful, who's maybe panicking. Then you can follow the broken twigs, scuffed plant stems, trail of crushed leaves. And his field biology will come in handy—Ed talked to him about watching what the animals were doing for any sign of disturbance.

Slowly, the five searchers crawl through the brush, watchful, alert, scanning the forest floor for any tiny sign, any disturbance in the field.

"UPSTAIRS, YOU," Martha says, shooing Luke toward the loft ladder. "Get some warm clothes on."

"I'm hungry," he says.

"I brought groceries. Get dressed and then we'll make some breakfast."

"Pop-Tarts?" Luke asks.

"Put some clothes on and we'll see." Luke climbs the loft ladder slowly, trying to eavesdrop on his mother and grandmother.

"Thank you for coming," Anne says, leaning in the doorway.

"It's easier than worrying at home." Martha waves one hand to shoo Luke up the ladder. "Coffee?"

"I saw filters around here somewhere." Anne crosses the kitchen and opens a cabinet with a yank. A small avalanche of tea boxes, spice bottles, and packets of sauce mix pours out across the counter.

"Here," Martha says, reaching over her shoulder and catching a bottle of maple syrup. Anne's hands are full of bottles and packages. Martha takes them from her, then gently grasps Anne's shaking hands in her own. "It's going to be okay," she says, and cups one hand along Anne's cheek. "We'll get through this."

Anne nods, staring at her feet. She can't speak, because if she does, the tears that have welled up in her eyes will spill over and she'll give in to the urge to throw her arms around this woman she loves, this woman who has always come to her aid when there's trouble, and bawl as if she were Luke's age. Anne can't speak, because she's afraid that once she starts crying, she might be swept away on an endless river of salt water.

"Sit here." Martha steers Anne into a chair. "I'll make coffee and some breakfast, and we'll figure out what to do next."

"I have to go look for her," Anne says.

"You should probably let the searchers take care of that." Martha pours grounds into the filter. "Don't you think?"

"I can't leave her out there," Anne says. "I left it to them yesterday, and look where that got us."

Martha looks at her for a long minute. "You think they're not doing a good job?" she asks.

"They haven't found her yet, have they?"

"Whatever you do," Martha says carefully, "you're going to have to live with for a long time."

"That's why I have to go up there."

"They'll try to stop you."

Anne's up out of the chair and halfway to the door.

"I'm worried about Luke," Anne says, gesturing toward the loft with her chin.

"Leave him to me," Martha says. "We're used to waiting together."

The two women stand there, silent for a moment.

"Be careful, okay?" Martha asks.

"I will." Anne pauses in the doorway. "Thank you."

"Go," Martha says. "We'll be fine."

Anne pulls the baseball cap low over her eyes and heads for the sandy gravel trail that leads back up through the pine forest, back out onto that bare granite, and up and over the lip of the cirque to the place where she last saw her daughter. She feels like a boxer hopping from foot to foot in the corner of the ring, centering himself for the blows to come, gathering his energy to one crucial focal point, the only point that matters, the blow that will knock out his opponent. Anne gathers herself, feels herself zoning in on her daughter, sensing her presence in this space, listening for her loud breath through the wind in the trees. Maggie is out there, and Anne leans into her stride, nearly running as she heads back out to hunt down and vanquish the invisible force that has taken her daughter from her.

"HOW ARE you this morning?" Steve asks when Richard and Jane enter the bus.

"All right," Richard says. "Is there any news?"

"Not yet," Steve says. He gestures Richard over to the map

143

table. The three of them pause, looking at the tangle of grease-pencil marks on plastic that delineate the history of Maggie's absence.

"The helis have come up with three suspicious warm spots," Steve says. "One down here in the trees, and then these two—one up by the PLS, and one over here near Grouse Lake."

Jane hands them each a cup of coffee.

"Thanks," Richard says. He's still not entirely awake and is trying to grasp this helicopter thing. "Could the warm spot be Maggie?" he asks.

Steve's radio crackles, and as he turns to answer it, Jane says, "The helis have trouble down in the trees like that. It could be Maggie, but it could also be a number of other things."

"At Aloha?" Steve asks into the radio as Jane and Richard pause a moment.

"Since they pick up anything warm," Jane continues. "It could also be an animal, or a hot spring."

"We'll send someone right over," Steve says, signing off.

"What was that?" Richard asks.

"A boy in the campground over at Lake Aloha claims to have seen Maggie early this morning, before anyone was up."

"Aloha?" Richard asks looking at the map. "She went over the ridge?" He can't imagine Maggie up in all that talus, climbing up and over the top of the mountain behind the twin lakes.

"Look, this could be anything," Steve cautions. "These kid sightings are notoriously unreliable. We're sending someone over in the heli to talk to the boy. Remember, this has been all over the TV news. In the meantime," Steve continues, turning back to the map, "our best shot is still down here in this area. We've got a shoe and a suspicious spot on the heli infrared. . . . The POD is pretty high, as opposed to these other spots."

Richard gets suddenly dizzy looking at the map and holds on to the table edges. POD, infrared, helicopters, footprints, television . . . *It was only a day hike.*

"Where'd mom go?" Luke asks as he jumps from the fourth rung on the ladder. Martha nearly reaches out to spot him, but he's too big for that now and she finds herself stifling the urge to snap at him to be careful. She hates it when parents carp at children about ordinary risks.

"She went to look for Maggie," Martha tells him.

"By herself?"

"Mmhmm," Martha says. "Come on, there're groceries in the car that need to be carried." Luke follows her to the car and she's glad she thought to get food. There doesn't seem to be much in the cabin. "Here," Martha says, handing him a brown paper grocery sack. "Careful, it's got eggs in it."

"Mom keeps leaving," Luke says.

"What do you mean?"

"She doesn't want to stay in the cabin. And she *hates* the bus."

"Why do you think she hates the bus?" Martha asks.

"I don't know, but she ran out of there yesterday like it was on fire or something," Luke tells her. "Dad says it's because she's scared."

"We're all scared, Luke," his grandmother says, following him up the cabin steps.

"I wish she didn't keep leaving, though," Luke says, putting his bag on the table.

"Well, let's just hope they find Maggie soon so we can go home," Martha says.

"Will you come home with us afterward?" Luke asks, unpacking the sack. "Yes!" he says pulling the box of frosted strawberry

145

Pop-Tarts out of the bag. "Can I have one right now—I'm starving."

"Sure, sweetheart," she says. "But only one envelope, okay?"

ANNE STOPS at the trail register. Warily, she approaches it and flips the pages back. There they are: Richard's square architectural handwriting, and just below, Maggie's undisciplined scrawl, the *g*'s written backward. She'd insisted on signing, stomped her feet and shouted while her brother rolled his eyes and said, "Just let her sign, Dad." Anne runs a finger over the pencil marks. The people who signed this register seem separated from her by a greater distance than two days.

Hiking back up this trail is a very strange experience for her, every corner and boulder marked by some shadow of that first hike. The place Maggie fell chasing the jay. The place Luke hid from them and leapt out, scaring his sister so she shrieked in delight. The place where Maggie refused to get out of the creek. The graduated boulders the kids climbed, leaping from one to another until they were much too high, the dicey moment when it looked like Maggie was going to jump and her father was sharp with her.

There are pieces of fluorescent surveyor's tape tied to twigs on either side of the trail. Anne comes around a corner and sees, at the end of a flat gladed stretch of trail, a crowd of searchers milling around. There must be forty of them. She shrinks back, retreating a few steps back down the trail. She can't go out there. They'll ask her all sorts of questions and try to send her back to the cabin, try to make her go sit in a corner and wait while they fail to find Maggie and then tell her there was nothing she could do.

She cuts into the woods to her left. The creek is down there— if she crosses it, she can bushwhack up through the boulder field.

Maggie would have followed the creek; they had to pull her out of it three times on the way up. She was obsessing over stick boats, floating them downstream until she couldn't see them anymore, then breaking another twig, starting over. When Maggie gets in that mode, that hypnotic state, it's tough to pull her out of it, and she was determined to keep playing. Anne climbs over a downed tree. There is thick underbrush, and she pushes alder branches out of her way. She finds herself at the edge of a mini-canyon; it's probably a twenty-foot drop to the creek below. Anne ducks through the shrubbery, working her way upstream to a point where she can jump across the creek.

Maggie's not in here. Anne's not sure how she knows this, but the woods have that same vacancy that the house does when Maggie is not in it. She's out in the boulders somewhere, Anne's certain. So she climbs up out of the creekbed and out onto the bare rock.

She's shocked by the number of people up here. She can see four search teams working their way in lines across the landscape just from where she stands. Somehow, although she'd seen them all below, seen them lined up to get supper, or crowded around the picnic area Steve uses for group meetings, she hadn't thought there were so many, or that they'd be everywhere like this. And they've all left their jobs for this—hundreds of people using up their vacation days because Anne and Richard were stupid. It's horrifying.

She figures she can either hide from them or act as if she's entitled to be there. She chooses the latter because she learned long ago that it's the only way to deal when the "experts" have tried to shut her out of decisions affecting Maggie. She's not going to go ducking behind rocks, sneaking around like some fugitive. She's looking for her daughter. She has every right to be here.

147

Anne stops for a moment to take stock. She's in a terrace sheltered by four large boulders. The terrain is stairstepped with these sandy flat spots between boulder groups all the way up to the lakes where Maggie disappeared. Anne begins climbing, one set at a time, stopping to listen to her sense of Maggie's absence. Is it getting stronger? Weaker? Can she feel herself honing in on Maggie? She's following her instincts, turning left or right accordingly, as if following some sort of maternal magnetic field, a vein of energy and attraction that will lead her to her child. Maggie doesn't feel like a separate person who has been lost, but, rather, as if a piece of Anne's own body has been torn from her and flung into this vast jumble of rock and dirt and tangible sky. Slowly, through the hazy heat of midmorning, Anne climbs and pauses, then climbs on.

FLORIDA'S SO fucking far away, Ed thinks as he crawls through the woods. They're in open ponderosa forest with light understory, not the dense brush that sets in a few hundred feet lower in elevation. They've been moving right along for almost fifteen minutes now. Why does Amy need to take him all the way to Florida? She says it's nothing personal—she just doesn't want to live in California anymore, doesn't want to live with him. Nothing personal? Ed remembers when she said that on the phone. He can't figure out what happened. It was only a vacation. She was only going back to visit her folks.

She'd been out here going to school when Ed met her. Everyone was worried that she was so young. Shit, Ed had worried about it. She was only a couple of years older than Jennie, Steve and Jane's daughter, and at first he couldn't figure out why she'd want to be hanging out with him. She was a triathlete, spent all the time she wasn't in school training, and weekends he, and sometimes Steve, if he wasn't working, would go watch her race. Ed loved to see her come out of the water, the black numbers written on her leg, and run, stripping off the goggles and bathing cap, hopping into her shoes, then racing out of the bike pit. She'd raced even when she was pregnant with Aaron. The doctor had said it was okay up till about the sixth month or so. She laughed at Ed's worries, claimed to be training the baby young, claimed she was going to make a champ out of him.

Ed stands for a minute, looking out across the line of searchers. He shakes his head as if to shake out these thoughts of Amy and Aaron and the mess he's made of his life again. This little girl can't afford to have him distracted; he's got to stay on track. He can't see most of his team members, which is a good thing—means they're all down close to the dirt, doing their job. Ed scans the terrain, then checks his topo map. He's looking for a convergence of lines, a gully, or drop-off—some place she could be hidden down inside, someplace that the dogs and the helicopters wouldn't be able to find her.

Then he's back on his hands and knees again—back into the enclosed world of unbruised brush, intact wildflowers, and heart-breakingly untracked dirt.

CONFRONTED BY a boulder too big to climb, Anne circumnavigates it and is startled by bright fluorescent flagging—concentric rings of tape flags that lead, she sees, to a small space, entirely ringed by pink tape, in the center of which is Maggie's shoe. Careful not to disturb the tape, Anne climbs over it, scrambling toward this tangible sign that Maggie is really out here somewhere. The shoe is tipped on its side, as if left behind by someone fleeing great danger. Anne thinks of the drifts of shoes in the

149

concentration camp museum; shoes, old now and brittle—the leather cracked, the tops folded at unseemly angles.

She wants it, wants to clutch this talisman to her chest and not let it go until she has Maggie back again. Anne reaches to touch it, then stops. Her hand hovers mere millimeters above the shoe.

Scent. She shouldn't ruin the clue. Jane said there were more dog teams coming in today.

It's Maggie's shoe. Anne crouches, her palm mere centimeters from the shoe. Eyes closed, she tries to feel Maggie's presence through this lost object. Maggie, where are you?

The shoe tells her nothing. It's simply a shoe—inert. This frightens Anne more than she can say, and she stands, backs away from it slowly, as one would back away from a beloved animal turned suddenly vicious.

Anne turns in a slow circle. She sees white granite and a flat white sky, high clouds blocking the blue. The only sounds are wind and the trickle of water through the outlet creek.

"I'M SORRY," Richard says, staring down at the tangled map. "I'm going crazy with nothing to do." He starts to pace again.

"Look," Steve begins cautiously. "I've explained why we don't send parents out on searches."

"Steve," Jane breaks in. "What about sending him up on those talus sections with the high POA?" Steve looks over at her, and she nods once, slightly, at him.

"POA?" Richard asks, looking bewildered.

"Possibility of absence," Steve answers automatically.

"I can't stand just doing nothing," Richard says.

Steve looks at the map. "Letting you do this," he says, "requires that you stop acting like her parent and agree to be a searcher."

"Of course," Richard says. "Anything."

"What this means," Steve continues, knowing he's asking the impossible, but also knowing that if he's going to take this kind of risk with his searchers, he's got to be somewhat sure he's not sending a loose cannon up there, "is that you absolutely *must* agree to obey your search team's leader. We can't have you bolting off every time you think you see something."

"I know," Richard says. "Don't worry—I'll do whatever you want me to do."

Steve still isn't sure this is a good idea, but Richard has guide experience, he's a reliable outdoorsman, he ran a good hasty search with his family, and he was exemplary on line searches that first night out.

"Really," Richard adds. "I won't be a problem."

"I'll send you up on Jake's squad," Steve says, pointing to a section of the map heavily covered in grease pencil. "They're doing one last grid search on this quadrant." Steve points to the map. "The POA is eight-five percent up there right now, so we're going to run a man-heavy grid search to make sure."

"Have they left yet?" Richard asks. "Where do I meet them?"

Steve is looking at his watch. "They left about twenty minutes ago. If you hurry—"

"Thanks," Richard says, halfway out of the bus.

Steve watches after him for a long moment.

"He'll be fine," Jane says. "He just needed something to do."

Steve looks back at the map.

"What is it?" Jane asks.

"If the dogs don't pick up something soon . . . " Steve says.

151

"There's a storm system moving in, temperature's dropping, cloud cover's building." He hesitates, looks over at her behind her cup of coffee. "If it rains like they've been predicting . . ."

"You're doing your best," she says. "That's all you can do."

Steve has a bad feeling about sending Richard up there. He trusts Jane's instincts, but . . . It was a years ago now. A toddler disappeared out in the rice fields north of Sacramento. It was winter, and raining like a banshee, so they sent divers in to check the culverts. Steve was chest-deep in water when they handed the kid to him, and when he turned to pass the body to the next searcher, he found himself putting that limp child into his father's arms. Steve's never forgotten the look of horror and grief in that man's face.

There," Luke says, pointing to the helicopter that rests, blades drooping, in the center of the gravel parking lot. "Will you ask them? Please?"

"Okay, sweetheart," Martha says. "You stay here."

"Tell him it's *important, Gramma,*" Luke says as she walks into the clear space.

"I will, I will," she says, waving one hand behind her as she approaches the big machine. Luke's urgency worries her, but she supposes it's only natural, under the circumstances. Identifying herself to the man leaning against the machine, she points to Luke standing by the tree. Looking at him through this stranger's eyes, he looks like a much smaller child, one who perhaps needs a rest room, but the man smiles and waves Luke over.

"My name's Scott," the pilot says to Luke. "Now, the first

thing you need to know about helicopters is that you *never* approach a helicopter unless the captain gives you permission. Why do you think that is, Luke?"

"So you don't get hurt if the blades start turning," Luke says quickly. "I watched you guys all day yesterday. I want to see inside." He stands on tiptoe a little to see in the high door. Martha wonders what he thinks is in there, what he's so set on.

"Okay, buddy," Scott says, opening the door. "Climb on in." He holds the door for Martha as well, but she declines.

"No thanks. I'll stay out here," she says. "I'm not real fond of tight spaces."

"Well, I'll leave this door open and you can see just about everything from where you are," Scott says.

"Thank you," Martha replies. She watches Scott explain to Luke about lift and momentum, about the radio, about loading and unloading safely.

"What about the red thing?" Luke asks.

"The red thing?" Scott asks.

"Yeah, you know, the thing that lets you see Maggie," Luke insists. His face is tense and there is a moment of strained silence as Scott tries to figure out what Luke's talking about. "You know," he insists. "The thing that shows where she is, because she's warm."

"Oh—the infrared," Scott replies, and Martha can see the relief in his face. Who wants to disappoint the boy whose sister is lost? "That's actually attached to the outside of the plane, and it's called an FLIR."

"A what?"

"FLIR—forward-looking infrared."

"Where do you look at it?"

"Here," Scott says pointing to a small television screen. "The

154

FLIR detects the difference in temperature between objects," he explains. "Like, say, the difference between Maggie and all that rock up there. Then it shows up on this screen. It looks sort of like a green-and-black TV picture of a person."

"Can you turn it on now?" Luke asks.

"No." Scott says. "It only works when we're flying. And the reason I'm on the ground right now is because it works best at night, or early in the morning when the ground temperature has dropped. See, now that it's warmed up outside, the FLIR doesn't work so well."

"Oh," Luke says, looking at the dead gray screen.

"Why, Luke?" Martha asks, looking in at the little boy.

"I wanted to see Maggie," he says. "Dad told me they could see Maggie on the helicopters."

An urgent voice bleats from the radio transceiver: "Clear channel. Clear channel."

Steve whirls from the map, grabs the mouthpiece. "Clear twenty-four," he replies. "All units, clear twenty-four." He turns the receiver dial, clicking it until the red LED display reads 24. Jane's hand has strayed to her face. The clear channel command is reserved for urgent news—victim or body recoveries, usually—for messages not meant to be overheard by family members, or the media.

"Command, this is George. Do you read me?"

"You're clear," Steve replies. "What have you got?"

"It's the mother."

"What about her?"

"She's up here," George says. "I'm right above the PLS, at B-four, and she's down in the rocks . . . probably about C-three or so."

Jane's hand floats down, rests against her diaphragm in relief. It's not a body.

"What's she doing?"

"Looks like she's searching," he replies. "What do you want us to do about her?"

Steve runs a finger down the coordinates they've drawn across the topos. She's in the rocks between the PLS and the shoe. He looks to Jane for her take on this.

"It's your call," Jane says. "But as long as she's not impeding the search, or in danger of hurting herself, I'd be tempted to leave her up there."

"Christ," Steve says, looking back at the map.

"Steve?" George's voice says out of the transceiver.

"I'm here," Steve says. She's in the rocks, where she'll be highly visible. He can tell the teams to keep an eye on her, but one of the first rules of searching is to contain the victim's family.

"She'll be okay," Jane says. "She's got plenty of experience."

Steve nods, then says quietly into the handset, "Leave her alone."

"Just let her wander around out there?" George asks. "You sure?"

"Yeah," Steve says. "I'm putting out a call on the open channel to keep an eye on her but not to disturb her. If she looks like she might get hurt, call me before doing anything."

There is a long silence on the other end of the radio.

"George?" Steve asks.

"Ten-four," George replies.

Steve can hear the tension in his voice. "Your search quadrant is your primary responsibility," he assures him. "She'll be all right out there."

156

"Let's hope so," George replies.

"Are we done with this conversation?" Steve asks.

"Ten-four."

"Back to open channel, then."

"Back to open channel."

Steve rubs his hands across his face before switching the red numbers on the dial and giving general instructions to the group.

As the team leaders send in their affirmations one by one, Steve looks across the map table at Jane. "This search is getting less and less orthodox by the minute," he says. "It's beginning to make me nervous."

"What's more important?" she asks. "Running a by-the-numbers search or taking the best care possible of these people?"

"Finding the kid," he replies.

RICHARD HIKES up the trail as quickly as he can, grateful for the ache in his calves, the ripping sensation of air filling and emptying his lungs, the painful clunk of the water bottle in his pack against the hard ridges of his spine.

He passes through the forest and the trail gets suddenly steeper as he climbs into the granite high country. Leaning into the ache in his legs, Richard pushes himself, seeking the haven of physical exertion.

Maggie sunshine. Maggie the difficult. Maggie the Hun. Her reign in their lives has been that of a benign tyrant. "Oh," people say with that simpering look on their faces when they hear his daughter is Down's. "Those children are so sweet." Yeah, he thinks to himself, you should have seen her clock that kid with her lunch box when I picked her up at preschool yesterday.

Retarded. He remembers how the word hit him. Once as a boy, his horse butted him in the back so hard that he lost his breath; he never quite trusted that horse again. Those dead-eyed, shuffling children on the country school bus. Tormented for letting their noses run long past an age when even the littlest first graders knew about boogers. Tormented for their big soft bodies, for looking back with those bovine eyes, just hurt and dim, not even puzzled, which would have implied wanting to find out *why* they were being tormented, but just sad, taking the taunts, the occasional sneaky blow, the pinches that left welts on the fat pink arms.

His baby was going to be like that? Clinging to the phone like a life raft, his mother on the other end. "Our baby, Mom. Please come." Anne crying because the baby couldn't nurse, because this seemed like the first in an endless chain of things this baby wouldn't be able to do. The social workers and counselors who quietly mentioned that the baby could be given away, if that was what they decided. Anne, wild at them in a hospital nightgown, IV pole in her hand, chasing them out of her room, then collapsing, weeping, into the bed, waving him away when he tried to help. She was twenty-seven years old and beautiful, an artist, successful. How could she have produced something wrong, something damaged? Crying, "Where is my baby?"

Richard stops a moment, breath ragged from the pace at which he's been attacking the trail. One hand resting on a boulder, he bends nearly double, gasping for air. And even now, he thinks. She can't see how Maggie's disappearance affects the rest of them. She walks right past that scared "I didn't mean to" look in Luke's eyes. He should have married someone sensible, like his mother, someone who could cope. Richard's ragged breathing settles, his heart ceases to pound so heavily, and shrugging on the day pack, he begins again to walk up the trail toward the place where Maggie disappeared.

ANNE KNOWS that they are going to start telling her Maggie is gone. Gone like that scarf she finally gave up looking for, the one that disappeared out of the underwear drawer where she was sure she had folded it, where she clearly remembered placing it next to the sexy underwear she bought as a surprise for Richard, the lace so stiff and scratchy that she doesn't wear it, not even when the laundry needs to be done. They are going to try to tell her that Maggie is like that scarf, just gone, and that she should accept it, move on, pack up the car and drive down the mountain, back to the house. That she should pack up Maggie's room because Maggie is lost and cannot be found.

Anne knows they are wrong, as they've been wrong so many times about Maggie. She's not gone. Anne would know if Maggie were dead, and what she knows with utter certainty is that although Maggie is not dead, something very strange has happened, something that has silenced her noisy girl. For even as an infant, Maggie was the sort of baby continually chugging out a little stream of noise, as if to say, Here I am, here I am. I'm your baby; I'm over here.

The wind blows steadily into the container that is this valley as Anne stands on a rock, looking out into that volume of emptiness, the negative space in which her child cannot be found. Picking her way uphill into another empty sand terrace between boulders, Anne can't imagine what else to do. Maggie is out here, and her mother will search for her as long as it takes to find her. *Maggie will be found.* She lets the phrase repeat itself in her head like a mantra. *Maggie will be found.*

MICHELLE CALLS out quietly, "Ed, come look at this."

And there they are. Footprints. Two of them, in the mud. Heading downhill, on the bank of the Secret Lake outlet creek. Ed crouches to see them better; holding his hand over the prints, careful not to touch them, not to contaminate the scent, he measures. Heel of the print to heel of his hand, the toes reach to the first joint on his index finger.

Ed stands and is momentarily blinded by the rush of blood falling to his feet. In the pool earlier this summer, he and Aaron goofing off. Ed had crouched, Aaron's feet in his hands, then rose quickly to full height, throwing the boy into the air. Aaron squealing with the sudden rush of it, rising from the water, launching into the hot valley air, then the splash, his big dad fishing him out of the water so they could do it again. Aaron had those things on his arms, orange floats so that when he hit the water his face didn't really go under. His feet fit in Ed's cupped hands, his toes curling into the base of Ed's fingers.

Ed shakes his head to clear his vision, tells himself to keep his thoughts on the search. Turning back to the small feet imprinted in the mud, he asks, "How fresh do you think they are?"

"Hard to say," Michelle answers. "At least a day," she says, waving for Jonathan to come closer. "See, look at the crust on the mud, the debris that's blown into them." When Michelle points, her index finger is nearly as long as the foot.

Ed turns away, pulls the radio from his chest holster. Dog teams. Steve's going to want to send in the dog teams, and while Ed knows this is procedure, part of him regrets it, is afraid the dogs will just mess everything up like they did yesterday. He can't figure out why he feels so strongly about the dogs; he's never had

160

this much trouble with them before. As Steve answers his call, Ed reminds himself to ask if she's scared of dogs. Maybe that's it.

RICHARD TWISTS his way through a section of trail that winds between narrow boulders taller than his head. It's a strange little gully of a place, and the first time they came through here, Luke and Maggie ran ahead and hid. Anne and Richard could hear them giggling from their hiding place, but like good parents they jumped, claiming to be scared to death by the surprise of two children leaping at them from behind large rocks.

He thought they'd come out of the woods, his family, that they'd made it to some safe glade of sunlight after the darkness of those unbearable days right after Maggie was born. Her Down's was a total surprise. They hadn't had an amnio—it hadn't seemed worth the risk of miscarriage. Anne was young and healthy; Luke had been a normal pregnancy; there was no history in either of their families. And then the terror when the doctors whisked her away for tests and more tests, that first scary surgery where they put the shunts in her nose so she could breathe while nursing, and they were bereft on that floor full of happy families. Normal families who had guests arriving with balloons, stuffed toys, lining up at the nursery window, checking out the babies like loaves of new bread in their boxes. Their friends didn't know what to do, those who came anyway, who hadn't heard—their faces falling at the news. Anne's resolute will periodically dissolving in angry tears. Then like an angel dropping through the operatic storm clouds of a Baroque ceiling, Kathy appeared. Her baby was three, she explained. She brought pictures of a cute black-haired child laughing from a swing. She brought books, explained that their children had more hope than those scary kids they remembered from school. Explained about

161

infant brain development, and that the idea was to get as many circuits activated as possible. That with lots and lots of exercises, stimulation, input, their child could have bright eyes, learn to count, to read, go to school in mainstream classrooms. She visited people, Kathy said, because she had wanted to kill herself after Timmy was born, because she felt like such a failure, felt she had done something wrong.

Richard emerges from the narrow cleft of rock and blinks at the bright glare of the high granite landscape. His group is up above the lakes, and one hand over his eyes, he scans for them. There are at least five groups he can see from the place he stands, and for a moment he's afraid he won't be able to tell which group he's looking for. Steve said they'd look for him, that they'd signal, so Richard begins to hike again, trying to have faith that he won't fail in even this simple task.

Looking back on Maggie's early days, Richard thinks of those old-fashioned captions that played between the scenes of silent movies: *The narrow escape.* Everything changed for them after they found Kathy, the parents' support groups, the right doctors—they could see a way through. Richard took on more work to pay for Maggie's doctor bills, to set money aside for her, to pay for the specialists and all the help. Both he and Anne had some money of their own, but Richard held a rancher's sense of the imprudence of dipping into the capital, of going into debt. He'd come home at night, his head full of lumber estimates, blue lines on sandy paper, and the house would be littered with bright toys, Anne on the floor, singing and moving Maggie's limbs, Luke hopping up and down. "Maggie! Maggie!" he'd chirp in his little-boy voice. "Look, Dad! Look! She followed me with her eyes!"

Anne's enormous efforts paid off, and once they saw Maggie through the terrifying surgery, the endless winter infections, she grew, she developed. Richard thinks of the stuff he never expected from her, the sense of humor, for one. She's sly, Maggie girl, and likes to tease people. Richard remembers his surprise the first time he saw her pretend to be more retarded than she was. It was in an airplane, seated next to Luke; she let her tongue hang out of the slack jaw, her eyes went vacant, and the stewardess slipped her an extra package of cookies. Then the shocking transition: Maggie giggling with Luke, their heads together, Luke opening the cellophane so they could share their booty.

And now, stopping to catch his breath, leaning one arm against that ever-present white granite, now what? He thinks of Luke, ahead of them as usual: "Dad, are we going to have to leave her here?"

Richard pushes away from the rock and hurries faster toward the search team he's to join. They'll find her, he tells himself. There're thousands of them.

"OH, SWEETHEART," Martha says. "I think your dad meant they could *look* for Maggie on that screen." Scott is looking at her like a man who has unexpectedly found a tiny bird in his hand and is afraid of crushing it.

"No," Luke insists. "He said they could see her." He sits back in the passenger seat hard, as if to express his rage at the unfair nature of the adult world.

"Well, sport," Scott says, "part of the problem is they think your sister's down in the trees. And trees are warm, too, so it's hard for this thing to tell the difference between a warm tree and a little girl."

"Trees aren't warm," Luke says, looking resolutely out the front window of the helicopter.

"Yes, they are," Scott says. "Well, at any rate, they're warmer than stone—anything alive is warmer than something like stone, which isn't."

"So what *did* you see?" Luke asks.

"Well, we saw trees . . . and a couple of big marmots . . . and that was about it."

Luke continues to stare out the window.

"I'm sorry, son," Scott says quietly. "We're trying our best, but if she's down in the forest, or under a pile of rocks in a little cave, we're not going to find her using the FLIR."

The three of them sit for a moment looking at the machinery. Martha can see Luke is close to tears. She exchanges a look with Scott, who climbs down from the pilot's seat. "Come on, Luke," she says. "Let's go find some lunch."

He climbs out of the helicopter and his disappointment is clear in the line of his shoulders, the droop of his head. It seems to have settled on all three of them.

"Can you thank Scott for showing you the helicopter?" Martha asks. Disappointment is no reason not to be polite.

Luke nods. "Thank you," he says, holding out his hand like he's been taught.

Scott takes the boy's hand. "You're welcome, son. Don't worry," he adds with a hand on the boy's shoulder. "We'll find her somehow. If it's not the helicopter, it'll be the dog teams, or the trackers. You'll see."

Luke nods and looks at his feet.

ANNE HAS made her way up and over the little ridge that delineates the cirque and has slowly found her way back to the PLS. She could see it from the cusp of the ridge, ringed with tape flags, the colors looking even brighter in the overcast light. Reluctantly, as if drawn by some outside force, she found herself picking her way down through the boulders to this place. She looks to the sky—high cloud cover. If it doesn't rain, this will be good, will keep it from getting so cold at night. As long as it doesn't rain.

She walks past the empty rings of flagging, which tell her nothing, this empty center, back to the spot where she'd been laying out their lunch. After Luke had run up, Anne climbed a hump of rock, trying to see where Luke and Richard were looking for Maggie. The wind had blown down out of the cirque behind her; she'd put a hand to her face to hold the brown hair back.

What was I thinking? she asks herself. I just stood here trying to do the right thing, more concerned with being good, with not making a scene, with not panicking than I was with finding my daughter. I *knew,* she thinks. I knew she was in trouble and I didn't do anything but stand here on this stupid rock, bleating out her name like some sort of helpless ninny. Why didn't I go after her? Why did I let Richard and Luke go when I *knew* she was in trouble?

She'd thought it was like all those times she'd searched the house, frantically opening closet doors, lifting dustruffles, until flipping up the hamper lid she heard that rough breathing, found Maggie, head fallen back, mouth open, snoring gently. The fantasy flashes through Anne's head that Maggie is at home, that they left her behind, that she's sleeping safe in her bed, under the mountain of stuffed animals that she insists on piling over herself each night.

I couldn't have left the lunch spot, she tells herself. Someone had to stay put. What if I'd left and Maggie had come back? Then she would have cried, and I would have run to her, and it would have been another minor trauma, another moment of anger and relief mixed with the endless frustration of trying to teach Maggie to behave. But instead, she just stood there, one hand shading her eyes, every bit of willpower poured into resisting her instincts, resisting that voice in her head that was screaming at her that something was really wrong this time, that Maggie was in serious trouble.

Anne buries her face in her hands and listens. She is absolutely certain she'd know if Maggie were dead. Something would happen—like that night years ago when she'd been walking home from the library and had seen her father, incongruous in his pinstriped formality on that Boulder street of India prints and long hair. He'd been waiting for a streetlight and she'd only had time to think, But where's his driver? before he was gone.

Walking the three blocks to her house, Anne had felt a sense of loss so acute, she might almost have been back on that plane from Singapore. She'd walked those blocks on the verge of tears, feeling as if it had all been pulled out from under her. The street had looked suddenly unfamiliar. She was lost, like one of those dreams where your ordinary world becomes unrecognizable. Then her mother's voice on the machine, the message sprinkled with "dearhearts" and "darlings," telling her her father was dead, in Singapore, so far away. Anne had stood looking out her window toward that streetcorner for a long time, hoping for another glimpse of his heavy, stoop-shouldered form.

Anne stands listening, but she hears nothing.

"WE'VE GOT prints," Ed says, trying to keep his voice calm. "But they're not fresh."

"How old are they?"

"Michelle thinks they're at least a day old."

"Where are you?"

Ed unfolds his map, crouches to lay it flat so he can read the grid coordinates. "Looks like we're at about A . . . A-five," he answers.

"The nearest dog units are over on B-three," Steve replies. "It should take them about fifteen minutes to get to you. Is there any other sign?"

"Not much," Ed says. "We secured the area to ten feet, and I'm only letting Michelle in there to check it out. But it's pretty bare. If she was here, these look like they're the only sign she left."

"What's the measurement on them?" Steve asks. They'll check it against the shoe dimensions. The problem with footprints is that they might not be hers. Although Ed doesn't think there could have been too many other barefoot little girls this far off the trail.

"Six and a quarter by two and a half inches."

"That's about right," Steve replies.

"How much time did you say we have until the dogs get here?" Ed asks.

"About fifteen minutes."

"Any way you can give us half an hour?"

There is a long pause on the other side of the radio.

"I'd like the chance to really check the place out before it gets hammered," he adds.

"I'll tell them to take their time," Steve says. "But I can't hold dogs off a live clue."

"We won't know it's live until the scent matches," Ed says. "But thanks, that'll give us a chance."

"If the scent is live, it's going to get crowded over there," Steve says.

"I know," Ed answers. "The POAs will all change. At least if

167

she's headed into the woods, though, she's got a better chance at keeping warm."

Ed replaces the radio in his chest holster and walks over to where Michelle is crawling in a slow circle around the footprint.

"Anything?" Ed asks her.

"Not yet," she says. "Except she's lost both shoes this time."

LUKE IS mad. His grandmother said they should go do something useful and not just sit around worrying, so she volunteered them to help clean up lunch and make dinner. Now Luke is stuck dragging a green garbage sack around to all the picnic tables and picking up the plastic forks that fell in the dirt, and the old napkins that got left behind. He has to wipe off the tables, too. He doesn't like touching the bits of food and things that were left behind and he wishes he had another kid to do this with so they could make a game of it. He and Maggie would have made a game of it—he'd have made Maggie crawl under the tables to get the things that fell in the dirt, because he doesn't like that part, and she would have done it if he'd told her to. She almost always does what Luke tells her. She would have pretended to be something—the dog, probably—and he would have had to yell at her not to carry the dirty things in her mouth even if she *was* a dog.

Luke thinks she's hiding in that scary place, but he doesn't know why. Steve told him they'd looked, that she isn't there, but Luke thinks maybe she fell over the edge, that she slipped on the dangerous green algae. She's not very careful about things like that. But if she'd fallen and was hurt, he'd have heard her crying. Not if she was knocked out, though. She wasn't knocked out, he thinks as he ducks under a picnic table to pick up two crumpled napkins. She's hiding in there. She's doing this on purpose just to make trouble. He can nearly see her crouching behind a bush, her hand over her mouth so no one will hear her giggle, watching the dogs and the helicopters and all the grown-ups go by. She did this so he'd be left alone. It's her fault.

Luke climbs under a picnic table to get the three forks and a spoon that have fallen under there, and for one terrible long moment he knows that this is what it will be like if Maggie is really gone. That it will just be him alone with all the grownups and no other children. Luke stays under the table for a long time, pretending to pick up napkins while this thought grows in his stomach like a black raincloud, long fingers of cold seeping into his limbs, paralyzing him there in the dirt.

*W*hat are you doing?" Richard says, horrified. He's come around a bend in the trail, and there's Anne, right in the middle of the tangle of tape that marks the PLS.

"Looking for Maggie."

"Get out of there." He points to the tape flags. "You're going to mess them up. They could be important."

"They're just tape flags." She steps across them, her long legs moving like a heron's in deep water.

"Why are you up here?" He's furious. She shouldn't be here, shouldn't be in the middle of the marked-off area, shouldn't be acting like this. "Why aren't you with Luke?"

"Luke's with your mother," she says. "He's fine."

"He's *not* fine." Richard can't believe her. "Have you looked at him? He's terrified."

"Why are you yelling at me?"

"Because you're not making any sense."

"I'm trying to find Maggie," she says, looking at him like *he's* the one acting irrationally.

"They're going to throw us off the search if you don't start playing by the rules."

"Luke will be fine." She retreats into stubbornness. "I'll talk to him as soon as we find Maggie."

"We're not going to find Maggie if you don't start listening to the search guys." He's astounded by her pigheaded blindness. He knows that bulletproof look she's taken on again, like the world just damn better well order itself according to her plans. That look that says she's not even considering that it won't.

"Fuck that," she says. "I *did* listen to the search guys. I sat on my ass all day yesterday like the good little mommy, and where did that get us? Did they find Maggie? No—they just kept saying that the dog teams didn't turn up anything. *They can't find her, Richard.*"

"And you can? Alone?" He hates it when she swears.

"I *know* her."

"What good is that going to do?" he asks. "There are thousands of trees and rocks and holes here. She could be in any one of them. How are you going to search them all?"

"I don't know," she says. "But I have to do something. I can't just sit down there. What are *you* doing here, anyway?"

"Steve's sent me up to join one of the search crews." He hates it when she's irrational like this. He has to get her to hike out. He can't have his wife wandering all over the site like some sort of Shakespearean witch, thinking she's going to conjure up Maggie. "It's only a quadrant where they want to check one last time, someplace they're pretty sure she's not."

"Great," Anne says. "Why the fuck aren't they searching

171

where they think she might *be* instead of wasting their time on sections where they think she isn't?"

"They're not wasting their time," Richard says. "They're just being careful."

"Careful isn't working."

"And this is?" he asks. "Mucking up the tape flags, ruining what scent evidence is left, wandering around up here like some sort of crazy person?"

"What do you want me to do?" she replies. "Sit there knitting like some little wife?"

"You know that's not what I want," he says. "Grow up, Anne. Stop wandering around out here thinking you're going to find her just because you're her goddamn precious mother."

THEY'D DONE perimeter searches in concentric rings out from the footprints for almost twenty minutes. The dogs will be arriving soon, and Ed is afraid they aren't going to find anything, that this is going to be another blind lead.

"Hey," Jonathan calls out. "Look at this."

As Ed crosses the area, taking care not to crash through the brush, not to ruin clues they may not have found yet, he's trying to shake that vision of Aaron out of his head. He can't get distracted now. They don't have much time until the site gets overrun and everyone will be talking at once, running off into the woods after the dogs, ruining what clues might be left.

Jonathan points to two large mushrooms knocked over and slightly crushed. You can nearly see the impression of toes along the edge of the slimy brown caps.

"Good job, Jonathan," he says. Maybe he isn't so useless after all. He might turn out to be a good searcher with a little more practice.

"Suillus tomentosus," Michelle says, poking at the spongy underside of the mushrooms. Ed's long since gotten used to Michelle muttering the Latin names for plants, birds, trees. He hardly notices anymore.

"She's veered to the left," Ed says, looking back to the tape flags surrounding the footprint. He marks it on his map. "Anything out in front of it?"

Michelle is a few feet ahead, crawling delicately through the sparse underbrush. Ed scans the area. What turned her? There's nothing obvious, no large boulder or a clump of trees. If they're wrong in thinking that she'll go straight until turned by an object blocking her path, they're in a lot more trouble than they thought.

Ed walks back over to the footprints. They are clearly pointing downhill. If she'd kept walking in that direction, she would have continued along a slight downward slope through an open glade of lodgepole pine. Nothing to block her path.

But she veered left, uphill, heading across, rather than down, the drainage. Ed walks back over to the mushrooms, now encircled by lank tails of orange surveyor's tape. It's fifteen paces for him, probably about thirty for her. What distracted her?

"Any luck?" he calls to Michelle.

"Not yet."

"We've only got about five minutes until the dogs get here," Ed calls to her.

"Put them on the prints first; that should buy us a little time."

Ed stands in the woods, looking from one sign to the other. What was it? An animal? Is she following animals through the woods? Or is her blood sugar so low, is she so dehydrated that she's getting loopy, staggering around out here?

If that's the case, she's probably close, and the dogs should be able to find her. If she's dug herself in under the leaves, trying to keep warm, the dog teams are probably her best shot.

Ed tries to get a sense of what's up with this girl, but she's opaque to him. He can't get a handle on her. It is this as much as anything else that distracts and upsets him. Maybe it's because she's Down's—maybe that's why he can't figure out a pattern to her, any sense of why she might be making the decisions that keep her lost. She doesn't seem to be hiding from them, but she's not trying to save herself, either. As far as Ed can tell, she's slipping past them somehow. Without a good imaginative sense of the victim, of what the victim is doing, how she is thinking, Ed finds himself missing signs, clinging to obvious leads instead of looking past them for that one oddball clue that will invariably open up the puzzle that is a lost person.

MARTHA, HATING to be at loose ends, has asked Steve what she can do to be useful, and he's sent her to Penny, the unit cook. Martha recognizes Penny as one of those women who has spent half a lifetime cooking for small-town events: church suppers, high school award dinners, and Elks Club meetings. Martha'd hardly had time to explain who they were when Penny had given her an apron, had given Luke a chore. Now Martha no longer felt like the two of them were at sea, helplessly waiting for something to happen. Luke is sulking a little, still upset about the helicopter. Martha keeps one eye on him as she sets to work.

They're chatting about families, and it turns out they both have people along the Front Range. Penny's folks, like so many, had come to California during the Depression, but she still has aunts and uncles and cousins all up and down that part of Colorado.

Martha watches Luke sling the garbage bag of lunchtime trash into the Dumpster. He nearly misses, the bag teetering for a moment on the edge before tipping in at last. He slouches toward them and collapses against the picnic table, as though picking up a little trash has completely exhausted him.

"Have I got a job for you," Penny says, capturing him in a white restaurant apron, spinning him to wrap it around twice, then tucking it up at the waist so he doesn't trip. She tugs him by the tied apron to a nearby picnic table. "What we need you to do is to get the cores out of these heads of iceberg lettuce so we can shred them for the burritos and use them for the salad."

"All those?" Luke asks, looking at the three teetering paper grocery sacks full of lettuce.

"It's not like work at all," Penny says, grinning conspiratorially at the sulking boy. Martha is grateful for her efforts to cozen him out of his mood. Disaster or no disaster, she hates sulky children.

"First you unwrap it." She hands one to Luke and swishes the plastic wrap off her head of lettuce with a flourish. Luke, still determined not to let her jolly him out of his mood, unwraps his reluctantly.

"Then you hold it over your head." She raises her arms high over her head.

Luke raises his a few inches off the table.

"Nope," Penny says. "All the way up."

Luke sighs and raises the lettuce above his head.

"Now," she says, "you smash it on the table." She crashes the lettuce on the splintery pine boards of the picnic table. Luke hesitates a moment, then whacks his lettuce on the picnic table. He looks infinitesimally happier to have smashed something but is trying hard not to show it.

"Okay," she says. "Now turn it over and the core comes right out." She demonstrates by pulling a hard cone out of the base of the lettuce.

175

"Uh-huh."

"Your mission," Penny says, "is to core all these lettuces. Once you've cored a lettuce, dump it in this garbage can." She points to the black trash can on wheels. "When you're done coring them, you're going to wheel the can over to that spigot and wash them all. You can just fill up the whole can with water, bob them around in there a little, and then drain them." She points to the drain plug at the bottom of the can. "Then open that and the water will drain out. Okay?"

Luke nods as he unwraps a lettuce. He holds it over his head and bangs it on the table. Martha and Penny play the appreciative audience for a moment. He tries very hard to look nonchalant about the task.

"That should burn off a little energy," Penny says to Martha.

"It's a good trick," she agrees.

Turning back to their conversation, and the burrito filling they're making, they watch Luke out of the corners of their eyes. It's not long until he's making full-blown karate-chop noises as, one by one, he kills the lettuces, then tosses them into the big black trash can.

"THEY *CAN'T* throw us off the search," Anne says to Richard. "We're her parents."

"Of course they can," Richard says. He's waving his hands. She loves those hands. A flash of memory—Richard's square wrists buckling his ski boots on one of their first dates. The way her heart thumped at his quiet competence, at the line of his body turning toward her in the lift line. He only waves his hands like that when he's really upset. "It's out of our control now, Anne—there's police down there. Steve has total jurisdiction over this whole thing."

"Well, you're the one who did this," she says, the memory gone and anger flaring up. "You're the one who brought all these strangers into our business." She hadn't wanted them. If they'd just kept looking, they could have found her.

"We can't find her by ourselves, Anne." Richard is shouting now. "Why is that so hard for you to accept?"

"And these people can? They don't even know Maggie!"

"They've got dogs, and they're going over the place systematically, in grids."

"Systems. Grids. Dog teams," Anne says. "That's a lot of crap. We lost her. We have to find her. These people can't find her—they don't even know who they're looking for."

"So what? They have numbers on their side. They found the shoe, didn't they? What are the odds of finding a shoe out in all this broken rock?" He's got that look that says he just doesn't understand her at all, that she's not making sense. "They'll find her. We just have to get out of their way and let them do their work."

"But that's what I'm saying, Richard—they found her stupid shoe, but they can't find Maggie. They're looking for the wrong thing. They're looking for her like she's some object, but she's not—she's our funny Maggie, our mysterious kid who doesn't act like anyone else on the planet. How are they going to know that? How are they going to find her if they don't know that?" Anne is close to tears.

"By being rational. By walking in lines across the area. By keeping track and being careful. They'll find her, Anne. I know they'll find her if only we can stay out of their way."

Anne turns and stares out into the middle distance. He's wrong. She knows he's wrong, but it's always been important to him to believe that Maggie *is* like other kids, that she's not so

177

different. Anne knows better. Maggie is absolutely unique and different and strange.

"You think Luke's not okay?" Anne asks him. The anger has gone out of her. She doesn't know what to think. Maybe she's only being stubborn and Richard's right; maybe these people *can* find Maggie with their lines and their dogs. Looking at him leaning against the rock, she doesn't want to talk anymore; she just wants the weight of his body against hers.

"Luke thinks this is his fault," Richard says quietly. She can see he's worn-out, too, and the fight is suddenly over in that strange way fights have of simply ending, both parties too exhausted to yell at each other anymore. "Because he was supposed to be watching her."

"He can't think that," she says.

"He's afraid you're mad at him."

"He told you that?"

"Pretty much."

"Oh God," Anne says. "And I keep leaving him. I thought he'd be okay," she says. "He's with your mother."

"He needs you."

"I'm afraid to leave her," Anne says. "I'm afraid if I go down, I'll never see her again."

"They'll find her." Richard pushes the hair off her face, tucking a long strand behind her ear. "There are so many of them and the area isn't that big. We have to let them do their job."

STEVE IS hurrying across the open space between the bus and the press bull pen. He's late, and he waves people off as they move to stop him, ask a question. There are nearly four hundred people here now, and while most of them are out on crews searching, there are still a lot of people milling around, signing in, getting instructions, unloading gear. There's an equine team from Salinas unloading, and he's careful not to spook the horses as he dashes past, ducks under the tape flagging just as the newscaster, on the air already, turns to him.

"With me is Steve Griffith, who is in charge of this increasingly serious search and rescue mission. Steve, what are this little girl's chances?"

"Her chances are good. We have nearly fifteen teams of highly trained searchers up here, and six dog teams." Steve hates the way these TV guys keep emphasizing all the wrong aspects of search and rescue.

"But she's spent two nights outdoors. Can you tell us what the average temperature has been?"

"It's late in the season, so the temperature has dropped into the forties."

"How does a small child survive in that kind of cold? I understand she's dressed only in a T-shirt and shorts."

"We believe she's found herself a sheltered spot where she can keep warm. If she'd been out in one of the areas of exposed rock that characterize the terrain above seventy-eight hundred feet, we feel we would have found her with the infrared detectors on the helicopters." These TV spots would be such a good opportunity for community education, but all they want is high drama. Will she survive? What are her chances? Steve's seen himself on tape, knows he comes off stiff and deadpan, but he just can't buy into the hyperbole of it all.

"How is her family holding up?" the reporter asks.

"They are understandably upset," Steve says. "But they have extensive wilderness experience and remain confident that we will find Maggie."

"The KRNT Weather Center forecasts a storm system

179

moving in from the coast. How will this affect Maggie's chances for survival?"

"Poor weather conditions are the biggest challenge we face," Steve answers. Steve wouldn't do these interviews at all if he had the choice, but he's had too many incidents of false information being fed to the press to leave them to subordinates anymore. "But we have found some strong clues and are hopeful that with dog team support we will find Maggie before the storm system moves in."

"In poor weather, the survival rate for children drops considerably, does it not?" the reporter asks. Steve knows where he's being led, tries his best to head it off.

"The statistics are not good in poor weather," Steve concedes.

"What is the survival rate for children in stormy weather?"

"It ranges from forty-four to sixty-six percent," Steve answers. "However, the weather is currently holding steady for us, we have several excellent clues, and our dog teams are on the site. We fully expect a positive outcome to this search."

"Thank you, Commander Griffith." The reporter turns back to the camera. "This is John Slaughter signing off for KRNT breaking news, at the site of the life-and-death search for little Maggie Baker, missing for nearly two days in this rugged wilderness area. Stay tuned for updates throughout the broadcast day."

As the red light on the video camera goes dim, the reporter turns to Steve. "Thanks again for speaking on-camera," he says.

"No problem, John," Steve replies. "Just remember, anyone talks to a searcher or family member without my explicit permission, I'll have the sheriff's deputies escort you to the roadblock."

"I know, I know," John replies. "We know the drill by now."

Steve flips his radio back on and heads over to the bus. He wants to check in with Ed and find out what the dogs have turned up at that footprint. Until they get a scent confirmation, they just can't assume it's actually her print, and with this weather moving in . . . well, he just hopes to God that it's her print and she's dug in under the vegetation somewhere nearby.

"MY FIRST husband died of a heart attack," Penny says. She's halved three heads of red cabbage, is slicing them crosswise into shreds for the salad. "But it happened at work. I never knew anything until he was gone."

Martha fries the onions and garlic in an enormous pot. Her eyes stream tears. She knows people will think they are for Maggie, but really, they're only onion tears. They'll either find Maggie or they won't, and her tears can't make the least difference.

"Now what do I do?" Luke asks, bobbing the lettuces up and down in the garbage can full of water.

"Are they all washed?" Penny asks, waving as Jane approaches with grocery bags in her arms.

"I think so."

"Open the spigot at the bottom to drain them, and then you can tear them up for salad," Penny says, slicing big bunches of green onions, sliding them off the board into a plastic bowl. "But save at least two," she adds. "We'll need to shred a couple for the burritos."

"Hi," Jane says. "I got those groceries you wanted." She glances at Martha.

"Onions," Martha says, nodding into the pot.

"What can I do?" Jane asks.

"You could start chopping vegetables," Penny answers.

Luke's watching the water stream from the open spigot at

the trash can's bottom. He's playing, Martha notices, using a big stick to divert the flow. They've got how many mouths to feed tonight—250, 300? Something like that, Martha thinks to herself.

"You were the one who found him?" Penny asks Martha, startling her slightly.

"Mmhmm," she says, stirring the onions. Somehow they've gotten onto the subject of dead husbands. Martha's not sure if she wants to change it or not. The onions aren't quite golden yet.

"Found who?" Jane asks, neatly coring tomatoes with a big knife.

"Hand me the chili powder, would you?" Martha asks. Jane hands the tin across. "My husband, Martin," Martha answers, sprinkling red chili across the white onions. "He was out irrigating," she continues. "The heart attack must have caught him just as he got out of the truck. He managed to call the house. I was in the garden. Came back in and found the message light blinking." The rank smell of cumin rises; it smells like sweat.

"It looks like all the water's gone," Luke calls out.

"Okay, wheel it over here, then," Penny answers.

Jane listens quietly, halving the tomatoes.

"You remember when I lost Hal," Penny says to Jane. Then turning back to Martha, she asks, "So what did you do?"

"Called nine-one-one, started doing CPR. It was nearly an hour before they came." She pauses, stirs the fragrant food in the deep pot, remembers how the blackbirds trilled in the cattails that day. It was spring; they were setting up nests. "I knew he was gone, but once you start . . . you know," she says, nodding at them. "They tell you that you can't stop compressions until a doctor says, or until you're so exhausted that you can't go on. That was probably the hardest part," Martha says. "Knowing he

182

was gone but feeling like I had to keep going. In case there might have been a chance to bring him back."

Martha doesn't like to dwell on Martin's death. Despite missing him every day, despite never having grown accustomed to sleeping alone in their bed, despite his constant presence in her life, she tries not to dwell on it. She's had friends say she's lucky, he could have lingered, she could have been saddled with an invalid. "At least he went quickly," they say. But Martha's not so sure. It would have been real hard on Martin, losing his dignity like that, so Martha thinks it's probably selfish of her to wish she had him with her, invalid or no. At any rate, what's done is done, and nothing Martha wants is going to change that. She tries to trust that God has a plan, that this trial is for some purpose. Most of the time, though, she just misses him.

She stirs the onions. It's about time to add the beans, she thinks, looking into the fragrant pot.

RICHARD WALKS along in line with the others, a much tighter line than the search he'd been on the night Maggie disappeared. He was so embarrassed—by the time he found his team, they'd been searching for nearly twenty minutes. Everyone had to stop while he spoke with the team leader, then got on the line.

Anne. She makes him so crazy sometimes. Doesn't she remember their raft guide training? It was the first summer they lived together; they'd gotten jobs guiding on the Arkansas. All that talk about managing the victim's family—how could she not realize they could be thrown off the search? He remembers one day on the river, looking back for her, and there she'd been, hung way out of the boat on a wide sweep, but perfectly on line through a tricky drop, the guests oblivious and having fun. He'd been overcome with happiness and love, thought himself the luckiest guy on the river.

He sighs and rubs a hand across his face. He needs to concentrate on *this* day, this problem. There are more searchers on this line than on the one he'd joined the night Maggie disappeared. This time, there are fifty people or so, each only five paces from the next, moving across the stone landscape. They walk slowly, halting the line whenever a searcher comes across a small pocket in the rock that might hold something. The pace is excruciating for Richard. There is nothing here, just rock, and wind. Richard looks toward the sky—high opaque cloud cover, clear evidence that a storm is creeping up on them from the coast.

"Search!"

The cry from that first night, Richard remembers, had passed from mouth to mouth down the line. When his turn to shout had arrived, Richard had felt a nearly physical relief. He wasn't calling alone anymore, Maggie's name fluttering solitary in the still air of her lostness. He'd thought with gratitude of their legs, the pairs of eyes, dividing like amoebas to cover this multiple space of rocks and trees. Why doesn't Anne understand this? he wonders. Why can't she see that the searchers are the only hope we've got?

Richard crosses the naked landscape, staring into Maggie's absence. He thinks of those children who fall through the ice in winter—pulled out cold and blue after twenty, thirty minutes, an hour even—they look dead, don't breathe. But at the hospital, they can thaw them out, do CPR, and they come out of it, wind up okay, not even brain-damaged most of the time. "Mammalian diving reflex," they call it.

Oh God, Richard thinks, *brain damage.* Maggie brain-damaged on top of everything else.

That first night, when they'd sent him out on the line search, hoping the sound of his voice would reassure Maggie, convince her to come out, Richard had found himself deep in the willow thicket, panicking. He's not panicky by nature, and at first he couldn't figure out the shortness of breath, the racing pulse. He'd thought he was having a heart attack, like his father. The idea of keeling over in the middle of the search was more horrifying at that point than the thought of actually dying.

Take a deep breath, he remembers telling himself. Calm down. Think about something useful. Where would Maggie hide? He'd asked himself this as if the question hadn't been loping along the backtracks of his mind all afternoon. Where? Where? Where? She likes small spaces, he remembers thinking—when they went to his office—when he took her in to his office sometimes on a Saturday—she liked the cubbyhole beneath the reception desk. He'd found her there asleep sometimes, when he'd gotten distracted by a set of plans.

Luke, on the other hand, liked the tall stools and the drafting tables. The electric erasers—he'd drawn intricately shaded pictures for the pure pleasure of wiping them out with the drill-like spinning eraser.

Richard, bent over, struggling for breath, in the dark heart of the willow thicket, had calmed himself by imagining Maggie asleep, curled inside a willow, a willow somehow lined with sturdy gray industrial carpeting. A clean, warm willow.

A shout halts the line and Richard's heart jumps. He watches a searcher stoop, lower the upper half of his body into a large hole. For a moment, only his legs are visible, and it feels like the whole line holds its breath. Nothing moves. Then the man bucks a little, backs himself out of the hole, shakes his head no, nothing. Another shout rings through the barren air and they begin to walk once more, slowly.

"Now what do I do with them?" Luke asks, dragging his trash can full of wet lettuces across the gravel. He's a nice kid, Jane thinks. Every once in a while, she thinks maybe they should have had more children. Steve would have liked a boy. Not that he doesn't love Jennie, and if they'd had a boy, he might not have spent so much time doing things with her. It's been hard having her gone this year, but she's only down at Stanford, still close enough to come home for a weekend now and then.

"It's getting cold, Luke," Martha says, noticing that he's only got a T-shirt on and he's all wet from the lettuce washing. "Why don't you run back to the cabin and put on a dry shirt?"

"I'm okay," Luke says.

"Go on Luke," Martha tells him. Jane hears that firm tone in her voice that means it's not a suggestion.

"All right," he says grudgingly.

"And grab a sweater while you're at it," Martha calls after him. "Penny, can you hand me the beans?"

Penny carries the industrial-sized cans over and she and Martha pour them into the steaming pot.

"So what do you do?" Martha asks Jane as she stirs the food with an enormous wooden spoon.

"I'm a pediatric nurse," Jane says. "Oncology. At the UC Medical Center."

"That must be hard," Martha says quietly.

"Mmm," Jane replies, slicing the tomatoes into quarters, eighths, small chunks. "Sometimes it is."

"Do you ever get used to it?" Martha asks.

"No, not really. I think to do a good job, you have to *not* get used to it." Jane slides a pile of tomato chunks into a bowl. "Most

186

of the time, it's great—they come in so sick, and you take care of them, and they get well and go home. Lots of times, parents will bring them back to see us, on a birthday, or a graduation or something. That's always a kick."

"There aren't so many jobs anymore where you can feel like you've done something useful," Penny adds. "Maybe it's one of the reasons I like doing this. . . . "

Jane pauses over the cutting board. "It even feels useful being there for the ones who don't make it."

"How so?" Martha asks.

Jane pauses. It's always so hard to explain this part. "Well," she says, "it seems sort of . . . Knowing you did your best to make sure they were comfortable and not alone at the end." She stops for a minute. "I lost one this weekend," she adds quietly. "A boy I've had since he was really little. He nearly beat it, was in remission for over four years."

The women are silent, each thinking of her own losses, and of Maggie out there alone. Of the possibility that she might wind up one of the nearly saved. One of the ones they miss.

Jane's thinking how peaceful Joey finally looked. The way the pain and tension and fight went out of his body. She's seen so many go, and what always surprises her is how different each one is. We die as individually as we live, she thinks. Jane and Sheila and Jim stood silent for a long time over his bed while Jane unhooked the respirator, the tubes, revealed their boy to them again. He looked so young, all the wise guy gone out of him, like the little kid he'd been the whole time under the weight of all that sickness, all that being funny and brave.

She'd left his parents there alone in the room with him. People seem surprised when she tells them that parents don't usually get hysterical, that they're quiet in their grief. With these ones, by the time the end comes, there's been such sustained and unrelenting pain that it's a relief to see them free of it. It's later that the heartbreak comes, when the relief wears off and the funeral is over and the casserole dishes have all been returned. When the room's been packed up and the house is still, months later, empty of the presence of their child. When it begins to sink in that never is a very long time.

PICKING HER way down through the boulder field, Anne is thinking about God and Martha. Martha, Anne knows, really has faith in God, a personal God, a God who is intimately involved in their lives. It's one of the things Anne finds comforting and trustworthy in Martha, one of the many things she's grateful to Martha for. Most women she knows are horrified at the idea of a mother-in-law spending as much time with their family as Martha spends with her and Richard, but Martha has never meddled in their lives. She's just shown up when there's a crisis and quietly done what needs to be done. When Anne's tried to thank her, voice tight with emotion and tears filling her eyes, Martha's patted her shoulder, waved the thanks aside, and said, "What else could I have done?" Of course she came to help. Anne's mother tries; she offers to come and help, but she's so untrustworthy, all tears and melodrama, that much of the time, Anne just doesn't tell her things until there's no choice.

Oh God, Anne thinks. I'm going to have to tell her I lost Maggie. The thought of her mother's dramatics on top of everything else is more than Anne can bear.

Anne stops to negotiate crossing the creek. She's avoiding the trail, avoiding having to explain what she's doing up there. Or, worse, the searchers who don't know who she is, who ask her if she's seen a little girl about this high. They stand there sincere and well-meaning, staring at her inability to speak.

The creek flows across flat, sloping stone, not even in a proper bed like the creeks of her Michigan girlhood. Anne has decided, for no particular reason, to stay to the right of it, and so she skirts a thick clump of alders, thinking of how they've told her—nurses, teachers, total strangers—that God will take care of Maggie, that God won't give her a burden she can't bear. How could any God who is good, who is, as Martha has tried to explain to her, wholly love, let this happen? What could be good about this? She tries to be polite, hides her incredulity. Faith, she has learned, is expected in mothers of the handicapped.

Anne knows she can't keep faith with that God—the one who sets up tests like hoops for us to jump through, but she can't conceive of a universe without some sort of pattern or meaning. For Anne, whatever concept of God she might have is tied up in that beauty that lives in the angles of her children's limbs; in the poppies on the sunny windowsill, bottom of the jelly jar stained the same luminous orange as the petals; and in that moment when they're all at dinner, and Maggie wants something she can't have, and Luke has tipped over the milk, and Richard's wiping the spill as Anne explains to Maggie that this is the dinner she gets and they're all there together, like a many-limbed organism, in a strange sort of chaotic harmony.

Anne stumbles over a rock. *Luke,* she thinks. She craves his body like salt. She'll have a good long talk with him. She sees herself sitting with Luke at the picnic table, or maybe walking down the shore, holding hands; then she shakes her head, tells herself to get real. This isn't a Hallmark commercial. This is her very real, very frightened son, the one who has *always* felt too responsible for Maggie, no matter how they try to shield him from that burden. Her boy, who picks on his sister when it's just the two of them at home but who she finds defiant in the

189

principal's office, saying, "But Mom, that kid called Maggie a retard."

Anne tries to think of all the kind, sane, motherly things she'll tell her son about his missing sister. How this is an accident, that accidents happen, that the searchers are working very hard and are well trained to deal with this sort of emergency. All the things Richard's been telling her—that there are all these people and they'll find Maggie and it will be all right.

But Anne's connection with Maggie seems broken off and she's terrified that Richard is wrong, that Maggie is gone forever. She has to prepare Luke for at least the possibility that . . . She has to somehow explain how dangerous this is. It's not like he doesn't know already, she thinks. And they've never lied to him about important things. They're not the sort of parents who think they can shield their children with ignorance—Anne, who was so often lied to as a child, insists on this. But how on earth is she going to tell Luke that his beloved, maddening sister may be lost?

Anne finds herself jogging now toward the campground. She hurries toward Luke as though the bony elbows and knees of him, as though the way he squirms away, saying, *"Mom! I'm not a baby!"* as though his towhead and ears and the line of his jaw will somehow give her the answer to this question.

LUKE'S WALKING back from the cabin with his sweater. The lettuce thing was okay, he thinks. But he doesn't want to hang out with the ladies. He wants to see the stuff. It was better yesterday, he thinks. When no one was watching him. Yesterday, he got to hang out and build that fort in the sand, instead of picking up stupid garbage and smashing lettuces.

Luke ties the bright blue fuzzy around his waist and takes the long way back to where his grandmother is cooking. He saw a

TV truck on his way to the cabin, and he wants to see the cameras. He's never seen a TV camera up close. He sneaks around behind the truck. There aren't any people here, just a fascinating tangle of black cables and big metal boxes. Luke's hoping he'll find a camera just sitting around that he can look at. He doesn't want to have to talk to anyone; all the grown-ups here are like that stupid helicopter guy. They all talk to him in that syrupy voice, like he's Maggie or something. He only wants to look at their stuff.

Luke sneaks around the cables and boxes, but he can't find a camera anywhere. All he finds are these big metal boxes. He's afraid to open one; it might make a noise, or something might fall out and break. He's edging around the back of the truck to see if there're any cameras out where he can see them when he sees two men leaning against one of those big cases.

"How much longer you think we'll be up here?" the one with the cigarette asks.

"Not long," the tall man says. Luke's seen him on TV. He's a news guy. "The kid's history, we just have to wait for them to call it all off."

"What do you think?" the smoking man asks. "Tomorrow morning?"

Luke's frozen. The TV man looks over and sees him. Luke can see it take him a minute before he figures out who Luke is.

"Hey, buddy," he says in that fake friendly voice.

"What did you mean?" Luke asks. *She's history*.

"Nothing, bud," he says, reaching toward Luke.

"Oh shit," the smoking man says quietly, dropping his cigarette, grinding it under one foot.

"Come on," he says. "You want to see how a TV camera works?"

When he touches Luke's shoulder, Luke screams "She's *not* dead! My sister's *not dead!*" and starts hitting.

Luke's never hit a grownup before, but he hates this man. He wants to hurt him and he's furious. Luke's screaming over and over that Maggie's not dead and hitting him as hard as he can. He feels the man saying, "Hey, hey, buddy, it's all right."

And then Luke's crying and furious and the man gets him in his arms and he can't move. The man says, "Whoa, *I'm sorry.*"

RICHARD'S SEARCH team is on the high bench above the twinned lakes, creeping across the fractured talus, checking each crevice and hollow between the shifting rocks. The weather has turned raw; the wind has an edge to it like sandpaper, getting into his collar, chilling his hands numb. There are a few breaks in the cloud cover, patches of blue like a Renaissance ceiling, but the underbelly of the clouds is that heavy gray that suggests weather. She's only got a T-shirt on, Richard thinks, turning up the collar of his sweater, snapping it into a stiff cone around his neck.

She may not make it. It's the first time he's allowed the thought all the way into his head, and it terrifies him. They may not find her in time. Richard is grateful that they're moving so slowly, because he's suddenly dizzy, stunned by the realization that Maggie might *die* out here.

He's even more frightened by the whiff of relief that this thought carries with it. Life without Maggie would certainly be easier: Luke could have friends over without that constant vigilance, the parental eavesdropping so that playtime doesn't turn mean, so that Maggie doesn't become the weak link where a kid could turn on Luke, make him a playground outcast. Anne could paint full-time, take those teaching gigs that come up every so often, go to New York for important shows. And Richard could build something other than tract houses for the money.

He stumbles over an uneven place and nearly falls. He glances around, and he realizes he's not really searching, that he's just here walking with these people, that they're humoring him by giving him something to do. This isn't like that first night when they'd searched the alder swamp and Richard had shouted and shouted, his voice cracking with exhaustion and fright, calling his daughter's name into the depths of that wet thicket, hoping beyond hope that she had not been flung by some unseen force into that gully of wet, rotting plants. Finally, Ed had yelled for him to stop, said that they needed to listen. Standing ankle-deep in wet muck, Richard had heard nothing, nothing that counted, just the eternal rustle of leaves, the scritching sound of Gore-Tex jackets, the whine of an airplane passing high over the night Sierra.

That's how the house will be without Maggie, he thinks.

Richard has never quite realized before now that Maggie is not only Anne's big love but is the beating heart of the family, the one who pulls them each out of themselves, asks for more than they can give. Over and over, Maggie asks them to give more, be more for her, and they do. They each rise, one by one, to the occasion, and in the process, she's come to define how they are a family.

Richard stares across the barren granite and thinks this is what their life without her will look like: cold and white and hard and dead.

"LUKE!" MARTHA says, her voice full of question and alarm as Luke walks back to the cooking place with Steve.

"What?" he says. He wishes everyone would stop making such a big deal about it.

"He did *what*?" she asks Steve. Steve's just told her about finding him hitting the TV man.

"He overheard a newscaster making an inappropriate remark," Steve is saying. Luke wishes they would just forget it. It wasn't that big a deal.

"What sort of remark?" Martha asks. Luke can feel her giving him the "I'm disappointed in you" look. He plays with the dirt, drawing designs with his toe. Steve's still got a hand on Luke's shoulder, and he'd shake it off, but he figures he's in enough trouble already.

"Luke?" Penny says. "Why don't you come over here and I'll make you some hot chocolate."

He looks to his gram and she nods yes, it's okay, so he follows Penny. Over his shoulder, he can hear the grownups talking.

"The guy made some stupid crack," Steve says. "Don't be too mad at the boy. I felt like hitting the jerk myself."

"Who was it?" Jane asks.

Penny takes him over to the kettle of hot water they keep going for the searchers who drop by on their way in or out of the field. "Minimarshmallows or plain?" she asks.

"Marshmallows," Luke answers. He's still trying to hear what the others are saying.

"That newscaster from Sacramento. He was talking with his cameraman, and he didn't know Luke was there." Steve's radio begins to squawk. "I've got to go. . . . "

"Of course," Martha says, waving him off. "Thank you for bringing him back here."

Steve reaches out, touches Jane on the shoulder, then leaves. Gram walks over to Luke.

"You want to tell me what happened?" she asks. Penny and Jane go back to what they were doing.

"Nothing," Luke says.

He can feel Gram looking at him. He just wants to forget it, especially the part where he was crying and his nose was running and that man had him and was being nice, saying over and over, "Hey, buddy, it's okay. It's okay. Your sister's going to be fine."

"Okay," she says. "We'll talk about it later."

Luke looks up and sees that she's not really mad at him.

"He said Maggie was dead," Luke blurts out, trying not to cry.

Gram bites her bottom lip and looks very stern. "He said what?"

"He said, 'The kid's history,' and the other one just nodded and I didn't mean to hit him, Gram, but he shouldn't have said that about Maggie." Luke looks up at his grandmother. There is a movement at the edge of the clearing where they are cooking, and Luke glances over. It's his mom coming through the woods toward them.

Luke's off the bench and running as hard as he can. He crashes against her and he's crying even harder than when the man finally got him to stop hitting, and his mother says, "Hey, what's this?" and he's crying and he can hear them, over his head, Gram telling his mom, and he doesn't care. His mom. He's got his mom.

THE DOG teams have engulfed Ed's site like a wave, and it is chaotic and noisy where just minutes before all there was was the long light of late afternoon slanting through the trees. Michelle bends over the mushroom sign, then cocks back on her haunches, scanning downhill, looking for the odd shadow cast by an upturned leaf, a telltale signal that she's heading in a consistent direction. Ed's three places at once—filling in the dog trainers on the two signs, yelling at a clumsy searcher not to compromise the footprint by falling through the goddamn tape flags, for Chrissakes, radios squawking, the noise of Gore-Tex rubbing against itself, the ready, set, go excitement of dogs picking up a scent and bounding off into the woods.

Somehow, it is this energy level that is getting to Ed. Usually as much of an adrenaline junkie as the next guy, he counts on that rush to keep him going through the long hours of searching. Ed's surprised to realize that it's getting in his way this time. He thinks she's close, this one, and hiding, and he can't help but be convinced that what he needs is quiet to find her. But he can't very well go calling off a dog search just because he's got a hunch. Look at them—they're running hard; he can hear the trainers crashing after them. They've got a scent trail, so there must be something out there. Just because the dogs came up empty yesterday doesn't mean they aren't going to find her today, he thinks as he walks back over to where Michelle is crawling across the ground just downhill from the crushed mushroom. Maybe she's got an idea.

Ed closes his eyes for a minute, trying to get a bead on Maggie. She's only a little girl, about Aaron's age. Where would she go? If she's not going in a straight line like they thought she would, what would she do? Ed thinks of this girl's white-blond hair in the photo they've handed around. A running girl with that bright flag of hair. What he sees is Aaron as a baby, hurling down the long back hall by the bedrooms in their house—that tipped-forward baby run, shrieking with the sheer joy of being up on his own two legs and running, and Ed scooping him high into the air, the smell of his hair and the noise of that baby giggle ringing through the house.

Ed opens his eyes as the dog teams emerge from the woods. He's got to stop thinking about Aaron and get his head back into this search. The scent ran dry on the dog teams and they're starting over again. Maybe, he thinks, I'll go fishing after this one's over. It's been one long goddamn year of searching.

THEY'VE MANAGED to get Luke to stop crying, or at least slow down enough to gasp out to his mother about the man and how he didn't mean to hit him, but he said that about Maggie. She sits on the bench, one arm around Luke, and takes the Styrofoam cup of instant rice and beans Martha hands her. It's not really food as far as Martha's concerned, but probably as good as she can hope for at this point. Penny pours Luke another cup of hot chocolate to replace the one he flung as he bolted off the bench for his mother, and they all stand around while Anne waves a hand at them. "Stop fussing," she says. "I'm fine."

"What do you say we go for a walk?" she says to Luke.

He nods, gripping her hand, not about to let her get away without him this time. "Thanks for keeping an eye on him," she says, and Penny and Jane nod, chime in with "Of course" and "No problem." Martha just nods to her; she and Anne have long since worked out that Martha will be there, whenever they need her, and for however long. But still, she thinks, it's nice to hear it.

The three of them are silent as they watch Anne lead Luke away. It's time to tell Luke this might not be okay, that this might, in fact, not work out at all, and none of them envy Anne the task. How do you explain this to a little boy?

"Poor bunny," Penny says, watching them walk down the path toward the lake. "This has got to be really hard on him."

"Mmhmm," Martha agrees, turning back to the beans. They're cooking fine on their own, but stirring them gives her something to do.

"It can't be easy," Penny adds, "having a handicapped sibling like that."

"What *is* easy?" Martha replies.

There is a tense silence between them.

"I don't mean that the way it came out," Martha apologizes. "I hate that sort of talk. Luke has a handicapped sister. Richard lost his father when he was only twenty-one. Anne had a rotten childhood. Life is hard," she says, stirring the thick beans, both hands gripping a long wooden spoon. "That's just the way it is."

Penny is quiet. Martha feels that maybe she's offended the woman. "That sounds much harsher than I meant. He's my son. . . . She's my granddaughter. . . . I wouldn't be here if I—"

"No," Jane interjects. "I know what you mean. . . . "

"You must see a lot of it," Penny says. "What with your job and all."

"People take it all kinds of ways," Jane says a little evasively.

"When did we start expecting that life wasn't going to be hard?" Martha asks, stirring the heavy beans around and around in the pot, careful not to let them scorch.

Silently, the two other women go back to chopping. There's nothing really that any of them can say. Martha worries that she's been too blunt, but it seems to her that once you accept that life is supposed to be hard, then you're not always surprised, not caught off guard. If you know it's going to be a challenge, you can prepare, whereas the other way, all you can do is cry like a child who's had its toy taken away, mewling that it's not fair. Seems to her life isn't fair, or easy, or good. It just is, and she's always believed that it's the way we take the blows, and the kindnesses we manage to mete out to one another despite them, that define what kind of a person we're going to be.

Anne sits on the tailgate of a Forest Service green pickup truck, holding a tin mug of coffee. She presses her fingers to the hot metal until they scorch, then moves them slightly. Despite the pile jacket and the hat, she can't seem to get warm. She blows steam off the top of the coffee, sips, burns her lip, and flinches, spilling scalding coffee on her jeans.

"You okay?" Richard asks.

She nods, rubbing the coffee stains on her leg. His presence is comfortable beside hers, this afternoon's fight behind them. It's enough having his warmth beside her, his body. Funny, the way she loves the bodies of her family—she's got sketches upon sketches of their limbs, their torsos. When she and Richard were first going out, he was shy about letting her draw him. He'd sit, hunched into his tall frame, self-conscious. They're some of her favorite drawings—the near boy he'd been then—long limbs and big hands, the body language that said, All right, if you want me to. She leans against his shoulder a little, keeping one small point of contact between them.

Placing the mug on the tailgate to cool, Anne pulls the Polaroid out of her jacket pocket. It is the photo of Maggie's shoe; there is a branch of manzanita in the upper-right corner. The shoe takes up most of the upper-left to lower-right diagonal. Anne strokes the photo with her index finger.

She once did an entire project with Polaroids. In art school. She took pictures of her friends, and then, using a Bic pen with the cap still on, distressed the images as they developed. Everyone came out with halos, exclamation points, cartoon embellishments. Then she painted these very dark acrylic canvases, and dropped the portraits in like punctuation—a sort of group self-portrait. Her Abstract Expressionist period. The part she'd liked best was distressing the Polariods. It was a lot like the process of working with gold leaf she'd been experimenting with in this last series. Maybe, she thinks, she'll combine the two things—set photos in gold leaf like icons.

Then she looks down at the photo in her hand—the photo of her daughter's empty shoe—and wonders how she'll ever make art again.

Even as the thought is crossing her mind, she knows that no matter what happens to her, that art-making place in her will continue, heartless in its ability to make something out of nothing.

Steve gave her Maggie's actual shoe this afternoon, when she came down from the high country. They didn't need it as a scent object anymore; he thought she might want it. She tucked it in her pocket, because she couldn't very well say, No, no, I don't want it. But she doesn't want it; it frightens her—this shoe that wouldn't speak to her when she stumbled across it earlier in the day. Anne prefers the photo of the shoe; the photo shows one of the places Maggie has been. There is information in the photo; the shoe is simply empty.

The shift debriefing is underway beneath the picnic shelter; Anne hears the rise and fall of Steve's voice threading through the steady noise of the gasoline generator. She cannot make out the words—it's that underwater effect again, as though everything is happening somewhere else. She glances at Richard, who is listening intently. She's glad he seems able to hear, to take this information in, because one of them will have to know what is being said.

Anne begins to shiver, deeply afraid in a new, deeper way than she's been since they lost Maggie. She thought she was scared before, but this is a whole different league. The dog teams have failed for the second day in a row. Maggie is spending the night outside, for the third time. She had to take Luke on that walk by the lake this afternoon. She didn't know how to bring it up with him. How do you tell a little boy that you might not be able to find his sister, that you've lost his sibling?

"You know what the man said?" she asked, steering Luke toward a big log they could sit on.

"The TV man?" he asked. His eyes were still red, and he had that swimmy look little kids get when they're still not far from tears.

"He might be right, Luke," she says as gently as she can. "They might not be able to find Maggie in time." She was sitting on the log; he stood between her knees.

"You mean she might die?"

Anne nodded. She couldn't say it.

"All by herself?"

Anne nodded again, her eyes full of tears.

"But she can't die all alone out there!" Luke was crying again. "Make them *do* something, Mom!"

"They're doing everything they can, sweetheart," she said. Luke was standing in front of her, his hands in fists by his side, and she pulled him to her. Her gangly boy wrapped himself around her and she rocked him as if he were little again, rocked him while he cried, and she cried, crying until they were both left gulping for air and swiping at runny noses with their sleeves and finally had to stagger back down the beach, clinging to each other like people rescued from drowning.

Maggie. Her Maggie, her flesh-and-blood child, is out in the woods for the third night in a row and there is nothing that her parents or this enormous collection of people seem able to do about it. "Make them *do* something, Mom!" Anne grips the edges of the tailgate with both hands, desperate to stop the spinning feeling, the feeling that the bottom is dropping out of her life and there's nothing she can do to stop it.

IN THE borrowed bed, Luke stares at the ceiling and cries quietly. The tears well up, then run down the sides of his face and into his ears, and he rolls over and buries his face in the pillow because he's afraid his grandmother will hear him making crying sounds, and he doesn't want another grownup to tell him it's going to be okay. It's not going to be okay. Maggie is going to die outside in the woods all by herself and scared, and he can't do anything about it and it's all his fault.

They keep telling him it's not his fault, but they don't know. Luke was so worried this afternoon, especially when they told his mom about him fighting the TV guy. Luke thought he'd be in trouble for sure over that. But she wasn't mad, and they went to the lake and she told him that the man might be right. They cried for a long time, Luke and his mom, and then she pulled him away from him and said that he mustn't think this is his fault; that it was the grownups who should have been watching Maggie and that she and his dad are the ones who are responsible. She made him look her right in the eye and repeat it to her: "I know it's not my fault that Maggie got lost."

But it *was* his fault. He knew when Maggie bent over to check that his eyes were closed that she was going to be bad. He always knows when Maggie's going off; he can just tell. The grownups don't usually see it until she's really pitching a fit, but Luke can tell, and she'd been a pain all morning. It's his fault because he ignored it, and didn't watch where she was going, and he should have. Because he knew. He knew she was planning something.

Luke's sorrow is a black wave that catches him, and he is tossed deep into the darkness. His sister, his other half, his fellow child in a universe of grownups, has run off and left him. He's abandoned her; they've violated the crucial rule of childhood—that siblings might fight among themselves but always, always band together against an outside force. He didn't protect her; he didn't look when he knew he should have, because he was mad at her. He was mad at having to play with her when he wanted to keep tracking lizards. He was mad that she's Maggie and a pain. Luke buries his face into the pillow and sobs, past thinking now, past everything except this terrible ripping grief.

ED LISTENS intently to the debriefing. Somewhere, he thinks, in the middle of all these stories is a child, one we can still find. This is definitely getting scary, but children have survived for longer periods of time than this without food or shelter. Those babies in the Mexican earthquake, newborns they pulled out of the rubble five, seven, ten days after the building collapsed. They were dehydrated, and scarily quiet, but alive. Blinking at the rescuers as though to say, Where have you been? We've been waiting.

Ed remembers reading somewhere about an anthropologist who'd done studies and hypothesized that babies and small children are hardwired to scream in the night because on the savannas, where humans evolved, to be left alone at night meant the child would be eaten by a hyena. He also remembers that the same anthropologist, noting the silence on wards full of very sick infants, came to the conclusion that if the babies' cries are not answered, they will go silent, because if their mothers have really abandoned them, their only chance of survival is to wait, very quietly, in the hope of being found.

Ed thinks of this little girl out there alone, three days now. She's certainly gone silent on them. Retarded or no, Ed figures this kid isn't stupid. She's taking care of herself out there; that's the problem. She must have gotten cold, and Ed's pretty certain she's dug herself in under a half-rotten fallen tree, inside a manzanita thicket, anyplace she can wrap something around her to keep warm. She's been moving, at least within the last twenty-four hours, because they found the footprint, the mushroom sign, and the dogs ran the scent a good five hundred yards farther into the forest before they got stopped again.

Steve's talking about the Aloha sighting. Ed can't imagine she would climb up and over that talus ridge to Aloha. Her parents said she was afraid of the talus, that she didn't like the way it shifted beneath her. That boy over there hadn't seen the TV reports, though; his family had been camping the whole time. It wasn't until the Forest Service guys went and put up missing-child posters that the kid came forward. It's possible, Ed thinks. Not likely, but possible. Steve's reporting that they checked it out and are treating it as a false sighting.

Ed sees that footprint floating before him and can't figure out why they couldn't find her. What has he missed? Ed only half-listens to Steve debrief; he's racking his brain, trying to identify that one place she's hiding, that one place they can't find.

"I'M HEADING back," Anne says to Richard as she slides off the tailgate.

"You don't want to talk to Steve with me?"

Anne waves at the crowd, the people watching them—*the parents*. "I can't."

"I won't be long," he says.

Leaving the half-full cup of cold coffee on the tailgate, Anne slips out of the circle of light and into the comforting darkness of the gravel road. Moonlight shines through the trees like strips of carpet across the bare, campground-smooth forest floor. Anne's relieved to be walking; it's the only thing that makes any sense to her. She needs to get away from the crowds, the people watching her. She knows she shouldn't keep creeping off like this, that a real mother would stay, tend lovingly to Richard and Luke, but they didn't get that wife, that mother; they got her, and she can only do what she can do. She can't stay there anymore, with everyone looking at her, everyone wanting something from her. Maggie is gone, and Anne doesn't even know how to begin to make anyone feel better about it.

As she passes along the edge of the lake, the moon ducks behind a cloud and the sheen runs out of the surface in one long disappearing streak—the lake is suddenly dark and soft and black. Stopping for a moment, Anne looks across the water. She feels the suffocating shadow of the hemlocks looming behind her as she looks up toward the high basin in which Maggie is lost. The dark clouds are edged with a silver gleam. The storm is near;

205

Anne can feel it in the air, in the wind beginning to blow off the peak. Putting her hands in her pockets to ward off the cold, she's startled by a lump. She pulls Maggie's shoe out of her pocket. It rests on the palm of her hand, silent. Is this really it? Is this all I'm going to be left with? The pain of the thought that she might be left only this hateful, defective shoe knocks the breath out of her.

Forcing herself to breathe, Anne stands in the middle of a dark, wet gravel road and stares at the hump of mountain above her. Inhaling, she remembers reading once that the Sierra batholith may be six hundred miles deep. Granite floats—inflated by air and water molecules, the white quartz floats above the molten core of the earth. A huge floating island of granite. Her Maggie is floating up there on six hundred miles of granite, floating in a crevice, behind a tree, in some small cavern hidden from the infrared radar beamed from the helicopters.

THE LIGHT shines up from downstairs, where Gram sits at the kitchen table. It's in his eyes. Luke's not crying so hard now, just leaking tears, but he can't sleep, and it's making him even more unhappy than he already was. He doesn't like the lights on when he sleeps; that's for babies like Maggie.

She hates the dark; it scares her. Sometimes she comes and climbs in bed with him. Luke doesn't like sleeping with Maggie because she scratches him with her toenails in her sleep, and she snores really loud. He knows she can't help it because her nose didn't work right when she was born, but when it's right next to your head all night, it's a pain. He likes it that she needs him, though. That she's his Maggie.

Sometimes when she gets scared, he has to make her laugh. Once, going into San Francisco to the Exploratorium, she freaked out on the bridge. She'd never gotten freaked out by a bridge before—and she was starting to cry and scream, and to try to get out of the car, when Luke made up a rap about "Maggie-baggie goin' to the ci-tee," and through her tears she started to giggle. She looked at him with those big eyes, like Ooh, look what Luke's doing. . . . Then she started to laugh at his nonsense rhymes. His mom made the thumbs-up sign and his dad grinned in the rearview mirror as the rap got sillier and sillier, not even words anymore, just goofy sounds to make Maggie laugh. They wound up giggling in the backseat, helplessly, giggling because they were giggling and it was so funny. Luke saw his dad give his mom this look, like What are they doing?

And now he's lost her and they can't find her. He flops over in the bed. The light is in his eyes. He can't sleep. What if she is dead? What if her dead body is out there on the ground somewhere? What if there are bugs? Luke squeezes his eyes shut. Maggie can't be dead out there. He tells himself that she's just being bad. Luke knows this isn't true, that this has gone beyond being bad. Maybe, he tells himself, she's hiding in a cave and can't hear them all calling to her. He clings to the image of her safe and warm, because the image that dances on the edge of his imagination, of Maggie sprawled across the rock, not moving, cold, is too terrible to let into his head. Luke desperately focuses on an image of his sister curled up in a little cave, her knees pulled to her chest, like when she's watching television.

STEVE KNOWS everyone's numb with disappointment after the footprint this morning. It was a real hopeful sign, then nothing. No scent for the dogs. They ran shoulder-to-shoulder searches in a one-half-mile radius from the point of discovery, and found nothing. No child. No clothing. No scent. Nothing. At least they know where she's not. Then the Aloha sighting, which got everyone off track. The boy saw something over there, but it doesn't seem to be Maggie.

Steve rubs a hand over his eyes and looks back down at the map. If this rain comes in tonight like it's supposed to . . . This is the hard part, the part he tries to explain to the new ones during training. They show up, eager to save someone, thinking the job is all grateful hugs, tearful smiles, and a shot on TV. He tells them that the real job is failure; that you will have to tell people their child is dead. This, he tells them, is the reason for the protocol, the rules, the order. Organization is the key, he says. If they are careful enough, orderly enough, they just might pull it off, just might avoid the fatal mistake, might pull the victim back into the land of the living, the found. Of course, they never believe him, the new ones; never believe that *they* will fail, until they do. Until they come back after a failed search, Steve's not sure he can count on them.

One by one, he lifts the shift transparencies off the map, as if trying to peel back time, peel back the search. Where did they miss her? Where is the hole in the search? There has to be a hole. She can't have disappeared bodily. Steve slowly smooths the transparencies down once again. Saturday night, Sunday morning, night; Monday morning, night. Grid lines fall into place, blacker and blacker grease-pencil lines, until the map disappears under their weight.

"Mr. Baker?" the man asks Richard as he's trying to work his way through the crush of people leaving the debriefing.

"Yes?"

"Is your little boy okay?"

Richard recognizes him. He's the TV guy. Jesus.

"All things considered," Richard says. "Yeah, he's okay."

"Look," the man says. "I had no idea he was there. I've got kids of my own and I would never have—"

"It's okay," Richard says. "He shouldn't have been there; you didn't know."

"I feel terrible about it." The man pulls a business card from his back pocket. "Here's my card," he says. "If there's anything I can do . . ."

"It's okay," Richard says, taking the card. "Thanks."

Richard turns away from the man and a wave of anger washes over him. Asshole. Richard feels years and years of anger welling up in him. Anger at all the people over the years who have recoiled from Maggie, the ones who pity them, say stupid things like "You're so brave" and "If you'd known, would you have had her?" As if he could wish this child he loves unborn, as if he wanted her gone or better or different. She's a pain in the ass, his Maggie, and it's been more difficult than it might have been with a "normal" child, but she's their *daughter*. She's the only Maggie they've got, and those stupid, stupid people who think they'd rather never have had her, that she'd never been—Richard stops, one hand on a table, his heart breaking with the knowledge that those people are about to win, that he and Anne are about to be people who do not have Maggie in their lives. Who will have to live without Maggie. Breathe, he tells himself. This isn't helping.

ANNE APPROACHES the cabin. It looks so cosy, lit from within like something out of a fairy tale. She can see Martha sitting at the table, knows Luke is upstairs tucked in his bed.

And Maggie is out here somewhere, out in this cold night.

She can't go in just yet. Anne stands silent in the gravel outside the cabin for a long, long moment, and then very quietly, like a kid trying to sneak in past her curfew, Anne creeps up the stairs, slides around the side of the cabin, and settles into a weathered silvery Adirondack chair on the deck. She can see the mountain from here, the lake shining below her pale and silver in the moonlight. *I'll just sit here for a little bit,* she tells herself; *then I'll go in again and be the mom.*

Sinking into the chair, Anne fits her fingertips into the curves of her brow bone. She is so tired, her sandy eyelids seep tears. Sleep—they all want her to sleep, but how can she sleep? "But she can't die all alone out there!" She's going to think she's been abandoned, that they didn't come for her. Anne's never left Maggie, has been there for everything. And Maggie can't figure this out.

If everything had gone the way it was supposed to, they would be pulling into the garage about now. She should be leaning into the backseat, unbuckling Maggie's sleep-heavy body, rolling Maggie's sweat-sticky head onto her shoulder, scooping her up behind the knees, noticing yet again how gangly those floppy legs are getting, smiling through the backseat tunnel at Richard, who's waking Luke. "She got your legs." Anne should be leaning back on her heels, careful of Maggie's head against the doorframe, Maggie almost but not quite too heavy. Anne was this way about Luke, too; she's possessive of her ability to carry the bodies of her children, reluctant to let that go, knowing that once gone, she'll never heft their weight against her body again. They'll be launched into the world. Anne hitching Maggie's heaviness more securely into her arms, turning to nudge the car door shut with her hip, crossing behind the car to where Richard holds the door, gold light spilling out in a rectangle across the garage floor. Richard's "Have you got her?" and his indulgent smile when she nods yes, she's got her. Then up the stairs to the pink-and-white room, the pyramid of stuffed animals spilling out of the corner, the flop of body onto bed, and the struggle to get the clothes off. First the shirt, up and over the sleeping head, Maggie curling in sleep to protect herself from the stripping. The struggle to get the wet pants off, new thick underpants pulled on, the furry yellow sleeper, then the heft of body once more while bedclothes are pulled back, the sleeping girl tucked in, the curl and snuggle of her into her bed, fetal. Anne leaning over to kiss her forehead, whisper, "Good night, sweetcakes." The Maggie smell. Then Richard in the doorway, his arms around her as she leans back against him, her head in his shoulder, enveloped in the sense that this life might not be what they'd expected, but it is good. The sound of Luke peeing from the bathroom. Another body grown out of her arms, another sleepy child to tuck in, kiss on the head, the snuggle and nuzzle of boy arms, smell of his hair, a groggy "Fun trip, Mom."

The hard moon slides out from behind the cloud and glares off the lake. The wobbly reflection shines flat and silent back up into the irrevocable night sky, shines through that blackness, beams of light passing in the dark like airplanes. Anne holds the shoe to her belly and shivers as the shadows of the forest slide over her, shadows she watches run out from the shore and dive into the deep, cold water like some sleek animal.

"LOOK," STEVE says right off. "I'm sorry about that thing with the reporter this afternoon."

Richard waves one hand to dismiss it. "It's over."

"Well," Steve says. "We try to prevent these things. . . ."

"He'll be okay," Richard says. "I think."

The men fall silent.

"What can I do for you?" Steve asks.

"That priest you mentioned?" Richard says, looking into the

middle distance. "I think it's probably time. . . ." He pauses. "I know Mother will want him here, at any rate."

"Sure," Steve replies. "First thing in the morning."

"I just wish—" Richard's voice cracks. He holds his hands out like a man carrying an invisible loaf of bread.

Steve nods, and they stand there for a long moment, silent.

"It'll break, you'll see," Steve says, putting a hand on Richard's shoulder. Richard is fairly sure Steve's lying to him. He's been up there. He's seen that they can't find her. But Richard's tired, and he clings to the lie.

Richard nods, then scans the crowd as he turns to go.

"How's Anne holding up?" Steve asks.

"She went back to the cabin," Richard tells him. Steve can see that he's so tired, he's unsteady on his feet. The two men stand there for a long, awkward moment, saying nothing.

"Go on back to the cabin, Richard," Steve says, keeping a hand on his shoulder.

Richard knows his gaze is stupid with sleeplessness and grief. "Thanks," he says. He looks around, encompassing in his glance the scene, the searchers, this small village that still cannot find his daughter, then shrugs, turns, and walks down the dark road toward the cabin.

MARTHA SITS at the kitchen table, a cup of tea steaming between the palms of her hands. She's thinking of that Chagall drawing she saw years ago in Paris. It was a pen and ink drawing of Job, very small, maybe eight inches by ten, like something out of a sketchbook. Job, bent over in his sorrows, is unaware that an angel floats above him, watching. The curve of Job's back and the curve of the angel's torso are the same; they mirror each other— the same but reverse. And in his travail, Job can't see the angel.

It was a simple drawing—the gently curved surface of the earth, Job's bent form, the hovering presence. The picture has stuck with her. She's thought of it often over the years, thought about the way that regardless of Job's feelings toward his situation, regardless of the fact that he'd given up hope, that angel was still with him.

It's how she thinks of faith, that the angel is there regardless of whether or not you believe in it. Despite the fact that she goes to Mass more mornings of the week than not, dragging herself out of bed in the dark, climbing into the cold truck, and rattling the ten miles into town, it's not because she has faith, but, rather, because she doubts. Martha's faith lies with the mystics, the doubters. She takes great comfort in the thought that because God is outside of creation, we can't know anything substantial about the actual nature of the divine. It's outside our ken; we just have to have faith, and wait to see what it is we're trying to believe in when we get there. It seems so much less limiting that way.

She remembers how annoyed she was with all those folks who told her she'd be reunited with Martin in heaven, as though it were a big party, where you get to see all the people you liked. Martha thinks it's probably a lot less personal than that, that all the idiosyncrasies that make us individual fall away and we're subsumed into that essential light that is the divine. But if she said that at a church supper in her hometown, they'd think she'd gone daft out there alone on her ranch. She talks about it with the priest sometimes; he's young and they share books. But mostly, she keeps it to herself.

Luke flops over upstairs in his bed. I'll have to try to get him to talk, she thinks. If he's as like his father as she thinks he is, he's decided somewhere in his heart that this is his fault. That he lost Maggie. That he killed her. And if they're not careful, in ten or twenty years some shrink will tell him he really wanted Maggie dead, wanted his rival, his competition—and not a fair competition, either, since Maggie's needs were so pronounced, so clear, so needy—out of the way. Some shrink will go telling him he did it on purpose, subconsciously wanted her dead, suggested she "get lost."

The problem with those people, she thinks, is that they can't accept that sometimes there are no answers, no first causes, no reasons for the things that happen in life. Things happen. Her husband collapsed on a sunny spring morning, died alone with the blackbirds singing. Maggie hid on an afternoon hike and cannot be found. What she's praying for there on her knees every morning is the strength and courage not to forsake God, the courage to have faith that it is as the nuns taught her, that God is merciful, that God will not give us a burden we cannot bear.

Head in hands, Martha sits at that kitchen table, not praying exactly, but hoping, asking for the strength to get her family through this, to get them off this cursed mountain. And if it be without Maggie, to give them the strength to make a home without that light at their center.

"GOT A minute?"

"What's up?" Steve asks him. Ed's got that bullheaded look on his face that Steve knows so well.

"I'm going back up there."

"I called the search, Ed," Steve says as he rolls up the maps, slides them into their black plastic tube.

"I know you did," he says. "But I'm going out anyway." Steve starts to object, but Ed waves him off. "Don't worry, I'm not taking anyone with me."

"It's still a protocol problem, Ed," Steve says. This is the last thing he needs right now. "It sets a terrible example."

"So I won't tell anyone."

"What's this about?" He knows that no matter what he says, Ed will be up there all night anyway. If Ed's got something up his sleeve, he wants to know what it is.

"I've got a hunch," Ed says. "That's all."

"Want to clue me in?" Steve asks, leaning against the table.

"There's nothing to say yet," Ed answers. "I just think we missed something where the footprint was. Something's bugging me, but I don't know what it is."

"I'll need you in the morning, you know."

"Since when has lack of sleep kept me from doing my job?" Ed asks.

"Take your radio," Steve says. He's too tired to argue with Ed. "Call me if you find anything."

Ed waves as he heads out into the shadows. Steve should be tougher with him, but he can't really figure out the point. It's not like the search guys don't all know that Ed is Ed and they shouldn't necessarily emulate him. And maybe, just maybe, he'll find the girl.

Heading for the path to the lake, Steve notices Anne's coffee cup. He stops, dumps the cold coffee into the gravel, and carries the cup back to the picnic table. They lose so much stuff when they have to run an operation this big. Seems like the ropes and mugs and flashlights sprout legs and walk off by themselves.

Steve looks around, checks one last time that things are in order before stepping off onto the little path behind the truck. It's always toughest on the mothers, he thinks. You'd imagine people would be a little more understanding, what with mothers working these days, fathers spending more time with their children. But something goes wrong and they all blame the mother. Even his people—he's seen the looks aimed her way, had to speak to a couple of searchers about keeping their mouths shut. Seems it's worse if it's a handicapped kid. All the second-guessing, the blame—just a way to convince themselves it couldn't happen to them. Half his people, he knows, are here for the sense of superiority that searching lends them. Thing none of them wants to admit, he thinks, is that these people did nothing wrong—it's just luck. There's as much bad luck as good luck in the world. Just depends on what you run into.

"MOTHER . . . " Richard says as he enters the kitchen. "You're still up?"

"Do you want some tea?" she asks, rising from the table. "I think the water's still hot."

"Did Anne go to bed already?"

"She's on the deck," Martha says, holding up the teakettle like a question.

"No thanks," he answers, looking out the window at Anne's shadow in the chair.

"She'll be all right," Martha says. "She'll come in when she's ready."

"You think so?" he asks, sitting heavily across from her. Martha nods, joins him at the table. They are quiet for a moment.

"Steve's going to call the priest," Richard says quietly. "He's down in South Lake. Should be here in the morning."

They sit with this information for a few minutes. Richard thinks of the night he drove up from school, after the call that his father had died. He got there late; the kitchen was full of covered dishes, food piled on the counters. His sisters finally collapsed, went upstairs to sleep in their childhood bedrooms, and he and his mother sat together, drinking coffee at the kitchen table. Richard can still see the little gold squares, like glitter—the swirling pattern of them in the white plastic. The hard metal edge of the table like a containment, a boundary. They were mostly quiet; she told him what had happened. He listened. They played cards that night, because his mother couldn't sleep. She didn't say it, but he imagined she didn't want to go upstairs alone to the bed she'd shared for forty-one years. Gin rummy. Hands of gin until the sun came up.

"What are they telling you?" his mother finally asks.

"It's what they're not telling me that counts," he says.

"And what do you think that is?"

"That they're probably not going to find her alive."

She holds her breath a moment but does not speak. What is there to say? Richard thinks, pushing his chair back from the table.

"I'm going to bed," he says, looking into the woodstove. "Tomorrow's going to be a long day." He stuffs a big log in, closes the door, shuts the vents down close so it will burn quietly and slowly.

"What about Anne?" Martha asks.

"Like you said." Richard rubs his eyes. "She'll come in when she's ready." He kisses her on the cheek. "Good night, Mother."

"Good night, dear," she says, placing a hand on his face in return. He's stupid with exhaustion, and he's grateful that he's too tired to think beyond the terrible sentence he just said aloud. They think they won't find her alive. For now, these are only words, but he feels their weight hovering above him, knows they will descend.

ANNE HEARS the door, then Martha's footsteps across the deck. Staring into the pale mountains above, Anne hopes she will go away.

217

"I brought you some tea," Martha says, setting the steaming cup on the arm of Anne's chair. Anne watches the steam rise and thinks again about how cold Maggie must be out there.

"It's so beautiful here," Anne says, pointing with her chin at the mountains.

"It is, isn't it?" Martha stands beside Anne's chair, looking up.

"What do you suppose it says about a person?" she says, a thin wire of anger threading through her voice. "That she finds the landscape in which her child is lost . . . beautiful? What sort of sin is that?"

"Maggie being lost doesn't change what it looks like," Martha says gently.

"All my life," Anne says, "beauty has been the most important thing in the world to me." A short, harsh laugh escapes her. "When Maggie was born, what worried me first was that she'd be ugly—not that she'd have a hard time, or wouldn't learn things, but that she'd be ugly."

"But she isn't, is she?" Martha asks. "Maybe that's what Maggie's taught us, that beauty isn't always where we expect it to be."

"What am I going to do if they can't find her?" Anne asks, looking up at this woman she loves and trusts.

"You're going to do what you have to do," Martha answers. "You're going to get up every morning and take care of your family. You'll paint. You'll buy groceries. You'll go to Luke's parent-teacher conferences. You'll play tennis with your broken-hearted husband." She looks down at Anne just as the moon slides behind a cloud. Anne watches Martha's face disappear in shadow. "Eventually, you'll feel less and less broken, less like the pieces of your life are shards of glass rubbing against one another. You'll never get *over* it"—Martha pauses, looks up toward the gleaming white mountain above them—"but eventually, loss gets easier to live with."

Anne reaches up and takes Martha's warm hand. "I don't know if I can," she says.

"Of course you can," Martha answers quietly. Sitting on the edge of Anne's chair, she smooths the hair back off of her forehead. "It's like everything else you thought you couldn't do. It's like giving birth, or dealing with colic for the fifteenth night in a row, or like sitting up all night in the hallway of some hospital waiting for your baby to come out of surgery. You never think you can do it, and then you do. You do it because you don't have any choice, and because the people who love you need you. You do it because you're a grownup and it's your job."

For a long time, the two women are motionless, holding hands across the bright moonlight of their grief. Then slowly, Anne rises out of the chair, picks up her mug, still half-warm from the tea, and they cross the deck, enter the yellow light of the house.

ED'S HEADLAMP illuminates only a small area at a time. He'd snap it off, but he likes the way this makes him concentrate, makes him really look at the ground, the leaves, the signs that people or animals have passed this way. The moon's still out passing quietly in and out of the cloud cover, and he can feel the imminent rain in the air.

He's back at the site of the footprint, tracking her from the mushroom into the woods. He thinks she headed across the drainage, although he doesn't know why he thinks this. But Ed trusts his hunch, and he crawls through the dark woods, his big head swinging from side to side like a nearsighted bear taking in the scent of whatever strange creature has invaded its space. The faint yellow light sweeps across the underbrush, lighting up leaves, pine needles, small bushes beneath which no child hides.

219

Ed feels his concentration begin to settle, feels himself getting to that place where he doesn't have to *think* about searching, he just does it. He follows whatever signs the woods will offer up to him. This is the place he couldn't get to all afternoon, when there was too much noise, too many people, too much adrenaline surging through all their veins. It's quiet now, and Ed is searching, on hands and knees, with his headlamp, one small bush at a time.

ANNE ENTERS the dark bedroom and fumbles with her jacket pocket; cold fingers struggle clumsily with the snap. She sets the shoe carefully on the table, in a shaft of light coming through the window, and she sheds her clothes. The air in the cabin is warm, but Anne doesn't feel it against her nakedness or the cold floorboards against her feet. She slips into bed beside her husband, startling him awake with the iciness of her feet, her hands, the chill of her skin.

He rolls toward her barely awake, and takes her in his arms. Anne stretches the length of her body along his. Skin. She needs to feel skin against her skin, needs to feel the familiar length and weight of Richard's legs against hers. He catches the cold hands she runs along his sides in his and rubs them, blows on them. Anne's body feels wooden, feels like it no longer belongs to her. She pulls her hands from his and reaches for him. He begins to speak and she kisses him. She doesn't want words; she wants touch. Richard's hands branch across her back like the thready creeks of a watershed, like the bronchioles and alveoli of her lungs; like the capillaries, veins, and arteries carrying blood in and out of her pumping heart. He knows her body as well as she does. Slowly, like the first pain after frostbite, she begins to come back to herself. First comes the shivering. The pain is sharp and sudden and Anne sinks under the floodwater of her need as he rolls her up on top of him. Anne's body is warming now, and her skin feels electric against his. They move together to a place where they do not exist outside their skins, sensations, desires. Together, they rock each other into the heart of their grief, the dark seat of both their pleasure and their pain.

It is dark in the moonless cabin. Tree branches scrape across the tin roof. There is no lightning, no thunder, only the steady falling of rain onto the absorbent forest floor.

Day Three

Luke wakes from a dream of spiders. Maggie wrapped in spiderwebs, like a cocoon. That's all he can remember. He lies in bed, squinting into the loft, trying to figure out what was happening in the dream. There were white lines, diagonals, spiderwebs, and he was trying not to touch them or he'd get caught. And Maggie's head sticking out of a cocoon.

She's still alive, he thinks. That's what it means that her head was sticking out. She was talking to him. She's not really dead.

Luke hears Gram and his mother downstairs. A pan clanks and he sits on the edge of the bed. The dream is getting further away and he wants to figure it out, but now he has to go to the bathroom. Sleep weighs on him like the lead vest at the dentist's office. He can smell coffee and bacon downstairs. He's sleepy and it's cold in the cabin. He hears rain on the roof. He wants to snuggle back into the warmth of the bed and close his eyes. But the lines are still there. The dark place.

Luke goes to the top of the loft and looks down at his mother and his grandmother. They don't see him. The sound on the tin roof is rain. A dark place with spider lines across it. Rain on the roof. It's chilly in the cabin. Wet. Maggie's head at the top of a cocoon. The smell of bacon. The leaden sleepiness seems to have him still. He can't shake the cocoon. He moves toward the smell of bacon, morning, safety. His mother is cooking. His grandmother makes coffee. See, he tells himself. Mom is still here. The dark place shot through with lines.

STEVE WATCHES the search teams walk into the rainy morning and worries about safety. Their heads bent against the dripping; the single line of bright rain clothes glows like strange flowers in the dim light. Foggy rainclouds shroud the peaks, crags emerging from them like the prows of ships. It is one of those storms that could change, at any moment, from cold rain to snow. And when it does, Steve knows that the possibility for searcher injury skyrockets. They're three days out; everyone's tired and a little disheartened, getting desperate. It's when people make dumb mistakes, get hurt.

But Ed calling in around 4:30 with the other shoe has reenergized everyone. It was about one hundred yards past the mushroom sign, and slightly uphill. It's a great sign, but, like everything else on this search, it doesn't really make sense. There were two footprints in the mud yesterday, so they'd assumed she'd lost the other shoe already. Either she was carrying it, and dropped it farther on, or she'd somehow circled around and was moving back toward the campground, coming down the drainage toward them. Ed flagged the area and hunkered down to get an hour or so of sleep while Steve called in the dog teams, yesterday's tracking team, and several grid teams. He's going to dump as much manpower up there as he has this morning; they're running out of time.

As he leaves the picnic shelter where they debrief, Steve turns the collar of his jacket up against the rain. Everything is soaked through. It has been raining steadily since 3:00 A.M. This is great for the dog teams—nothing holds scent better than a soft rain, although if it comes in any harder, they'll be in trouble—a hard rain washes out a scent trail. But more importantly, if it goes to a hard rain, they'll lose her; even if she's been holed up these two or three days, even if she found someplace where she could conserve her body temperature, it's three days now and she hasn't eaten. With this wet, hypothermia will be setting in; she'll be getting sleepy, sluggish, losing whatever capacity she had to answer them. No food means no fuel to keep her warm, and growing children don't have the stores of body fat that adults do. Water. Would she have found water? They've searched all the bodies of water, and it's been dry up here the last couple of weeks. Her parents say she dehydrates quickly, is always thirsty.

The third day is always hard. Giving the shift briefing, he saw the exhaustion on their faces, the worries about jobs and families start to set in, the numbing disappointment of walking yet another quadrant and finding nothing. You can only look for so long. Sometimes people just disappear. There's no way to explain it. Steve thinks of his Irish grandmother, who blamed lost objects on the fairies—"They steal things," she'd say, "because they are jealous and spiteful. *They steal babies,*" she whispered. "You have to watch out for them."

Is it fairies, he wonders as he climbs into the bus, that send one suddenly, spinningly lost on a simple day hike? A game of hide-

and-seek turned into this? These days of walking, calling, following clues that lead only to dead ends? Scent tracks that peter out across bare sunbaked granite? A shoe, cast aside in a moment of haste, but no foot to put in it?

Steve shakes out his wet coat, sees the colorful jackets of the last few crews recede through rain-smeared glass. Is he being realistic when he plans how to tell the parents, the TV people, that if this clue doesn't pan out, if the rain turns to snow, that they'll have to deescalate? Is he making sound decisions—or only getting bored? Has the glamour of the search worn off? Are they all looking for reasons not to continue with a task that has become routine, like the lives they seek to escape by volunteering? Turning from the window, he searches the map again.

ANNE IS surprised and relieved that she feels okay this morning. The underwater effect seems to have lifted, and for the first time since Luke came running back to her on that granite slab, there's no buzzing in her ears. She even slept some—a dark, dreamless sleep—and awakened feeling clear in the head. The lead weight still hangs on her, but it's not overwhelming. Maybe, she thinks, it might be possible to live, to continue, as Martha said she would, to get up each day and live in this world in which Maggie is missing.

"Hi, buddy," she says to Luke as he slides, stocking-footed, down the loft ladder. "Want some breakfast?"

He nods, too sleepy still to talk, and slides into a seat at the table. Martha pours him some cocoa, and he just blinks, watching them.

Anne cracks an egg in the pan, watches the edges of the egg sizzle in butter, and she doesn't even feel nauseous as the egg white coagulates, goes opaque. She flips it, cooks the other side. Luke doesn't like it when the egg stares at him. Martha has made bacon, and although usually Anne can't stand the heavy odor of the grease, the way it settles on the surfaces of the kitchen, lodges in the weave of clothing, this morning it smells homey to her. The kitchen smells like a cabin kitchen is supposed to: coffee, bacon, woodsmoke.

She slides the egg onto a warm plate already set with two pieces of buttered toast, two strips of bacon. "You okay?" she asks Luke as she sets the plate in front of him. His hair is sticking up the way it does in the morning, and she smooths it down.

"Mmhmm," he says, mouth full of bacon. She watches him eat; he looks grumpy. She worries; he's usually a morning person.

Anne slips a piece of toast and a strip of salty bacon onto a plate and eats while standing at the counter. She feels a strange calm settle over her. They can find Maggie today; she knows this in her innermost heart. Despite everything they said yesterday, despite having told Luke that Maggie might die; today, this morning, when her head is finally clear of that panicked static, Anne knows that Maggie can be found.

Richard stumbles into the kitchen, hair sticking up, T-shirt untucked from his jeans. He looks like Luke's mirror image. "Hey," he says as Martha and Anne turn toward him. "Is it still raining out?"

Anne feels the edges of her calm crack like a mirror, jagged shards of resolve separating. It can't still be raining. It is warm and bright and homey in the kitchen. Maggie is out there. She turns from Richard, grasps the sides of the sink, swallows hard to hold back the bile that rises in her throat.

ED'S GOT that sinking feeling he gets when a search is going south on them. They've run tight grids across the entire area where he

226

found the shoe. They've followed the bounding dogs deep into the thickety forest. They've crawled through the heavy underbrush, the manzanita and blackberry canes, tall dried stalks of purple and yellow aster, and emerged bedraggled and wet and empty-handed.

Ed halts his tracking group and pulls out the laminated map he's been carrying. They're bumped up against the little ridge that runs downhill, into the forested flats below. On the topo, this ridge appears as a line of V shapes pointing to the southwest. They're all pointing to something. What?

Michelle comes over to look at the map, and Ed stops a minute, closes his eyes, so all he hears is the sound of rain on the hood of his jacket, the scratchy sound of Gore-Tex as the searchers shift behind him.

He's been up here a million times, knows the area like his own backyard. In high school, they used to drive up here for weekend parties in the campground, and he'd head off into the woods, away from the noise and the beer and the kissing, head off into the woods to be alone, away from all the people. Sometimes he just can't be around so many people; he's always been that way. He'd take his sleeping bag and head out, looking for a good spot, a spot that felt okay to him.

Maggie was looking for a spot, a dry place to curl up. She'd need something to hide against.

Then he sees her. Ed sees a vision of Maggie curled up underneath a big Jeff pine deadfall, nearly buried in behind it; she's found a spot behind some manzanita, and she's dug back in between the manzanita and the tree trunk. She's alive, looking out from her hiding space with those big quiet eyes children get when they've almost given up. She's just looking out at them.

"Let me see that map," he says suddenly to Michelle.

"Deadfall," he mutters, looking out into the gray rain. "Has there been a blowdown around here?"

"ANNE?" RICHARD asks. "You all right?" He watches her clutch the sink edge for a moment, the four of them frozen there.

"Yes," she says somewhat faintly into the porcelain sink. "I'm fine." She turns, her face pale. "Do you want some breakfast?"

Richard looks across the gulf that has become the kitchen, looks at his wife, sickness written across her face, and he doesn't know what to do. Crying isn't going to get Maggie back for them, and it isn't going to make anyone feel any better, either. He pulls a chair out from the table, "Breakfast would be great," he replies. Luke's fork is hanging halfway between his plate and his mouth. Richard smiles at him a little. "Your egg's getting cold, buddy," he says gently to the boy. They might as well act like a family, like a family who are normal except for the fact that they're missing their youngest child, a child who is outside in the rain, and has been for three days. Richard buries his face in his hands.

"Did you get any sleep?" Martha asks, setting a cup of coffee in front of him as Anne cracks two eggs into the pan on the stove. They hiss on contact. Martha sits.

Richard looks across the breakfast table to Anne's back.

"Hmm?" he says. "Yes, Mother, I slept fine."

"Good," she says. "You needed it, both of you."

Luke is wiping egg yolk off his plate with a piece of toast. It occurs to Richard to wonder where the food came from; then he remembers the brown bags his mother emptied from the rental car.

"Dad?" Luke asks.

"What, Luke?" Richard replies, watching Anne's shoulder

blade move beneath her shirt as she flips the eggs over in the pan.

"Will they still look for Maggie in the rain?"

"Sure," Richard replies as Anne slips the plate in front of him. "Thanks." He punctures an egg yolk with a toast corner. "They'll just wear raincoats."

"Maggie's scared of thunder and lightning."

Richard looks out the window.

Anne takes Luke's empty plate, asks him if he wants more. When he says no, she runs water in the sink. "It hasn't been thundering so far, Luke," she says. A hint of color has returned to her face.

"Where do you think she is, Dad?" Luke asks suddenly, urgently. "Is she out there in the rain? It's so cold."

"I don't know, sweetie," Richard answers, watching Anne scrub the clean plate with an SOS pad. She scours the shiny plate. "We just have to hope she's found a little cave or a dry spot out there somewhere, someplace she can keep warm."

"Maybe she's in a hollow log," Luke says, staring into the middle distance. Richard and Martha exchange glances. Her eyes are steady, carefully neutral, waiting to see how this pans out.

"ED," JONATHAN says tentatively. Ed's still looking at the map. "Ed, I think I know where that burn might be."

"What?" Ed looks properly at Jonathan for the first time since he'd chewed him out for stepping on the shoe two days earlier.

"Up here," he says, pointing to an area about two miles up the watershed from where they're searching. "It's just a little pocket up here between Secret and Smith lakes," he says. "I remember it from when my dad and I had to bushwhack down from Pyramid Peak a couple of years ago."

"Here?" Ed asks, pointing to the map. The spot is only two

miles from the PLS directly, but more like four or five by the time you walk around the high ridge that separates them.

"There's a lot of deadfall," Jonathan says. "And blackberries—we got real scratched up slogging through there."

Ed looks at the spot. It's a little area of forest, a small cirque really. He's not sure. Ed can't shake those eyes, looking at him from that manzanita, not even blinking, just looking and waiting. It is definitely deadfall, the place he sees her watching from.

"Well, Jonathan," he says as he picks up the radio to call Steve, "let's hope you're right."

Jonathan watches Ed call in to Steve and is amazed he can convince him that even though he doesn't have any real evidence, the kid is up there and Steve should allocate the resources, send them up. A little awestruck, Jonathan thinks that Ed is the kind of searcher he wants to be, someone completely dedicated to the task, someone who will go to any length to find the victim. He can't believe how lucky he is that Ed keeps letting him tag along. After all, it's only his first live search.

ANNE AND Richard walk down the dripping road toward the command bus. Anne seems strung together this morning like a marionette loosely wired, ready to fly apart at any moment, and he's not feeling much more put together himself.

"We have to talk about this, Anne," he says. "We need to talk to each other, not just to Luke, or Steve, or Mother."

"I know," she says, head bent against the rain, hidden in the hood of her jacket. "But I can't just yet."

He takes her hand and they walk through the silent tree trunks, fat droplets sliding off pine needles, plopping to the forest floor with small splats.

Richard thinks of a horse he had once, the summer he was fourteen. She'd been born on the ranch, out of his dad's favorite mare, and was so pretty with her perfect dark socks, matching mane and muzzle that they'd all spoiled her a little. She was the first horse he ever broke, and it took him weeks, sliding up to her, sweet-talking her in the high-sided paddock, slipping bits of tack on her one by one, then back, flat against the rails, while she exploded into the strangeness of the leather straps and buckles, trying to outrun the saddle strapped to her back, the bit he slid into her mouth. Slowly, as the summer wore on, she got used to her new clothes, learned to circle on the lunge line, then the heart-stopping day when he finally mounted her, both of them trembling with the newness of it, that strange moment when, one foot in the stirrup, he hopped a little, stood into the saddle, and she snorted, but stood for him. Quietly, as they circled inside that space they'd shared all those weeks, as they went one way, then the other, Richard saw his father watching from the barn door, saw the grin on his face, saw how he didn't wave for fear of spooking her, and the two of them grinned over the top of the rail fence, the boy on his horse, the man who'd given her to him.

"Later, then?" he asks.

She nods yes, and he tucks her cold, slim hand into the pocket of his raincoat with his own. They walk down the road toward the man who is going to try to convince them to give up hoping that their child will survive this rain, these three days lost.

"GO ON now," Martha says, shooing Luke up the stairs. "Get some clothes on you. . . . " She watches him climb the ladder to the loft, thinking how like his dad at that age he looks. It seems so strange to her sometimes, looking at little boys with their thin limbs, the shoulder blades poking out on their backs, that they grow up to be men, that men begin like this.

Martha turns to finish the dishes in the sink. Egg yolk and bacon grease. She tosses a toast crust in the trash can. She'll have to find out where to empty it, and if there's a place nearby they can wash the sheets before they leave.

Its all she can do, these practical things. The blackness hanging over them this morning seems so inescapable that she doesn't know any other way to cope with it. She knows there's nothing to do with grief except live through it, try your best to get up and go through the motions of being alive, because eventually, somehow, you actually do come back to life. She'll go into town and clean the linen. She'll take care of Luke and give Richard and Anne some time to figure out how to tell him. We can pick up some groceries, too, she thinks, putting the cast-iron skillet on the stove, heating it dry, watching the damp spots chase one another across the warming surface of the black metal. She'll have to ask Steve how much longer he thinks they might be here.

Martha looks out the window into the half-light of the morning. Gray mats of fog hover among the trunks of trees. She can hear a woodpecker's insistent tap; it runs a moment, then pauses, starts up again. Water drips from tree branches, falls from the cloud in that soft, nearly invisible way that saturates every surface. It is as if the forest has been submerged.

Luke startles her, slipping off the last rung of the ladder in his socks, landing with a thump on the kitchen floor. She whirls on him and they look at each other, silently, for a long moment. The kitchen hangs suspended.

"Is that pan getting too hot?" Luke asks, pointing to the cast-iron skillet, which is beginning to give off that hot metal smell, the burner on high.

STEVE LEANS to swing open the bus door for them. Richard hesitates a moment, and Anne steps forward, climbs the three steps into the long confines of the bus.

"There's some good news," he says.

"What?"

"Ed found her other shoe."

"Where?" Richard asks, leaning over the map.

Anne clutches the pole at the head of the stairs. *She's okay.*

"Here," Steve says, leaning over the maps. "About a hundred yards uphill from the mushroom footprint." He launches into that litany of statistics that still, three days into this, mean nothing to her. Possibility of detection. Possibility of absence. The numbers rise and fall with each search, each time they walk an area and find nothing. It's a sort of algebra of Maggie's disappearance. What interests Anne are the lines on the transparencies. The hatch marks that delineate search areas, the topo lines on the map that show cliffs, water, the edge of the forest.

"Anne, are you listening?" Steve asks suddenly.

"No," she admits. "I don't care about the numbers. All I want to know is when you're going to find her." Steve and Richard look a little shocked at this, as if by mentioning *finding* Maggie, Anne has somehow broken their bubble of guy talk, number crunching, all the acronyms they're using to cover up the fact that Maggie is actually lost.

"Well," Steve says slowly and carefully, "what I've been trying to show you here is that although this is a good sign, things are still pretty dicey."

"But you found the other shoe."

"We found the other shoe."

233

Anne nods. They watch her as if they expect her to fly into a thousand little pieces. The searing pain, as if she has swallowed a live coal, is back, the one she forgot about for a few blessed moments this morning. It's back, which means she has to carry it still. Anne will carry it as far as she needs to, because to give up this pain is to give up hope. Not yet. They found a shoe; they can find her child.

LUKE WATCHES the sheets go around in the Laundromat dryer. He likes the way they float, the way they seem to hang for a second, suspended between the rotating cylinder walls. It's too bad, he thinks, that you can't see into the dryer at home. Maggie would like watching the laundry go around.

One of the things he likes about his gram is that if you don't want to talk, she doesn't try to make you. On the drive into town, they just drove. He looked out the window at the tall fir trees, dark green in the river bottom, and thought about the place with the lines. It's stuck in his head and he can't get it out.

Luke's alone, waiting for Gramma to come back from the coffee shop next door. It's taking her a long time. He turns from the dryer and looks around for something to do. There's a paper on the table; he pulls it toward him and unfolds it.

Maggie's on the front page.

It's that silly picture of her running down the driveway, both arms out to her sides, wearing the funny sunglasses their other granny sent and that feather boa she loves. He leans across the table, looking at the photo of his sister, and starts to read the story. Their names are all there. It tells how she got lost while playing hide-and-seek, that she's six years old, Down syndrome. Search and rescue teams from six counties, three dog teams, helicopters from the Civil Air Patrol. Luke reads all this and looks at the picture of Maggie running—she'd wear that boa to school, but Mom won't let her.

Gram walks through the door with two Styrofoam cups.

"Hot chocolate," she says. "Careful."

"What's that?" she asks, looking over his shoulder.

"It's about Maggie," Luke tells her.

His grandmother picks it up and Luke can see her reading ahead.

"What?" he asks. "What does it say?"

"Nothing," she tells him, sipping at her coffee. "Drink up before it gets cold."

Luke slides back down into his seat. He thinks, from the frown on Gram's face, that the paper says something about the fact that Maggie might die. He'll sneak and read it later; after all, it's not like he's a baby anymore. He can read as well as anyone. As he sips at his chocolate, cool enough to drink but not too cold, he watches the sheets tumble slowly into a fluffy heap on the bottom of the dryer.

"Look, Gram," he says. "The sheets are done."

BACK IN the cabin, Richard finds the coffeepot still warm at the back of the woodstove. "More?" he asks, turning toward Anne.

"Sure," she says, reading Martha's note.

Richard pours two cups, then reaches into the fridge for the milk, which he dollops into his own.

"Maybe," Anne says, "we were wrong all this time."

"What do you mean?" Richard asks, pulling out a chair. "Wrong about what?"

"Wrong to treat her like she's any other kid," Anne says. "As if the Down's doesn't matter." Anne sees their last Christmas card in her head. The four of them posed along an overlook fence high above the Pacific. Maggie and Luke perched on the top rail, Anne's and Richard's arms around them. The cliff fell hundreds of feet behind, but all you could see in the picture was the mild ocean, stretching to the blue horizon. As if the cliff hadn't been there the whole time. As if they had never noticed the cliff.

Richard sips his coffee. "What else were we supposed to do?" he asks.

"I don't know," Anne says. "But maybe all those other people were right. Maybe we should have—"

"Should have what?" Richard answers. "Should have locked her up, made her one of those fearful children who aren't allowed to do anything?"

"Like she'd listen to 'No' anyway," Anne says, smiling a little, blowing on her coffee.

Rain drips down the windows, tats softly on the tin roof above them. Richard gets up and looks into the woodstove.

"I guess," he says. "We could have treated her differently. Been more frightened, kept her at home, not let her do the things Luke does, but really—" He breaks off, rearranging the log so it fits, doesn't hang out the end of the stove. "Is that the kind of life we wanted for her?"

"Past tense?"

Richard sits back on his heels, looks at her for a long moment.

"There's that other shoe," Anne says. "They found the other shoe."

STEVE PEELS overlays off the map. The grease-pencil lines lift off with each transparent sheet until finally he is looking at a pristine map, green areas of forest, buff amoebas of rocky terrain above the tree line, blue lakes, dotted lines for the trails. He couldn't tell them about Ed's hunch, about the team he's leading up to that unlikely burn site. It's too cruel to get their hopes up over something with no real evidence like that.

"I'm about ready," Jane says from the stairwell of the bus.

"So soon?" Steve asks.

"Mmhmm," she says. "I need to be back at the hospital by three, and with this rain . . . "

"Of course," Steve says, shrugging his wet raincoat back on. They walk together across the empty parking lot, toward her car.

"When do you think you'll be home?" she asks, leaning against the car.

"Hard to say," he answers. "If Ed's hunch pans out and we find her . . . Otherwise, we'll probably run body searches for another day or two, depending on the weather. I imagine I'll be home by Friday at the latest."

"Say good-bye to the family for me."

"When's Joey's funeral?" he asks.

"Today."

"Call me about it, will you?"

"I'll be okay."

"I know you will, but call me anyway."

"Okay," she says. Peeking up at him from under the hood of her rain jacket, Steve thinks she looks as beautiful as she did that day he first met her at that river-safety clinic.

They kiss, and he holds the car door for her.

"Drive safely," he says. "The roads in this weather—"

"Don't worry," she says, grinning at him. "And close that door; I'm getting wet."

Steve closes her into the little Japanese car and watches her pull out of the gravel lot. She'd waited up for him last night, when he'd come back from the debriefing. Steve was nearly wordless with grief and sadness. These people are probably going to lose their child and he's going to have to tell them he can't find her. He hates this part of the job. Jane had been there, quietly asking him what had happened, getting him to talk it out, being the one person he doesn't have to lead on this search. They'd still been up when Ed's call had come in, when that small flame of hope was rekindled.

He watches her car disappear into the fog. It was her hands, he thinks. She was so good with the knots. Hard to imagine it was over twenty years ago now, hard to believe they've got a daughter in college. Steve walks back to the bus, thinking not about trajectories and grid searches, but about the way the woman who was to become his wife had looked all those years ago, rigging z-drags from trees with climbing rope, pulling boats off imaginary rocks.

"GRAMMA?" LUKE asks, standing on tiptoe to keep the clean sheet between them from touching the floor.

"Hmm?" she hitches the folded sheet up to fold it in half again.

"Will Maggie be retarded in heaven?"

Martha lays the sheet flat on the Laundromat folding table. "I don't know, Luke," she says, looking thoughtfully at him. "I never thought about it." She folds the sheet over, smooths it flat. She thinks back to the nuns from her convent school; how would Sister Jo have answered this one? "Let's see," she begins. "Since we're all our perfect selves in heaven . . . I suppose not." She picks up another sheet from the basket. "Here," she says. "Take an end."

"Mom says that if Maggie wasn't retarded," Luke says, backing away until the sheet is tight, "then she wouldn't be Maggie, that she'd be someone else."

"She does?" Martha asks. "Other way," she tells him, shaking the sheet.

"Yeah," Luke answers, flipping the sheet longways, pulling it tight again. "She says that since Maggie's Down's is in her DNA, since it's in all her cells, that if she wasn't Down's she'd be a totally different person."

"Hmm," Martha says as she walks toward Luke with her end of the sheet. They fold the sheet twice more; then Martha turns toward the folding table. "Let's see, Luke," she says, stopping to think for a minute. "Maggie will still be Maggie in heaven," she tells him. "Because everyone is unique and special to God, so whatever that part of her that makes her Maggie—"

"Like how funny she is?" Luke asks.

"Sure, like her sense of humor, and how she always wants to hug people—all those parts of Maggie that are so special." Martha pauses. "Well, I suppose those are all the things God loves about Maggie, too, don't you think?"

"Yeah, that's the fun part about her," Luke says. "But what about when she gets mad and breaks things, or has fits about having to eat the wrong stuff?"

Martha sits on the edge of the table and looks at her grandson. "Doesn't most of that come when she's confused, or can't understand something?" Martha asks him.

"Yeah," Luke says. "She gets so frustrated sometimes."

"Well in heaven," Martha says, turning to the last sheet in the basket, "Maggie won't get frustrated like that."

"You mean she'll understand stuff?" Luke asks.

"Mmhmm," Martha says, handing him one end of the sheet. "She'll be able to understand everything."

"That would be good." Luke backs up with the sheet. "Because I don't think Maggie likes not being able to understand stuff."

"I'VE BEEN using the past tense?" he asks her.

Anne nods. Richard stands slowly, one knee clicking loudly. "Do you really think we did the wrong thing?" he asks Anne. "Do you think we should have . . . we should . . . rein her in more carefully?"

"I don't know," she says, tracing a shape with her finger on the tabletop.

"What kind of life is that for a kid?" he asks, pacing in front of the stove. "It's not the way we've ever wanted to live . . . being afraid of things. Would we want Luke to be afraid to try things? Afraid to take risks?"

"But Luke's not Down," Anne says softly, staring at the table. "Maybe we expected too much."

They hear the logs shift inside the stove, the cascading sound of coals sloughing off burning wood.

"Is that what you really think?" he asks, his voice very quiet. "Do you really think that it would have been better never to have let her out of that fenced-in backyard? That we should have kept her on a short lead, always snatching at her—'No Maggie. Don't do that, Maggie. You might get hurt, Maggie. . . . '"

"Maybe if we'd done that, she wouldn't be lost," Anne blurts out, looking up at Richard where he stands in front of the clicking woodstove, hands in his pockets. "Maybe she wouldn't be out there." Her voice breaks as she waves toward the wall.

"We can't know that," he says, crossing the room, sitting in one of the straight kitchen chairs. He spins her chair so she's facing him. Their knees are nearly touching.

"And you know where this argument goes," he continues.

"It's like when she was born. If we start what-ifing, we'll go crazy."

"We didn't have any control over her being Down," Anne says. "But this . . . we could have done something. . . . If I hadn't gone ahead to the lake, if you hadn't gone off to pee, if Luke hadn't closed his eyes . . . there are so many places we could have caught her."

Anne holds her hands before her as if she is trying now to catch Maggie, to snag her out of this nightmare free fall. Richard hooks her by those fingers, fingers that know him, fingers he's watched make intricate and sometimes frightening artwork, fingers that have held the babies they made together; fingers he's felt on his body and that still, all these years later, feel like a benediction and a grace to him, and as he pulls her by those fingers into his body, she begins to sob.

"We could have done *something*," she cries into his pile sweater. "We just let her go."

Richard feels as though he is being split down the middle by the knowledge that in some elemental way, she is right. Had they done things differently, their beloved, needy, maddening child wouldn't be outside in the slow rain, freezing to death. One big hand covering the back of her head, Richard holds his wife and rocks her a little, useless tears streaming down both their faces as they try to grope their way through this midday darkness.

Anne and Richard had stayed at that table clinging to one another for a long, long time. Then, just as the crying was subsiding, as they were sniffling and scrounging around looking for Kleenex to wipe their noses, blinking at each other incomprehensibly, trying to invent a way to live with this new reality, a world in which Maggie is simply and unimaginably gone, the call came over the radio that the priest Richard had called, the one from Lake Tahoe, was on his way over. Anne panicked. "I can't," she said to Richard. "I just can't."

Anne watches as patterns of wet leaves and sodden pine needles unfurl between her feet as she walks. It's one of the things she's most grateful for, that there is this space in their marriage, that he gives her room to bolt. That, unlike her mother, say, Richard's never taken it personally when she needs to be alone, needs to think or process through something. But how can she think through this? It's like a big black wall, a dead end.

"Accident," Richard had said over and over into her hair as they cried. "It's an accident. It's not anybody's fault." But she doesn't believe him. It was her fault, his fault, Luke's fault; it was even, in some strange stubborn way of hers, partly Maggie's own fault. Everyone failed for one fleeting moment and Maggie slipped through that net of their love. They let down their guard and Maggie fell.

Anne crosses the wet packed sand, hard almost like pavement now, hard like that white granite that looms above her, hidden in the fog. She walks down the thin strip of stone that juts into the lake, walks into a space that hangs between fog and rock, surrounded by the smooth surface of the lake, which shines softly, like an old-fashioned metal mirror.

It's the first thing you learn as a parent, she thinks, standing on the end of the spit, nearly in the water, water lapping gently at the toes of her boots. How could I have forgotten? You turn your back to stir the soup and the child falls on the kitchen tiles and bleeds. You turn your back to put the wash on and the child inhales a marble. You turn your back to load groceries in the parking lot and the child runs into the path of an oncoming car.

We were so stupid; we thought she was safe, Anne thinks. We thought we'd gotten her past the worst of it—the endless repetitive exercises of early intervention, the surgeries, the viruses and colds and flus she couldn't shake, the time she got giardia from the town water supply and no one figured it out for months, not until she wound up in the hospital, dehydrated and so sick. We thought that just because she was finally used to school, learning to follow the rules, learning to speak and read and count and not be disruptive *all* the time, that just because she could ski and swim and ride a bike, that she was safe, that she wasn't really impaired, that she was okay. Anne hunches deeper into the hood of her raincoat. The cold air seems half water. *Dead wrong.* The phrase takes on a whole new meaning for her. Peering out from under her rainhood, Anne can't tell if the rain's falling down or the water's rising up out of the lake, rising to meet the opaque clouds in which those malevolent peaks, those peaks that stole her child, are packed like fragile objects in a box of cotton wool.

Then Anne feels a stab of hope. For the first time in hours, she feels Maggie's presence, feels her as surely as if they were at home and Maggie were in the other room watching television while Anne cooks dinner. The shoe, she thinks. They found that other shoe. She's at the end of the spit of land, and she feels Maggie near her, so near, just out of reach. It's as though that coal she'd been carrying has flared up again, sent out one small flame.

The water, she thinks. She's behind the water. The water is a curtain, a veil that separates her from Maggie, and Anne feels her daughter's urgent presence, just out of reach, just beyond this scrim, this mask of water.

Maggie is *out there,* right beyond her reach. Anne knows this now, knows it with a wild certainty. If she can get beyond this scrim, she can punch through it, she can pull Maggie back into the world. Maggie came into the world through her mother's body once; why not twice?

Anne wades into the lake; it's just a little farther. She can see it. If she can reach that leg . . . Maggie's leg is right through there, if only she can stretch a little farther, she'll reach that ankle, that sturdy leg; she can haul Maggie back into this world like some heavy fish.

Ed surveys the little basin below them. It's the third ridge they've climbed over since they left the spot where he found the shoe. "Is this the one you meant?" he asks Jonathan.

"Can I see the map a minute?" Jonathan asks.

Ed pulls it out of his jacket and spreads it across a wet rock. The other searchers crowd around him.

"Yeah," Jonathan says. "This looks like the spot my dad and I slogged through. It's really thick in there."

As Ed looks across the brambles and deadfall, the blackened debris of a years-old fire, the first white flakes come floating down.

"Okay, folks, everyone listen up," Ed says. "We don't have much time; the temperature's dropping fast. And this snow's going to make it even more dangerous out here, so be careful. We're heading downhill over slick terrain, so if you need to slow up, then slow up."

He looks up into the snowfall. He'll have them search downhill, toward camp, and then they can start doing cross searches. Ed can see her eyes out there, see them just as real as the way he felt Aaron's feet in his hands when they found the footprint. She's out there, and they don't have long. She's dying. It's too cold.

Ed shouts for the line to proceed, and they plunge into the tangle of briars and downed trees like drowning people desperate to make it to shore, like people who know they've got only one chance.

"Drive *faster*, Gramma," Luke says, face pressed to the window. They're on the gravel road and his voice makes that weird vibrating sound from the washboards.

245

"I'm going as fast as I can," she says. "Why? What is it?"

"Nothing," he says, flopping back into his seat. He thinks Maggie is dead, but he can't tell his gram; he can hardly think the thought himself. It jumps around inside his head, trying to get out, and he has to keep it in until he gets to his mom.

He didn't think she was dead before, when he was goofing off with Gram in the grocery store. "What will happen if Maggie's dead?" he'd asked her. But he wouldn't have asked if he'd really thought she was dead. He didn't then, but now he does, and it scares him.

"To Maggie?" Gram had answered. "She'll go to heaven like we talked about before."

"All by herself?" Luke'd asked. "Who will take care of her?" It had been dark all around her in his dream. Maggie's afraid of the dark. Luke twinged his fingers in the metal rods of the cart and walked with his grandmother past the cold air coming off the meat coolers.

"The Virgin Mary will take care of her," Gram had told him. Luke loves it that his grandmother always has an answer for things. "Do you know about her?"

"She's Jesus' mother," he'd said. They'd been looking for the cereal aisle. "In the crèche at Christmas."

"She's like the mommy of heaven," Gram had said. "She takes care of all the babies and little kids whose parents are still on earth." Luke had thought then about Maggie with that serene-looking Mary from the Christmas display.

"Even the naughty ones?"

"Even the naughty ones, Luke," Gram had said, smiling side-ways at him. "Why?"

"She doesn't look fast enough for Maggie," he'd said. Luke had stopped in the aisle and imitated Mary's stance, head bowed, arms straight at his sides, palms out. "You have to be real fast to catch Maggie."

"Oh, Luke." Gram had laughed. "She doesn't have to stand like that in heaven; that's only in statues."

"Good." Luke had giggled. "Because she'd never catch Maggie like this." He'd rocked back and forth, waddling down the cereal aisle like a frozen statue trying to chase Maggie.

"You goof," she said, ruffling his hair. "What kind of cereal do you want?"

Luke had kept waddling down the aisle, pretending to be the Mary statue, calling in a falsetto voice, "Oh Maggie! Come back here right now! You naughty girl!"

But that was before, when he didn't think Maggie was dead, and now he knows she is somehow, and it scares him. If we can get there faster, he thinks, if we can get to Mom, then maybe it won't be true.

Martha looks at the small boy in the passenger seat. He's looking straight out the window, staring ahead, his face unusually pale. "Are you getting carsick?" she asks, slowing the car a little. It's a very curvy road.

"No!" he shouts. "Go *faster*. I'm not getting sick—I just want to get there!"

"Don't shout, Luke," she admonishes quietly.

He looks stonily out the window into the rain. There were those lines in the dream, like spiderwebs, like the kind you can't see that stick to your face when you're playing in the woods. Everything feels like the place with the lines. The place with the sticky lines that you can't see, that catch you.

RICHARD OPENS the door for the priest and is shocked that the man is his age, maybe younger. He doesn't wear a collar, just

247

ordinary clothes, and it isn't until he introduces himself that Richard even realizes he's the priest. He thought maybe he was a searcher, someone Steve had sent to the cabin with news.

"How can I help?" the priest asks. Richard offers him a seat at the kitchen table.

"I don't know, Father," Richard answers. "My mother's the religious one. She's gone to town to do some wash, get more groceries."

"Call me Kevin," the man says. "That is, if it makes you more comfortable."

We did call him, Richard thinks. Now what am I going to do with him? And when, Richard wonders, pouring coffee for the man, did I get to be the same age as the priest?

"Thanks," the priest says as Richard sets the coffee in front of him. "But you did ask them to call?" He seems a little confused.

"Yes," Richard says. "I mean, they're telling us they probably won't find her in time . . . won't find her alive. Seemed like . . . well, seemed like the time to . . . "

"The time to . . . " He seems, Richard thinks, like he's trying to gauge the situation.

"I don't know," Richard says. "It's not like I've been a regular at Mass or anything, but it seemed like maybe we could use some help."

Richard can't imagine anyone he knows having decided to go into the priesthood. They sit quietly for a moment.

"So," he asks. "How are you doing with this news?"

"I . . . well," Richard begins. "It's . . . it's complicated."

"Yes," he replies. "I imagine it is."

WAIST-DEEP in the lake, Anne reaches into the mist for Maggie's leg. She wades in with the heavy stride people use when they're hurrying through deep water. Maggie's so close. Anne can feel her the way she feels a painting that is *almost* finished, one where the elements are all in place but haven't quite come together yet. Maggie's right there, in the negative space she needs to make this right.

Anne's taking on the cold again, and she's back in that place where she knows that if she can only absorb enough of it, she'll be able to crack open the shell of this layer of reality, of this cold in which her Maggie is trapped, and there she'll find her, waiting. Maggie will be pink and warm and alive; her gangly-legged girl will squirm into her arms and they can both go home.

Then the bottom drops out and she's underwater in the black dark and it is colder than she could have imagined. The water closes over the top of her head and she jerks for the surface, feet flailing for the rock. Her rain jacket floats around her, slowing her arms, and she fights it, fights the icy water, fights for the surface, kicking with legs encumbered by wet jeans, feet entombed in sodden boots. Her clothes are dragging her down and the cold water forces the air out of her lungs. She sees bubbles flying past her toward the surface.

Anne kicks and claws against the black water. She can't drown now; Richard and Luke need her. She can see the the surface of the water shining above her like a mirror in a dimly lit room. She's not going to make it.

Her mouth opens to breathe water at the exact moment that her face breaks the surface, and Anne finds herself choking on a mixture of air and water as she flails toward shore. Her whole being is overcome by the panicky need to get out of the cold, out of the water, and there's no room for anything but this thought as Anne scrambles, finds her footing once more, and, hacking and coughing, afraid she's going to throw up, staggers back to shore.

Anne lies flat, her stomach pressed to the dark granite. The only thought in her head is to get enough air into her lungs, to expel the water she took in as she broke the surface. As her heartrate slows, she feels nothing but gray ash where the coal used to be, a powdery pile that crumbles as she reaches for it. The surge of desire that got her to the surface of the water, that burning desire to live, to return to the people she loves cuts her now like a knife. Maggie is cold and dead under a bush somewhere out there and Anne lies useless here on this rock, sobbing in the cold of heartbreak and grief, unsure how she'll get up and walk back into her life once more, walk into a life where she failed to save the one thing she loved above all else; Maggie.

SHRUGGING DEEPER into the hood of his jacket, Jonathan can't believe it's snowing. Means a good ski season, though, he thinks, and is immediately ashamed of himself. A good ski season. He shouldn't be thinking of such things at a time like this. His girlfriend would tell him not to be such a fucking Boy Scout, to lighten up, but really he thinks he should be concentrating on the search, on finding the little girl.

There's a couple in Jonathan's apartment complex who have a Down's kid; he sees them at the pool sometimes. He's a cute little boy; you'd hardly know he was retarded by looking at him. The mom will be down there with him sometimes when Jonathan goes to do laundry. They're always playing games, and last summer Jonathan was surprised to see him swimming—he's only a little kid, three or maybe four. He told the mother how impressed he was and she said she'd just feel better if she knew he could swim, felt safer, you know. Just like any other child. Not like when he was in school and the "retards" were kept locked away. Like it was contagious or something.

Jonathan checks to see if he's falling behind. The footing is tricky here. There were so many people this morning—if she's up there, they've got to find her. How could they miss her with this many people? Jonathan looks up to check how hard the snow is coming down, and that's when he feels his leg slip between the two logs; that's when he hears the unmistakable sound of a large human bone cracking.

"IT'S ALL my fault," Richard says. "I was supposed to be watching them and I left." He shakes his head. "Because I had to take a whiz. I wasn't paying attention. . . ."

"Richard," Kevin says quietly, "please don't do that to yourself."

"I'm the dad," he says. "I'm supposed to take care of them."

There is a long silence as they sit together at the table. Richard can sense the priest struggling for the right thing to say.

"Does it help," he finally begins, "to think that Maggie's in the arms of a loving God, in a place where she's in no pain, but enveloped in perfect love?"

"That seems like a fairy tale to me," Richard says, staring into the muddy coffee. "No offense," he adds.

"Of course not," Kevin says.

"How could this happen?" Richard says, suddenly angry. "What kind of a God lets this happen. *Look* out there. . . ." He stands and walks over to the sink, stares out the window into the gray drizzle.

"There's no good answer I can give you for that one," Kevin says quietly.

"It's *raining,*" Richard says. He'd always believed in God, not like his mother perhaps, but he's always believed that there was a presence out there, an underlying principle perhaps, an order

251

to the universe that sometimes, if you were very careful and very lucky, you could glimpse, or feel in passing. His God has always lived in the high country, but now, Richard looks out the cabin window and sees nothing in these mountains but meaningless rain.

"My child is out there," Richard says, turning to the priest. "In rain that will kill her because she only weighs fifty-six pounds and it's cold and she hasn't eaten in three days. What kind of a God allows this to happen?"

"The only one we've got," Kevin answers. "The one who promises us that no matter how bleak things look, we're always safe in his love."

"Safe," Richard says bitterly as he sits back down at the table. "I'm sorry, but nothing is safe anymore."

The two men sit silently together at the scrubbed wooden table. Kevin knows that sometimes the best he can do is to keep watch, to give witness to the searing reality of the pain, and to sit with it until it subsides enough to allow some small comfort an opportunity to reenter.

MARTHA LOOKS over at the little boy beside her, absolutely tense, face pale, rocking a little, as if he can hurry the car along by doing so. She's driving as fast as she can, skidding a little around the washboard curves of the late-season road. If he needs Anne, then she'll do her best to get him there.

Concentrating on the road, she thinks about their conversation in the laundry. "Will Maggie be retarded in heaven?" What a question. But he has a point. If Maggie weren't retarded, she *would* be someone else entirely. Anne's always been adamant that Maggie's handicap not be treated with pity, that everyone simply accept it as one of the basic conditions of her life, like her blond hair. It's a stance Martha's always admired; she's never believed in crying and moaning over something that can't be changed. Maggie is Maggie, and that means taking into account her Down syndrome: retardation, runny nose, heart trouble, and everything else.

Luke had been asking about heaven. Sometimes she really wishes these children had had some religious instruction, but since they haven't, she hopes she gave Luke a heaven he can trust in. Martha doesn't really believe in the version she told Luke about. But her abstract vision of heaven seems a little complicated for a small boy who needs to know his sister won't be alone. "She's all alone out there," he'd cried out at the breakfast table. Martha could almost hear their hearts breaking, one by one, around that table.

As the car climbs up and over the last ridge and the road levels out for its final stretch through the lodgepole forest, she turns to Luke. "We're almost there, sweetheart," she says. "Just a couple more minutes."

Luke looks stonily ahead out the window. He *knows,* she thinks.

ANNE HAS to get up. She's lying on the cold rock and she's wet. Her sobs have subsided, but she's starting to shiver and it's cold. She remembers the old movie from her high school Outdoor Education Class: "It's hypothermia, Uncle Marvin." For months they'd repeated it to one another in the halls, the high school nerds, into climbing, addicted to the smell of wood smoke in one another's hair. Oh shit, she thinks, flat on her stomach on a cold rock. I have to get up.

Richard. Luke. She left Richard waiting for the priest. Luke will be back soon. She feels her love for them flow back into her like a warm flush, like blood in her veins again. It hurts the way she remembers her fingers and toes hurting, years ago, when she'd gotten hypothermic in raft-guide training. Standing in a hot shower, crying as her feet and fingers swelled up, getting hot and tight like little sausages as the blood flowed back into her extremities. Luke and Richard need her. She needs them. They're the blood in her veins and she has to get up, walk back to them on these stumps before it's too late.

As Anne stands on that isolated spit of rock halfway between water and land, she feels like someone who has walked through a pane of glass, and now looks at her bleeding limbs with confusion, wondering how she came to this flayed state.

ED HEARS Jonathan cry out, and he stops, hands clenched at his sides. It takes every last molecule of self-control he possesses not to let loose a great long, howling cry of disappointment. This can't be happening—they were so close.

"The Stoke's!" Ed finally shouts. "Who's got the Stoke's?" He sprints uphill toward Jonathan, who, despite himself, is hollering like a man who's just broken his leg.

"I've got it," Joe yells, shucking his pack to unlash the aluminum-frame Stoke's litter.

"Let's get him out of there," Ed says to the team, which has gone into full rescue mode. Jonathan's thrashing back and forth in pain and they've got to get him out from between the logs before he compounds the injury. Michelle's talking to him, getting him to calm down while Ed takes a position behind him on the slick log and prepares to pull him out.

"You're going to be all right, buddy," he says. He's got one arm around the kid's chest and he lightly rests the other against his head. Jonathan has stopped shouting, but he rocks back and forth with the pain.

Joe's got the litter put together, and Michelle's got an arm down into the crevice, feeling along the injured leg.

"Is it caught?" Ed asks.

"Doesn't feel like it," she answers. Bits of wet log debris cling to her jacket and face.

"Okay, Jonathan," Ed says into the boy's ear. "Here's the plan. On the count of three, we're going to pull you up and out of there. Joe's got the Stoke's set up behind us, so we'll lay you out on that and take a look at that leg, all right?" Ed can feel Jonathan nod yes. "Can you get a purchase with your good leg? Okay, this is probably going to hurt," Ed says as he nods at the other searchers, who have set themselves up to spot in case he falls. They count to three and pull Jonathan out from between the slick logs.

The poor kid's that sick gray color people turn when they're really hurt, and it looks like a clear tib-fib break. Michelle and Hugo, who're both EMTs, get the leg splinted, and they start to pack Jonathan in a sleeping bag and a waterproof tarp before lashing him onto the Stoke's.

Ed takes a quick head count while scrambling for his radio. Jonathan probably weighs about 165, and he's got about a team and a half's worth of folks to start evac'ing him. They can probably get him down out of the snow zone before they have to stop and wait for reinforcements.

"MOM!" LUKE yells as he runs down the beach. The sand gives way beneath him just as he wants to go forward, to go faster. He has to get to his Mom, and the sand is holding him back.

She catches him as he jumps into her arms, buries his head in her hair, her shoulder. "Mom," he shouts, surprised to find he's crying. "Maggie's dead, Mom."

"I know," she says, arms around him. He wraps his legs around her and lets her carry him. It's such a relief to say it out loud. All the way up in the car, he thought it was going to explode out of him and he was afraid Gram wouldn't understand, that she'd try to explain it away.

"What are we going to do?" he asks into her neck. He's crying really hard now. He doesn't want Maggie to be dead. What's he going to do without Maggie? But he knows she's gone; he can't feel her anywhere anymore, and it's so cold and it's raining.

"Oh, sweetheart." She sighs, shrugging his weight a little higher into her arms. "I don't know." They're walking now, and Luke knows he's too big, knows he should get down, but he wants his mom to carry him while he cries and cries. He feels like he might never stop crying. "I don't know what we're going to do," she says into his hair as they walk across the sandy beach, walk back toward the cabin.

STEVE FINISHES sending three more teams up to help Ed evacuate Jonathan, and he looks to check the temperature. The red line on the thermometer has been steadily dropping.

A fifty-six-pound child dressed only in a T-shirt and shorts cannot survive a day of rain turning to snow as night is falling. Not when she's been out there three days with no food, no water. Steve knows this, just as he knows that Ed's team pulling out, having to reallocate resources, having had all of their leads dry up, means this search is going to fail.

This is the part of the job he hates. They can tell themselves all they want that they've made their best effort, that they did all they could, but a failed search means a dead person, a person beloved by family members. And a kid. It's always worse when it's a kid.

Steve makes a note to call the psych squad, set up some counseling sessions, a group debriefing. And this snow, it's going to wreak hell on a body search—unless she melts it off, residual warmth, decomposition. He'll have to get the cadaver dogs up here tomorrow; he talked to the trainer this afternoon. It's all lined up. There's one heli scheduled to fly back up tomorrow morning, if it clears off. If it's sunny and there's snow on the ground, he thinks, they've got as good a chance as any to find her body. If the storm socks in for a couple of days, well, they'll deal with that later.

Steve stands for a long moment looking out the bus window at the fat snowflakes floating down out of the sky. He thinks about Jennie, safe in her dorm room at Stanford, or safe as any twenty-year-old girl can be in a place where there are dark paths to walk on at night. He thinks of her as she must look through the window, sitting at her little desk, the lamp illuminating her blond hair, head bent over her books. Steve watches the snow; it's still melting on contact, he notices. It's coming down fast, though. Won't be long.

ANNE WALKS down the gravel road, carrying Luke in her arms. His sobs have subsided, but she knows from the sporadic sniffling noises, and the simple sadness percolating out of his body, that he's crying still. She's glad that he can cry out his sorrow, exhaust himself this way.

The cabin's not far now, she tells herself. Luke's heavy, and although she's grateful for his live weight in her arms, for the arms and legs that clutch her body, she's so tired, she's not sure

257

she's going to make it to the cabin with him. She'd hate to fall; it'd scare him. She jogs him a little higher in her arms.

"Mom!" he says suddenly, leaning back to look at her face. "You're all wet!"

"You just noticed?" she asks, smiling at him a little.

"Yeah," he says, snuggling back onto her shoulder. "How come you're all wet?" His voice is thick and getting sleepy from the crying.

"I fell in the lake," she says. Just then, she sees Richard coming down the steps toward them and feels her own eyes well up at the sight of him. He's running. She staggers toward him, willing herself not to stumble, not to drop Luke.

"Look," she whispers. "There's Daddy."

It's at that moment, as Richard runs toward her, concerned for her wetness, for Luke's too-heavy weight in her arms, that she notices the snow falling. Big flakes swirling down out of the dark sky like a scene from a storybook.

"I'M SORRY," Jonathan cries as they carry him down. "Just leave me here. I'll be okay. Go find the little girl."

"You've done a real number on that leg, son," Ed says, looking down at him. "I think we'd better get you to a hospital."

"No," he pleads. "Just leave me here until you find her. That was the right clearing. You've got to go back and find her."

"We've got two other teams going into that area," Ed says, lying to him. He can feel the other searchers on the Stoke's shrug Jonathan more securely into their grasp. "They'll find her, don't worry." Ed knows no one will be going back up there, that unless they stumble across her in the trail on the way down, the chances for a live recovery are next to nothing.

Jonathan pleads with them until finally he slips into that glassy-eyed shocky state that accompanies great pain. It kills Ed, having to leave the site like this, without even getting a chance to run one loose grid across it, but his first duty is always to his searchers. He shouldn't have been so careless, shouldn't have brought a searcher this green up here like this. It's his fault that Jonathan got hurt; after all, it was clear the kid was kind of klutzy. Ed should never have brought him up here like this.

"Rest!" he barks, and the team gently sets Jonathan down. While they rotate in two new people and switch sides, Ed gazes back up into the cirque. It's nearly disappeared in the snow squalls, but he can just make out the peak, like some granite ship's prow bearing down on them. Then, shaking his head as if to shake out that unbearable vision, her big eyes staring at him from under that lodgepole log, Ed bends with the four other members of his team and, bearing Jonathan's weight among them, heads back down toward the campground.

MARTHA STANDS in the open doorway, the young priest looking over her shoulder as Richard runs toward Anne, who nearly staggers under the weight of Luke in her arms. His lanky legs hang down to the back of her knees.

"She's wet," Father Kevin notes behind her. "I'll put some more wood on the fire."

Martha stands a moment longer, looking at them out there. They're going to be okay, she thinks. Well, maybe not okay; they'll never be really okay again, she thinks as Richard takes Luke into his arms. The boy's tired and weepy; he'll sleep soon. She watches her son take his son in his arms, then stoop to Anne, one hand on the side of her face. They're like people who've been cleaved down the middle, but who aren't entirely broken.

259

There's a cottonwood tree on the ranch that was hit by lightning years ago, when the children were small, and although it split nearly all the way down, the two parts continued to grow despite the black scar running its length.

"Father, could you grab one of those blankets out of the bedroom, please?" she asks over her shoulder, reluctant to turn from the doorway. "We'll need to get Anne warmed up."

"Sure," she hears him answer. And when she turns back to the three of them, who are nearly to the foot of the stairs now, she sees Steve in the distance, walking down the road toward them. He's hard to see through the snow, and then she's busy with Richard handing Luke to her up the stairs, Anne right behind, both of them cold and shivery and crying. Steve'll get here soon enough, she thinks as the cabin is swamped by a whirl of people, as water is boiled and blankets are draped around shivering bodies, as they get down to the encompassing business of taking care.

Epilogue

Richard walks down the section road with his mother and Luke. The feed bucket swings against his leg. As a boy, he'd walked this way nearly every day, had seen these fields in every shade of green, and brown, and white. The bucket against his leg, the smell of wet gravel, the early songbirds in the cottonwoods by the creek—all of this is as familiar to him as his own name, and yet to Richard, it doesn't feel like home anymore. Everything these days seems to be happening as though he's inside a tunnel of glass, and while he can see people talking and moving and living outside, he can't quite hear what they have to say.

At least winter is over, he thinks. It doesn't snow in the Bay Area, but every time there was a storm, those newscasters on TV reporting from Blue Canyon, white flakes swirling around their Gore-Tex jackets, cars creeping by on the highway, all Richard could think of was Maggie, out there somewhere. It made him wild; he'd wanted to hurl the set across the room. "Don't worry," they'd said to him, Steve and the others. "She wasn't in any pain. Exposure. Hypothermia. It's just like going to sleep." As if it were a comfort, the thought of Maggie out there getting cold and stupid, staring into the woods from which her parents fail and fail to come get her. Their most basic task.

Luke runs down the road with Pearl, Martha's old Border collie. The hay fields to their right are beginning to green up with last week's rains. The grass should be good this year, Richard thinks, despite himself, as he sees the dew sparkle in the long light of early morning.

"Anne seems to be doing well," Martha says. She catches one of the long, dry grass heads left over in the ditch from last season, pulls the furry seed head through the fingers of one hand as she walks.

"Anne?"

Martha glances at her grown son, watches his eyes follow Luke. Pearl's trying to herd the boy, nipping at his shadow as he runs. Luke holds out one hand, makes shadows to see her bite at the gravel road.

"Luke!" Richard shouts.

"What?"

"Don't tease her—she'll break a tooth."

"Okay." Luke shrugs and continues to run, the dog at his heels.

FROM THE kitchen window where she's elbow-deep in sudsy water, Anne watches them walk down the road. She stayed up late last night, playing gin with Martha, and she's feeling a little foggy around the edges. "I'm worried about Richard," she told her mother-in-law. "It's like he's not really here." Martha nodded, said that sometimes it takes time. Then they'd gone back to playing gin, two women up in the middle of the night, sitting together with their worry.

She fishes a plate up from the bottom of the sink, rinses it clean, and sets it in the drying rack. They keep fussing over her, because she's the mother, but really, she's all right. Well, not all right—she'll never exactly be all right again—but she's not shattered like Richard. Anne came out of that lake knowing that the worst thing she could imagine had happened to her, and since it hadn't killed her, she'd have to get up and go on. It surprised her, this certainty, this absolute knowledge that she knew what to do next. *Oh,* she remembers thinking. So *this* is what Martha was talking about. Maybe it was that moment where she kicked for the surface. She chose it, chose to return, so now, somehow, she has to find a way to live in this new place where she feels like she's walked through glass, like a layer of her skin has been stripped from her body, and yet, where she feels unafraid in a way that's totally new to her.

So it puzzles her, this fussing over the mothers, when at every funeral she's been to, it's the fathers who are done in. When their friend Andrew was killed in the avalanche, the receiving line at his funeral was full of men—his six brothers and father, enormous athletic men who raced cars for sport, men sobbing in disbelief and shock and sorrow. And in the midst of them all, Andrew's mother glowed; she radiated such love, such gracious concern for everyone else that she destroyed the few of Andrew's friends who'd made it through the service dry-eyed. "It's good to see he had such nice friends," she said. "It makes me happy to know he was loved."

Anne had thought of her at Maggie's memorial service. Not that Richard had sobbed; she'd almost wished he had. He'd stood frozen at her side, nodding at the people who offered their condolences, as though he didn't recognize them, didn't know why they were there. It was a weird event, half-terrible, seeing the grief in the red-rimmed eyes, especially those of the other parents, and half a reunion of sorts, the sharp pleasure of seeing old friends, people one had loved a long time back, and realizing that those currents of affection still held. Then the memory slamming down on them, why they were here, and the light going out of everyone's eyes. Maybe it was the lack of a body that had somehow softened it for Anne, that there was no small box at the front of the church. Although that's what is making this so terrible for Richard; she's found him up in the middle of the night sitting in the dark living room, staring through the glass doors into the cold, flat rains of northern California.

She fishes up a cereal bowl and wipes it clean. She wishes there was a way to pull Richard across to this shore, this place where she can stand bent but not wholly crushed by her grief. She's tried to explain this to him, but it never comes out right. "Missing" Maggie doesn't begin to describe the way she feels Maggie's absence throb like a phantom limb. There have been whole weeks she's found herself impersonating a live person—buying groceries, getting the car washed, nodding as Luke's teachers tell her he's had some bad days, but overall seems to be doing as well as can be expected. And there are long days spent crying in her studio, staring at the empty canvas, the oranges and fish arranged on the table, and wondering how just days ago they could have been suffused with a tender light, could have summed up all that is fleeting and beautiful in this phenomenal world, when today they just look like so much dead matter, and the fish is beginning to stink.

There's this intuition she has that Maggie is somehow always with her, that Maggie's presence, her existence, is embedded in the light, the objects, the very air through which Anne passes. Walking back down that road with Luke in her arms, she knew that although she'd never carry Maggie again, she could never *lose* her. She doesn't talk about it much, afraid she'll sound heartless, or like some crackpot who still sees visions of her dead child. Martha would call it "grace," and Anne guesses she'd agree with her—because it didn't come from her, this sense of solidity, this strange peace that she can't quite inhabit all the time, but which visits her, which comes down upon her, and which makes the rest of it bearable.

How she hates that psychobabble people keep throwing at her—those infernal "stages of grief." It's madness, Anne thinks, to presume the road through grief comes with some kind of a map, that all one has to do is to round the bases, tag the sandbags, and you'll be "done" with pain. She knows they'll never be done with this longing and emptiness, but she also knows, as she knew lying cold and wet and weeping on that granite slab in the Sierra, that they're not dead. They have to *live* in this after, and all she can do is be the mom, cook the food, keep the house, and watch over Luke while she waits for her husband, her Richard, to grope his way home to them, to wash up on the shores of family life again.

"WHAT'S EATING at you?" Martha asks as she squints across the back field, looking to see how far the horses are out in the pasture.

"Anne won't pack up her room," Richard says. "It's all still there, just like she's going to come home to it."

"Has she said why?" Martha can see the horses now, moving out from under the trees in the center of the field. Luke and Pearl reach the gate and Luke climbs up, hangs on the top rail while Pearl, skeptical that it is indeed okay for a boy to be hanging on a gate, looks up at him until it's clear he isn't coming down, then circles twice and flops into the dust to wait.

"She says it isn't time yet."

"Is she in there much?" Martha asks. The horses are moving toward them, in single file, neither hurrying nor lagging, but swinging along in that interested horsey way. They know there are oats in the buckets, know feed buckets mean halters and lead lines, the pleasure of currycomb and brush, mean the happiness of animal and human engaged in a common project. Although there isn't any stock to work on the ranch these days, Martha justifies keeping a few too many horses by coming up with interesting training challenges for them. She's been playing at a little dressage. It makes her smile to think of how horrified the proper Swiss riding master of her childhood would be to see her out here on stock horses, in jeans and old boots, messing around with leg yielding and countercanter. Frankly, some of her rancher neighbors would be just as outraged: sissying up her horses, ruining them for useful work. She likes the precision of it, though, the tiny shifts of weight, the quiet signals with rein and heel. And she figures it keeps them all from getting too decrepit in their old age.

"No," Richard answers, also watching the horses approach. "That's the thing—she hardly goes in there at all. Although," he adds, dropping his voice a notch, "we've found Luke in there a couple of times. Sleeping in her bed."

"Maybe it isn't time, then."

"I hate it," Richard said, skipping a stone into the ditch with more force than necessary. "It breaks my heart every time I look in there—the stuffed animals, her clothes." He swallows hard and concentrates on the line of approaching horses. It's the smell that really kills him, that Maggie smell that still permeates her bed, her toys. He's afraid if he goes in there, he'll go mad, crawl into her bed, wrap her absence around him in her blankets, and lose everything he has left, Anne, Luke, the house, his job.

"Come on!" Luke shouts from the gate. "You're so slow!"

"Hold your horses," Martha calls back to the boy. Richard sees him grin at his grandmother's corniness, then watches him turn back to experimenting with how far he can swing the feed bucket before the oats trickle out.

"Do you hate it so much you can't stand it?" she asks. Martha can see how terrible this is for him, but maybe, she thinks, it's better not to do like the old days, when a baby's things were whisked away while the parents were still at the funeral. Where they'd come home to an empty room, just as if there hadn't been a child at all.

"What do you mean?" he says, stalling for time. What's so much that he can't stand it? What's worse, her empty room or the fact that she's still out there somewhere? What can't he stand, the fact that he can't properly hear anymore or that he comes home and there's no Maggie, too big but hurling herself off the stairs at him anyway, trusting he'll catch her because he's her daddy and he has to catch her? He misses the edge of danger to it all, the wondering how long it would go on, if she'd be sixteen and enormous, still endangering him every night on the stairs.

"Well," Martha says, "maybe they think putting her stuff up would be like saying it never happened, that Maggie never happened."

"I want it never to have happened," Richard says, looking at his boots. "How I wish to God it had never happened."

"All of it? Maggie being born?"

"Of course not," Richard says. "But I can't see how leaving all her stuff there can do anything but remind us that she's not coming back." Richard thinks of those awful people, the ones who ask why they didn't have an amnio, as if it were a foregone conclusion that they would have chosen not to have Maggie, not to

267

let her tornado into their lives. Those people who hint that this is for the best, because, after all, what kind of a life was the poor child going to have? It takes every last ounce of strength Richard possesses not to pound their heads into the pavement, not to howl with the grief of having lost this child these people think was only damaged goods anyway.

"If it's important to Anne and to Luke, maybe you need to let them take their time," Martha says, squinting with one hand over her eyes, trying to see whether Doc's lame or just faking it to get out of working this morning. He's got a left hind leg that goes a little gimpy on him sometimes.

She can see the weight hanging on Richard's shoulders. Sometimes he looks so like his father, it makes her lonely and proud for him all at the same time.

"I'm sorry," she says. "I'm not trying to make this harder for you."

"I know, Mother," he replies.

He looks at his son hanging impatiently on the pasture gate. Flying out from California, they'd passed over the top of the Sierra. Luke had the window seat. "Look," he said to his mother. "Look how snowy it is." Richard heard the edge of panic in Luke's voice as he'd repeated it. "Mom, there's so much snow."

"I know there is, honey," she said. "But see, it's starting to melt in patches. A lot of that's not snow; it's white granite."

"Is Maggie under the snow?" Luke asked.

"Sort of," Anne said.

"Her body's under the snow," Luke repeated, as if to make himself believe it. "But her soul's in heaven, right?"

"That's right," Anne said, and rubbed between his shoulder blades as he looked out the window, his face plastered to the porthole.

While Anne had this conversation with Luke, Richard fought the urge to bury his head in his hands and weep. He stared at the magazine in his lap, unseeing, half-listening to Anne distracting Luke by explaining how Lake Tahoe was formed by block faults, how it's the clearest water in the world, how scientists come from all over to study it. Richard, frozen in his grief, unable to read or move or flee to the bathroom at the back of the plane, listened to his wife fill Luke's head with information to distract him from the undeniable fact that there was still foot upon foot of snow blanketing the area where their daughter had disappeared, where she had not been found.

ED WATCHES the new searchers try to sort themselves out. He's starting with a gear shakedown, having them all empty their packs so that he and Steve and Michelle can go through and see what sort of bonehead things they've packed. Most of it is pretty innocuous—heavy old metal canteens instead of lighter Nalgene bottles, stuff like that, but one guy seriously thinks he needs to pack in a big old ham radio set. It takes them a while to convince him that the walkie-talkies search leaders carry in chest holsters are going to be all the telecommunications they need.

Ed spent all winter poring over the maps of the site. He got Steve to request the NASA satellite shots for him, send them down to Florida. He's not sure the clearing where Jonathan broke his leg is the one, but he's nearly certain that she's somewhere in the triangle formed by Wright's Lake, Twin Lakes, and little Lake Sylvia to the south. It's wooded, high, away from the trails. There're a couple of spots on the satellite photos that look like blow downs. It would put her within the mile-and-a-half probability zone, and all the signs led off that way—the footprints, the mushroom sign. Ed pulls out his binocs and looks toward the high country. The big problem is going to be snow; it's still early. They probably won't find anything today, but at least he'll have a good shot at scouting out the terrain.

Ed's thrilled to be home, back in the mountains where he belongs. Florida is just so unbearably flat. He hates it there, the endless strip malls, the scrubby vegetation, the sterile white box of an apartment he'd rented. He'd taken off right after the search ended last fall . . . hadn't even said good-bye to anyone, just climbed in his old Bronco and started driving. It had taken him four days to get to Florida, and he'd pulled into Amy's folks' driveway early, just after dawn. He'd planned to hang out until they woke up, but Aaron must have heard the Bronco, because the next thing Ed knew, his funny leggy boy was running across the lawn in his Bert and Ernie pajamas, screaming, *Daddy! Daddy! I knew you'd come!"* and Ed was out of the car, crying with his kid in his arms. Sitting on the curb in goddamn fucking Florida, crying and holding the boy out so he could look at him. He must have grown three inches, Ed had thought as Aaron said, "Dad, why're you crying?" and he couldn't answer, so he'd stood and thrown his big boy up high in the air so he squealed, and then caught him, held him tight, happy just to smell his hair and feel those arms around his neck.

Things hadn't been so friendly when Amy and her folks woke up. Although everyone had been perfectly nice, Ed could tell they were a little alarmed to have their big grimy son-in-law show up after a week searching and nearly a week driving. First thing he'd done was take a shower and clean up; then they'd all had breakfast out on the back patio, Aaron chattering on about his new friend Donnie and trying to make his grandparents' old white fluff dog do tricks for bits of bacon. Ed had sensed the tension in the air as he'd perched on the white wrought-iron furniture that made him feel too big in nearly every direction. He'd always liked Amy's folks, and thought they liked him, no matter how skeptical they were about this wild man their pretty young daughter had brought home. But he could tell it was over. She was sitting right across the table from him, but it was as if he were still in California and she were a million miles away. My wife, he remembers thinking.

But he wasn't about to lose Aaron. That kid was the only wholly good thing that had ever happened in his life, and Ed wasn't going to be one of those dads you see at the mall, looking across a table at the food court as though these little people have become small aliens. So he'd stayed and rented that god-awful apartment, and got a job at a nice clean Volvo shop he found in town. Good thing about being a mechanic, he figures. You can get a job anywhere. It wasn't a bad job and he didn't have to talk to the customers much, and a couple of times one of the other mechanics had taken him out hunting birds on his grandaddy's place about an hour inland. That was okay, but most of the winter had been spent figuring out the custody and divorce agreement, and poring over the maps from the Maggie Baker search.

He'd dreamed about her. The first three or four weeks, she'd showed up in that feather boa, like in the photo they'd distributed. Running, always running. Sometimes across the bare rock up high, but mostly down in the trees. Classic stuff really, the lost victim always disappearing behind the next set of trees, always right out of reach. But sometime around Christmas, the dreams had changed. She wasn't there anymore. No, that's not right; it's just that he couldn't *see* her. But she was even more present than when she'd been teasing him in the earlier dreams. Mostly, he felt himself following her, wandering through glades that don't even exist in the Sierra, glades like he'd never seen before—tall, tall red pines with nothing but deep green moss beneath them. Shards of

271

light slanting down. All peaceful and quiet and always this sense that he's following someone he can't see.

Nights he didn't have Aaron, Ed had sat at the cheap folding table he'd bought to serve for everything—desk, dining table, map table—and followed the contour lines. He saw the clearing in the dreams, too, but always slantways, always as though he was looking at it out of the corner of his eyes. Sometimes there was snow—big flakes like those last three days when they'd de-escalated to the body search—floating down and filling the clearing. Dry asters poking up through the undisturbed snowpack, then covered over, buried like everything else in that little spot. Looking at the maps, Ed had thought the clearing might be over by those little lakes, Smith and Grouse, Lyons and Secret—especially Secret, which looked like a puddle, as if in a dry year like these last few, it was just a meadow, not really a lake at all. Because in the dreams, the clearing was dry. There wasn't a lake there, but on all the topos and the NASA photos, the only clearings he could find had water in them.

For weeks, he and Steve have been talking snowpack numbers on the phone. It was a dry winter, only five and a half feet at Tahoe; the ski people had been bumming all season. And it got hot early. Runoff's been high, Steve's been so busy with river rescues, he wasn't sure they could pull together a training weekend. But the search last fall was so high-profile, they've got a lot of new volunteers, people who don't know jackshit about searching or even being in the woods much. At least that's what Ed figures from looking at the random things they've brought with them. I mean, for Chrissakes, who needs a fucking ham radio on a search and rescue mission?

As ANNE tucks the remains of lunch into the saddlebag, she glances at her watch. Twelve-thirty. The plane isn't until nine, so they should be fine. Richard's boosting Luke up onto his horse as Anne puts one foot in her stirrup, stands into the creak of leather, and settles into the easy-chair feeling of the stock saddle. It's a long way from the flat saddles of her youth, and frankly, she likes it. It's so stable, she can look around, watch things, although she does miss being able to feel the horse like she could in her old hunt saddle. Anne runs through the time left, the things to do: ride out, trailer up and drive back to the ranch, clean up, get to the airport. It's more important than it used to be that things go smoothly; Richard's stretched so thin these days that little things do him in, frustration overcomes him, and he's scared Luke a couple of times. As the four of them swing the horses around, begin to head down the trail, Anne falls back. She likes riding sweep, and Doc likes to keep his nose close on the tail of Martha's Spy.

It's been a good day, she thinks. The first one in so long. They're up on a piece of property that belongs to an old friend of Martha's—ten thousand acres of foothill land with little canyons and creeks, bare ridgetops where they can see far out over the plains. The sky's been blue and the aspens are just leafing out, fluttering with that electric green they get in the spring. They'd swung companionably up a long drainage terraced by beaver ponds, chasing a pair of mallards up the canyon from pool to pool, then stopped to picnic in the driest of the little meadows they could find. Luke spent lunch telling them a very long story that involved water balloons, second-story windows, and a piece of rubber tubing used as a catapult. The horses grazed, ripping large hunks of new grass out of the soft ground, dirt clods dangling from their velvety mouths. They seemed like a normal family again and Anne almost forgot for a moment or two that Maggie is gone.

Martha turns a little, and Anne smiles at her, nodding toward

Luke and Richard, who ride side by side, Richard pointing something out on the ridgetop.

"He's getting to be a pretty good little rider," Martha says, and Anne nods back at her.

"He's a good athlete," she says. "You should see him on the soccer field."

Up front, Luke is concentrating on riding well. He's keeping his toes forward and trying to feel all of his weight sink into his heels. He's trying to relax the small of his back so he doesn't bounce in the saddle. Diesel is different out here; he isn't as plodding as he is at home on the ranch road. He keeps tossing his head up and down and trotting like he wants to go faster, and Luke is a little scared, but he doesn't want the grownups to know it. He's trying not to be too hard on Diesel's mouth, but he doesn't want him to take off.

Luke's dad points out a hawk up high, riding a thermal above the ridge, and Luke looks for it, but then he gets dizzy riding and looking up into the sky and Diesel does a little hop.

"You're okay, son," his dad says. "He just wants to get back to the trailer."

Luke doesn't want his dad to think he can't ride. Luke's dad says he learned to ride before he learned to walk, and he tells Luke stories all the time about how he and Luke's aunts spent all day on their ponies as kids. They'd had wars like cowboys and Indians, and for a while they even had a wagon they called "the buckboard," and there were a lot of stories about them chasing one another and falling out of it.

Maybe we should get him a horse, Richard thinks, watching Luke deal with Diesel, who really is acting up and trying to catch the boy off guard. We could sell the house and move a little farther out, he thinks. Maybe La Honda or somewhere, get a couple of horses. It's good for a kid to take care of something. We could play around with some team roping.

Martha watches Diesel giving Luke a hard time. "You're doing great, Luke," she calls to the boy. They're coming down into the long, flat stretch that leads back to the yard.

"What do you think?" Richard asks his son. "Want to let them out? A little lope might get the kinks out of him."

"I don't know, Richard," Martha says. Her son twists to look at her, one hand resting on his horse's rump. "They'll be okay, Mother," he says. "There's that nice flat run-out ahead."

Martha worries that she hasn't worked Diesel enough lately; he's spent an awful lot of time in the pasture this winter and he's pretty rank. But Richard actually looks happy for the first time in so long.

Anne watches her son's tense face. He doesn't want to, she thinks. "Richard," she calls out as her son nervously kicks Diesel, who takes off too fast, Richard just to the right rear. They'll be okay, she thinks. We've got to try not to overprotect him.

"That's it, Luke," Richard yells, encouraging him. "Sit into it and slow him up a little."

Luke leans back and pulls on the reins until Diesel slows down to a nice rocking canter. Luke's happy and his dad is right there telling him he looks good, that he's doing great. The road goes around a little bend and then uphill and Diesel starts to go faster on the uphill. Luke loses his seat and starts to bounce; he has to grab the saddle horn. At the top of the hill, the road levels off toward the ranch yard, where they'd started, and Diesel flattens out into a full run. Luke can hear his dad behind him telling him to sit into it, to slow down, but he can't. He's bouncing too hard and trying not to fall off and his feet don't seem to be in the stirrups anymore. He's going too fast and he really doesn't like it. He's scared.

Anne and Martha lope along right behind, and when Martha

sees Diesel kick into high gear on the little slope, she knows Luke might be in trouble. The women speed up. If they can all get in front of Luke, they can pull Diesel back.

Richard spurs his horse up in front of Diesel, who by now is really running away with Luke. "You're okay, Luke," he calls to him as he pulls ahead and slightly in front of his son's horse. "Sit back a little; there you go." Richard starts to rein his horse in, keeping him out in front of Diesel, who knows the gig is up and begins to slow down.

Luke feels the bouncing slow to the point that he can get his stirrups back, and then Diesel is actually slowing down when Luke pulls on the reins. They're trotting, and then, finally, walking. Diesel's blowing and still tossing his head a little, but he's stopping now.

"You all right, buddy?" Richard asks. Luke's face is pale and drawn.

"Yeah," he says. "I'm okay."

Richard looks into the tense face of his son and suddenly remembers the terror of being nine and streaking down the back road, his sister Sherrie chasing him. The heart-thumping terror of knowing the horse had you and you were out of control.

"You did really well there, Luke."

Luke won't look at him; he stares at the dirt and struggles to breathe normally. He doesn't want his dad to see him scared and crying. But the tears are running down his face as he walks Diesel back toward the trailer. He can't even go out for a stupid ride without blowing it and getting scared and ruining everything.

"WHAT DO you think?" Ed asks, surveying the little basin below them. It's the third ridge they've climbed over today, the third cup of snow and pines they've surveyed from above.

276

"Where are we?" Jonathan asks. "Secret Lake?"

"No, we're one over . . . see." Ed pulls the map out of his jacket and spreads it on a rock. Some of the trainees crowd around him. "We've just come over this little ridge here, and now we're heading down toward Lyons and Sylvia."

"We could have just come up that trail," one of the new searchers grouses. "Would have been easier."

Ed turns, stares him down. "We're not here to do things the easy way," he says evenly. "We're here to find the victim. If that's a problem for you, you might want to rethink your commitment to search and rescue." The guy doesn't say anything.

"Is that a problem for you?"

"No," the guy says, shaking his head. "Sorry, I didn't think."

"Well, then start thinking," Ed says, and sighs. He turns to Jonathan. "Okay," Ed says. "How do you want to approach it?"

He's training Jonathan to be a team leader. He's turned out to be a real good kid, Ed thinks. He kept calling from the hospital, sure Steve was going to kick him off the search for screwing up, wouldn't believe them when they told him it wasn't his fault. Wasn't anyone's fault, really; sometimes searches just fail. Ed watched him trace several approaches on the map, go over the pros and cons, ask for feedback from the group. He'd stayed in Ed's house all winter, he and his girlfriend, and they'd taken good care of the place, kept the house and the yard real clean.

"You think that's the patch of deadfall we've been looking for, right?" Jonathan asks. Ed nods. Last thing he wants is to tell a whole bunch of new searchers they're looking for a spot he saw in a vision.

"So let's go in from below," Jonathan says. "If she was coming up from over here, from the last footprint, she'd have dug herself in on the downhill side of whatever it is she's under. We've probably got a better shot at finding her that way."

"How's that leg holding up?" Ed asks.

"All right," Jonathan says. "But I'm going to be pretty sore tonight."

It takes them nearly forty minutes to get down into the lower part of the basin. Ed checks his watch; if they don't find her here, they'll have to pack it in for the day. It'll be dark in another three hours or so, and the last thing he wants is to be up here with a bunch of green searchers in the dark when the trails haven't melted out yet. They organize a line search, Ed and Jonathan on either end, and start working their way uphill. There's less snow the farther they get from the edge of the forest. Out here in the sunshine, it's pretty well melted out—a few patches on the downhill side of the bigger deadfalls, but enough open space that Ed thinks they might find her if she's out here. Ed knows this is the place he's been looking for—the light is right, there isn't any water, and there's a big patch of deadfall—probably blister rust killed them off before a summer storm knocked them over. The line moves uphill slowly, Ed and Jonathan warning the new guys not to go so fast, to take their time, to really *look* at the terrain.

They've been at it about an hour when one of the trainees stops the line.

"Hey," he calls out, looking real pale all of a sudden. "You'd better look at this."

"Everybody stay where you are," Ed says. "If it was a live search, you wouldn't want to ruin a clue." He catches Jonathan's head turning sharply and shrugs at him. "Sorry." He crosses the fifteen feet to where the searchers have nonetheless begun to cluster. Glancing uphill, Ed sees the tree, the one he's been look-ing for all these months.

Ed and Jonathan look at the leg.

"Oh Jesus," someone says behind him. "I wasn't ready for this."

It's a small leg, thigh and knee and ankle, that bare foot they'd been tracking so hard last fall. It's dried up and a little leathery, but unmistakable.

It could be worse, Ed thinks, looking up under the tree where the rest of her lies. She's not all in one spot anymore, but there's enough of her left to take home. He squats on his heels, looking up under the tree where she'd taken shelter. Her bright hair is right there, right where he'd thought she'd be.

"Jonathan," he says quietly, "find out who's got the body bag."

LUKE LEANS his head against the window of the plane and pretends to be sleeping. Ever since he got run away with, his parents have been treating him all weird—they've got that tone to their voices that means they're being careful with him, that they're worried. That means he's such a loser, he can't do anything right—ride a horse, watch his sister, go to a friend's house after school—without 10 million phone calls. At least his gramma kind of understands. He'd helped her clean up after they got back to the ranch. His mom and dad went inside to pack and she said, "Come on," and they went to the tack room to clean the bridles before putting them away. He was sitting on a tack box with a soapy sponge, trying to get the green stuff off the corner of Doc's bridle, when she told him he'd done a good job out there.

"No, I didn't" he said. "I got run away with."

"So," she answered, scraping at the corner of the bit with her thumbnail. "How'd it feel?"

"Bumpy," he said, and bounced on the box like he had in the saddle. Maybe if he made a joke, they could all forget about it.

She kept working at the bridle and didn't laugh.

"Scary," he admitted. "I was bouncing so hard, I couldn't do anything but hang on."

"Mmm," she said. "That happens sometimes." His grandmother stood to hang the bridle up, straightening out the head-stall on the hook. She likes a tidy tack room. "But you didn't panic. You would have been all right, you know," she said, turning to look at him. "You would have gotten your stirrups back, and gotten Diesel to slow up."

Luke looked at the floor. His eyes were filling up and he didn't want her to see, but she did and she came and sat next to him on the box and put her arm around him. Luke leaned his head on her shoulder and she talked into his hair. "You've got to try to believe, Luke, that things aren't always going to turn out for the worst."

"MAYBE WE should see about getting him a horse," Richard says, looking across Anne at Luke's sleeping head against the window.

"You think so?" Anne looks up from her magazine. She thinks back to her own adolescence at the barn, all those mean blond girls gossiping about whose parents had spent the most money on boots, ponies, trailers. "Where would we keep it?"

"I'm thinking maybe we could look for a place with a barn." Richard floats the idea tenuously. "Someplace a little farther out in the country, where we could have animals."

Anne watches her husband fold his hands carefully in front of him on the airline tray. Move, she thinks. He wants to move. "Can we afford something like that?"

"We can now," he says, then immediately regrets it. Now that we don't have to worry about supporting Maggie. How can he say that to her? He looks over, but she seems fine. She looks like she's considering the idea.

"My studio . . ."

"I'd build you a new one." He hates the pleading sound in his voice.

Anne reaches for his hand, which clutches the edge of the seat tray, and laces her fingers into his. "We could look at some places." She turns his hand over and runs her thumb across his fingernails. "If that's what you really want."

"It's what I really want," he says.

LUKE DREAMS about Maggie. It's the same dream he always has about her. They're in the city and Maggie has on her bunny pajamas—but she won't wear the hood. So she's got the bunny ears hanging down her back until they almost touch the great big powder-puff tail on her costume. It was originally her Halloween costume, but she wanted to wear it all the time, so it became pajamas. They're in the city and it's just the two of them and they're at Chinese New Year, but this time Maggie likes it and isn't scared of the firecrackers or the lights or the noise. They're running down a side street, trying to get to the main parade, and he has Maggie by the hand and he's yelling, "*Faster, faster—come on, Maggie—run!*" Then it's the busy street and it's all lighted up yellow and red and the dragon is coming. That's what they've been trying to get to, the dragon dancer. And it's a huge one that stretches on and on and on around the corner; it's so long, they can't see the tail at all. And Maggie's following the dragon head, dancing along with him, trying to weave and sway like she has a big dragon head on. All the people are laughing and clapping and even the mean-looking dragon man smiles at her. Then the firecrackers go off, firecrackers everywhere—so much noise, he can't hear anything. And there's smoke and the dancing dragon man, and he can feel Maggie's hand in his, but when he turns to make sure she's not too scared of the firecrackers, she's not there. She's gone and he's running and running and running, looking for her. He keeps seeing colors, but they're the wrong colors, red and yellow and black of the dragon dancers, and every once in a while there's a flash of pink through all the dancing legs and arms. But no matter how fast he dashes through them, he can never get to the pink.

STEVE WATCHES Ed emerge from the path that leads out of the woods, the small bundle that is Maggie Baker cradled in his arms. The other searchers file out of the woods behind him, then quietly congregate on the far side of the parking lot.

"You all right?" he asks Ed, who carries the black parcel like it's the child herself. He's cinched it down with gaffer's tape so she doesn't jostle inside the big bag, a bag made to house a full-size man, not the desiccated remains of a little girl.

"You call the coroner?" Ed asks. He's got that slightly dazed look he gets when he's trying not to take something too hard.

"Yeah," Steve says. "He should be here anytime now."

Ed called him from the site. The terrain was too rough to bring the coroner up, so they agreed he'd photograph everything, and one of the searchers who had good sketchbook skills would make a map of the scene before they brought her out.

"It's been long enough," Ed said into the radio. "We need to get her out of here." The coroner okayed bringing out the body, and then Steve called Jane to fill her in and ask her to start the phone tree. Searches like these, that last so long, people get real involved and no one rests well until they know how it ends. Even though they don't have all the details yet, haven't reconstructed what went wrong, they can at least let folks know she's been found.

Ed stands, looking around for a place to put her. He's not putting her on the ground.

"Over here." Steve points to a green Forest Service pickup with the tailgate down.

Someone's spread an old horse blanket in the back, and Ed lays the bundle gently on top of it, then sits on the tailgate. "You'd better see about the new guys," he says. "I think some of them are pretty shook-up."

"You going to be all right?"

"Yeah, I'll just wait here with her," he says. Steve sees him white-knuckling the edge of the tailgate. "I'm okay," he says, looking up at his friend. "It's hard, that's all. She wasn't in very good shape."

Steve rests a hand on Ed's shoulder, then turns to the group of stunned search trainees. He tells them that since they've started at the grim end of the search and rescue experience, there shouldn't be much they can't handle after this.

Jonathan limps over to a picnic table to take the weight off his leg. It's going to be a really bad night, but the doctors said it was important to keep at it, that weight-bearing exercise is the best way to get the bone to heal up on him. He listens to Steve ask the trainees for feedback on today's experience, listens to the halting attempts to describe the scene up there, and wishes he'd been there for the end of the search last fall. It had kept snowing, hard that first day, and then in unpredictable blinding squalls throughout the next two. Apparently, Ed had marched through it all like some counterforce of nature, his head bent against the snow, increasingly dogged as conditions worsened. He'd scared everyone; he wouldn't rest, he hardly ate—he was the classic example of the emotionally involved searcher, endangering himself and others in his desire to find the victim.

The coroner's van pulls up and his men unload a gurney from the back end. It bumps along the uneven gravel, ridiculously big for the small bundle Ed lifts from the truck. Everyone stops what they are doing, quietly stands at attention as Ed lowers the black bag onto the gurney.

"Careful," Ed says. "She's pretty fragile at this point."

"We just have to make sure she doesn't fall off," the guy says, gently securing the straps.

Then she's in the back of the van, and Steve's conferring with the coroner. Ed waves Jonathan over. "Tell them they can go home," he says. "We'll have a meeting later this week to debrief. Tell them to call if they want to go see the shrink."

"Okay."

"And Jonathan?" Ed calls after him. "Good job today. You're going to be a solid team leader."

"Thanks," Jonathan says as he crosses the silent parking lot to dismiss the trainees and to tell them about Dr. Lowe. She'd come by to see him a couple of times when he was in the hospital, after the initial Baker search. He'd been just wrecked about it, thought it was all his fault that they hadn't found her.

Ed spends about forty minutes with the coroner going over the Polaroids and the sketch of the site. It's not a suspicious death, but nonetheless, it's important to get an accurate account of what probably happened. "I'm thinking exposure," Ed says, and the coroner agrees, says he'll be surprised if they find anything different.

"Tell the parents to call us," he says, handing Steve a card. "It should only be a day or two before we can release her." Steve and Ed watch the van drive off, then turn to the parking lot, empty except for Jonathan and the Forest Service guy, who lean against the pickup, waiting.

"Anything else you guys want me to do?" Jonathan asks.

"Yeah, actually," Steve says. "Could you drop some stuff by the office for me? We're going to go tell the Bakers."

OUTSIDE ANNE'S window, the dark neighborhood scrolls past, the strip mall where she buys the kids' shoes, the supermarket, the residential streets, which are, as always, marked by anomalies—the ugly new condos that went up on one corner, a single-story house suddenly exploding upward into a much bigger and different-looking structure. On other nights, she and Richard might mull these over, weighing the pros and cons of various architectural choices while he sketches in the air above the steering wheel what it is that he would have done differently, how the line of a roof is slightly off, or why he'd have suggested different windows. Sometimes, if they see one they particularly like, they stop, get out, and take a look around, never too far from the children, crashed out in the backseat. They stop on the sidewalk, sometimes venture into the yard if the house is dark, or unoccupied, around the side perhaps, checking to see what windows, what finish details they would have chosen.

But tonight, they're both worn-out with travel, with the hassle of the airport. Airports are hard, haunted even more than most places by Maggie's absence. She loved airports, and aside from that one incident when she ran off, they're places full of happy visions: Maggie flirting with passengers; Maggie lying on the floor moaning for juice, as if she were dying of thirst in a desert, then giggling when a very stern man in a dark suit looked appalled; Maggie and Luke in a baggage cart that Anne, alone that time, was riding like a scooter, racing down the slanted concourse for an early-morning flight, before there were crowds, and the concession stand workers laughing and cheering them on. It's still strange getting off a

285

plane without Maggie's heavy unconsciousness to deal with, no Maggie to hand to Richard because in heavy sleep she's too much for Anne, no redistribution of bags among her and Luke and Richard. Once, they plopped her in a wheelchair and piled all the luggage on top of her—giggling at the aghast looks the people gave their small child, snoring loudly while buried in backpacks.

And Richard wants to move out of the house, their house. The last house where Maggie ever lived with them. A new place, a place Maggie's never been. Anne knows he needs this. He can't stand to be home anymore, can't stand Maggie's room. It was only Luke's face, pale at the idea of boxing up Maggie, that had stopped him. But Anne finds Maggie's door closed every time he's been upstairs, has seen him stare at the hall carpet to get past the door when it's open and she's there with him.

She loves their house. Loves the way the light slants through the skylight over the second-floor landing, loves the tree outside their bedroom, loves her sunny kitchen with the center island where the kids eat lunch. Her garden—after three years, she's just gotten the dirt in shape, her perennials are finally starting to look rooted, and her roses are getting fulsome. But it's her studio— finally she got a studio of her own. A converted garage, yes, but hers. Good light and a concrete floor she can hose down, all her paints and brushes in cans and baby-food jars. After they came home from the mountain, it had taken her weeks to venture in there, but when she did, she knew she'd be okay. When she could look at a canvas again and see something, see possibilities. "People without hope don't paint pictures," a teacher had once told her. Everything's in *use* in there—how can she pack it up?

Canvases prepped, some sketched out, others starting to come into focus . . .

"I'd build you a new one," Richard had said. He wouldn't ask unless he's drowning. She looks over to Richard just as he pulls into the driveway, hits the garage-door button and pulls into their lighted garage. Maggie's pink bike leans against one corner, the white streamers drooping from the handlebars.

"Home," he says, looking across at her. She notices his temples starting to gray; the lines around his eyes have deepened.

Anne turns to the backseat, shakes Luke's knee. "We're home, buddy," she says, to no response. "Come on, sweetie, wake up."

Richard pops the hatchback and walks to the back to get the bags.

Anne peers through the car at him. "I don't think he's going to wake up," she says. She's pretty sure he's faking, is in that state where they could get him to sleepwalk upstairs if they had to, but since Maggie, sometimes he needs to be carried.

"Let me get these bags and then I'll get him," Richard says, heaving the duffels out of the car. He slings one over a shoulder while he unlocks the door, and as the timer turns out the garage light, a rectangle of yellow light falls out across the car from the door to the laundry room.

Anne climbs out her side and, passing behind the car, grabs her shoulder bag and Luke's backpack, heavy with books and necessary plastic action figures, out of the hatchback. Richard steps down from the lighted doorway and, stooping into the backseat, unbuckles Luke. He's far too heavy for Anne, and nearly too big for Richard, as well. "Come on, buddy," he says as he shifts his sleepy son into his arms. Luke wraps his long arms and legs around Richard, his head heavy on his dad's shoulder. Richard hitches him up for a better grip, bumps the car door with one hip to close it before carrying his sleeping boy into the yellow light of the house.

STEVE ROLLS down the window as they drive through the humid darkness of the Central Valley. He can smell the feedlots out there, the tang of urine and fermenting hay. Ed's got the map light on, is trying to figure out how she got from the mushroom sign to the spot where they found her, trying to figure out how they missed her.

"She would have had to go over this ridge," Ed says.

"How steep *is* it?"

"Nearly vertical over here." Ed points to a cluster of topo lines. "But she might have been able to go around this way." He looks at the map for a quiet minute. "I'll need to check the satellite photos again," he says. "Lot of times, they show stuff you can't see on the map."

Steve looks at his friend. Ed continues to study the map, tracing likely paths the child might have taken, possible places they missed her. This is what they do. They try their hardest to make up for the things that happen in life, for the wrong turn taken, for the map forgotten, for the shortcut that doesn't work out. And sometimes, they have to take care of the unspeakable; they have to put on the surgical gloves and dig the remains of a child out of a snowbank, bundle her up, and carry her out so there can be a proper funeral, so the parents can go on with their lives, so the story can be closed.

And it's a story they'll make of this. They'll trace the maps and the photos, find the most probable line the child could have taken, figure out a time line and try to pinpoint how they missed her. Because if they can figure out this one, then maybe they'll be able to catch the next one before she slips through the cracks.

"At least we can tell her folks she went easy," Ed says.

"Hypothermia?"

"Yeah, looks like it. Nothing was broken, not that I could tell, anyhow." He pauses, looks out into the velvet darkness of the valley.

"How'd we miss her?" Steve wonders.

"I don't know," Ed says. "The underbrush is pretty thick in there. If she'd been hiding, it's possible we walked right past her."

"But you'd think the dogs would have found her."

"I think she was moving at night," Ed says. "And a child like that—her mother said she didn't have much of a grasp of cause and effect; she could have been going at odd angles, turning every time something caught her eye."

"We'll need to walk it," Steve says. "See if we can figure it out on the ground."

"Mmhmm," Ed says, tracing patterns on the map again.

When people ask him why he does this, Steve's never sure how to answer. Because he's good at it is what comes to mind. He's afraid that sounds sort of arrogant, but that's what it comes down to. He does it because he can. He's got the skills, and people need help. It's times like this that it gets hard, when you've got to surprise people in the middle of the night, tell them you've found the body of their child. But mostly, he does it because he can't imagine not doing it.

"What do you want to tell them about the body?" Steve asks.

"As little as possible."

ANNE'S UNPACKING the dirty clothes right into the washer and thinking that this isn't actually such a bad time to consider moving. Luke's nearly done with school for the year, and maybe it will be good for him to be in a school where no one really knows

289

about Maggie. If they get on it soon, they can probably find a place over the summer. Anne has a vision of Richard and Luke, road-tripping to Martha's to buy horses. It might be good for all of us, she's thinking when the doorbell rings.

It startles her, this late at night, and she figures it must be a lost pizza delivery guy or something. When she flips on the outside lights, she's scared for a minute; there's a very large bearded man outside her door. It's not until she sees Steve beside him, not until she recognizes the SAR logo on his cap that she realizes who they are.

"Come in," she says to the men on her doorstep. They seem awkward and displaced in town.

"Was that the door?" Richard calls from upstairs.

"You should come down here," she calls back. "Come in, come in." She ushers them inside. "It's so late—can I get you some coffee or something?"

Richard pauses on the staircase when he sees them. "What?" he asks. "What?"

"We found her," Ed says. "This afternoon."

"Hush," Anne says, pointing upstairs, where Luke's bedroom door is still open. "Let's go in the kitchen."

Richard is frozen on the stairs. Anne hustles the two men in front of her, waves for Richard to come on. He descends the last few stairs like a sleepwalker.

They stand silent and awkward in the cheerful yellow kitchen. It seems strange to be indoors with these men. Anne realizes she's shaking.

"We brought the map," Steve says. "Maybe you'd like to see?" Ed unfurls it across the kitchen island as Richard leans toward it. She still doesn't want to see that map.

"Coffee," Anne, says. "You probably want some coffee. It's so late . . . and you've been driving." She reaches for the coffeemaker and her hands tremble so, she can hardly pull a coffee filter from the stack.

She hears Ed behind her, pointing out places on the map, the footprints, the shoes, explaining that they found her up and over a ridge about half a mile from the PLS, that they're not sure yet how she got there.

"Where is she?" Anne asks, starting for the door. "Is she in the car?" The coffeepot full of water is still in her hand. "Did you bring her?"

"No," Steve says, putting an arm out to stop her. He takes the glass coffeepot out of her hands, pours the water into the machine, flips the red switch. "She's at the Placerville County Morgue." Anne notices he's speaking very slowly and clearly. "I have their card." He reaches into his back pocket, pulls out an old brown wallet, and, finding the card, hands it to her.

She stares dumbly at it. "Placerville County Morgue."

Richard leans on one of the high stools and stares at the map Ed's unrolled. "Here?" he asks, pointing at the cluster of markings.

"Is there someplace safe I can put that for you?" Steve asks.

"No," Ed says, tracing a line with his finger. "Actually, it was over here."

"I'll just pin this on the board," Steve says, tacking the coroner's card to the bulletin board by the phone. "Where it will be safe."

"When can we see her?" Anne asks.

"You might not want to do that," Ed says, his voice low and quiet.

Anne stares at Ed's face when he says this. She thinks for a moment about Maggie's body, outdoors all winter, and knows nonetheless that no matter how gruesome it is, she'll need to see her. She doesn't care how terrible it is. She's Maggie, and Anne can't put her in the ground without having laid a hand on her. Maggie can't go into the grave without a mother's touch.

A choking noise startles them all, and for one awful moment Anne thinks Richard's laughing. Then she sees how tightly he grips the edges of the island, and she watches as a wave of something that can only be a sob rises through his body. He's nearly convulsing, it's taking him so hard, and the first sob is followed by another, and then another as all the months of his fear and grief, all the months of his visceral horror that his baby girl was *out there,* rise through and out of him in ripping, tearing, racking sobs.

Steve and Ed stand deeply still. The kitchen is charged, not with embarrassment or shame, but with the strange intimacy of shared trauma. It is out of this calm silence that Anne finally moves, crosses the kitchen, and takes her husband's head to her chest. He leans into her, clumsily, his hands still gripping the countertop, and weeps the long, sad weeping of deepest grief. Anne rocks him slightly, one hand gentle on the side of his face. When she looks up, she sees that both Steve and Ed have tears running quietly down their faces. They share this space together, broken yet alive, living the pain that can only mean that one must, one will go on, despite the anguish of a universe that can contain such sorrow. Finally, Steve turns and soundlessly takes four cups down from the cupboard, begins to pour them each a cup of coffee, something hot to drink, some small comfort for the survivors.

Acknowledgments

Writing a first novel is such a quixotic and lonely task that each one must invariably come with a long list of thanks to those who loved and supported the author during the many years that he or she remained "promising" but not yet published. This book is, of course, no different. My most enormous thanks go to my oldest friend, Constance Woods, and her husband, Emil Chau, for believing in me, and for their astonishing financial generosity. For reading endless drafts and bringing me food and drink, big thanks to my beloved brother Patrick McGuinn and my dear friend Debra Francine. To Jack Hicks and the Art of the Wild community, especially Barbara Ras, James Houston, Gary Snyder, Alison Hawthorne Deming, John Daniel, and Louis Owen, I owe a deep debt of gratitude for early support and encouragement. Gary Short helped me to see the actual landscape of this book in a whole new way. Steve Dooley, Rick DeCastro, and Mike Larish as well as the entire SAR community on-line provided crucial technical assistance, and answered even my most basic questions with patience. Thanks go to François Camoin and David Kranes for asking important questions, and to Mark Doty and Katherine Coles for reading early drafts and giving invaluable notes, to say nothing of their words of encouragement when I most needed them. Katherine Stockton and Steve Tatum encouraged my academic work and continually pushed me to connect it to this book, and my stalwart friend Anna Vogt listened with infinite patience as I rehearsed the theoretical and theological positions that form its intellectual spine; I could never have completed the degree for which this serves as dissertation without her. Betsy Burton and Barbara Hoagland not only employed me and gave me wonderful places to write but also provided me with a stellar education in what it means to be a truly dedicated reader. Matthew Tolmach provided a much-needed sanctuary and unflagging faith in my project. Mary Lowe's spiritual guidance and the support of the entire Newman Center community, particularly Fathers Cassian Lewinsky and Bartholemew Hutcherson, were a real live godsend. Terry Tempest Williams came to the rescue with an infusion of faith and enthusiasm just as I was about to give up—without her, this book might truly have never happened. And to Jennie McDonald, who took a chance on my fiction and so enthusiastically represented it, and to George Witte, who made this book a reality, you both have my undying gratitude.